THE POISONED GARDEN

THE POISONED GARDEN

LEOPARD'S BANE BOOK 1

PHILL FEATHERSTONE

Cover design by Cathy Helms, www.avalongraphics.org

Typeset in Palatino by Opitus Books.

ISBN 9781739745547

Also available as an ebook, ISBN 9781739745554

Published by Opitus Books, Sheffield, UK.

www.opitus.net

❀ Created with Vellum

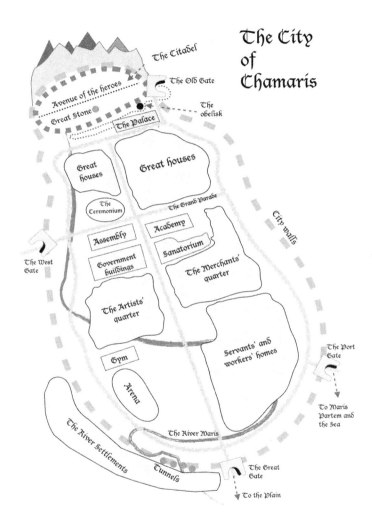

The City
of
Chamaris

The Citadel

The Old Gate

Avenue of the heroes

Great Stone

The obelisk

The Palace

Great houses

Great houses

The Ceremonium

The Grand Parade

City walls

Assembly

Academy

The West Gate

Government buildings

Sanatorium

The Merchants' quarter

The Artists' quarter

The Port Gate

Gym

To Maris Partem and the Sea

Arena

Servants' and workers' homes

The River Maris

The River Settlements

Tunnels

The Great Gate

To the Plain

1

AROUND MIDNIGHT

The girl shivered and pulled her cloak more tightly around her. It was a cold night and her breath was misty on the still air. She crept into the square and flattened herself against the wall, listening for anything that might mean a problem, maybe the bark of a dog or the distant tramp of a Guardian patrol. There was nothing, just the bell in the distant tower of the Ceremonium marking the hour.

She scanned the buildings. All were in darkness. They were the simple homes of small merchants, tidy and respectable, just the sorts of places that she had been told to target. She remembered the instruction. 'Leave the big houses at the top of the hill. They've all got high walls, and guards. Go for the ones in the middle town like you've been shown. Plenty of good stuff there.'

She thought she was eight but she might still have been only seven. She lived in a shack on the edge of the River Settlements but that was not home. Home was in another city far away, and she could still remember a big house, her mother, her father, her older brother. Now they were gone and there was just her.

She'd entered the city with a boy. All the gates had been locked at dusk, as they were every day. They would not open again until dawn, but there were other ways in, tunnels and passages built over the years and forgotten by almost everyone. She and the boy had been taken by a man they called Scorpion to a spot where the river passed under the city ramparts, emerging through a passage foul with sewage. It was so cramped that even though both the children were small they were only just able to squeeze through.

'Get in there,' Scorpion growled, pointing to the rank opening with his whip. 'When you get through, split up.' There was no need to say that, they knew from their previous raids that there was a better chance of avoiding the Guardians if they were on their own. The man bent down and stroked the girl's hair. 'Bring me something good,' he purred. 'You know what I like.' She was his best snatcher, a fast worker who always came back with a worthwhile catch.

The girl understood. She knew that to return empty handed, or even with something Scorpion judged to be of insufficient worth, would make him angry. Those who made him angry were beaten. If he was in a bad mood they might even be put in the pit.

Alone in the cold of the night the girl shuddered. She had got wet in the stream and was now paying the price in the freezing dark. She blew on her hands to try to get some warmth into them. She wondered about the boy. How was he getting on?

She slid along the edge of one of the buildings, silent

and smooth as a shadow, looking for weaknesses. There were none. The people who lived here had been robbed enough times to be careful, and everything was locked and barred. Then she spotted something, a single chink in the armour of the blank wall. It was above her head, a window where the wooden casement had warped and no longer closed properly against the frame. It was the merest crack, but that would be enough. She'd done it before: jump, grip, reach in, spring the catch, wriggle through. On the other side she would drop lightly to the floor and wait until she was sure all was clear. Then she would quickly grab whatever caught her eye and be out before anyone knew.

It would be easier if the boy was with her because she could climb on his back to help her get in. She was glancing around to see if there was something she could drag to the wall to scramble on to, when she heard a sound behind her, a faint, metallic whisper like a blade being drawn from its sheath. She froze. It wasn't the Guardians, they made much more noise than that. She peered into the dark. Nothing. She backed into a fold in the wall, crouching to make herself small.

Not small enough. Suddenly they were on her, five of them, each from a different direction. She made to run but every way was barred. One grabbed her hair, another her arm. She opened her mouth but her scream was cut off as the point of a knife speared her windpipe. Her knees folded and she sank to the ground, clutching her throat. Her eyes bulged with the horror of what was happening to her.

Her attackers made a circle around her, watching the swelling circle of blood, listening to the gurgle of her life ebbing away. Her bladder released, she convulsed, twitched, her chest gave one final heave and it was over. She was still.

Their leader poked her with his foot. His nose wrinkled in disgust. 'Phew. She stinks like she's been swimming in the sewer.'

'She probably has,' said one of the others. 'That's what the Settlement rats do.'

The group's leader took out a large hunting knife, a zirca, and stooped. With a swift hack he removed the little finger from her left hand. Then he wet it in her blood and drew on her forehead a symbol: the letter R. He took a rag from his waist pouch, wrapped the tiny finger in it and tucked it away. Finally he wiped his blade on her smock, sheathed it, stood up and looked at his companions.

'Well done,' he whispered. 'That's another of the vermin gone.'

'One more for the Rat Catchers,' murmured the young man at his side. 'We must be well ahead now.'

'At this rate we'll soon run out of rats to catch,' said one of the others. 'There'll be none of 'em left.'

The rest of the group laughed. In one of the windows a light appeared.

'Ssh. Split up,' whispered their leader. 'Same time tomorrow. Meet at the usual place. Go.' He held up his fist in a raised salute.

The five figures melted into the dark, each taking a separate route. None of them looked back.

The street was empty once more. The lamp that had been lit was extinguished and its lighter, unable to see anything amiss, returned to bed.

Time passed. The night passed. The sky lightened, dawn came and the searching sun crept along the wall, feeling out the frail body and the pool of blood, a crimson halo bright as a poppy on the frosty ground.

2

BROTHERS

'What do you think you're going to get, then?'
Peglar didn't reply.

'A fifth?' Ragul persisted. 'A tenth? A twentieth?' He sneered. 'Lost your tongue, runt boy?'

Ragul always called him that, even though Peglar had grown a lot in the past year and was now actually taller than his half-brother. However, he was nowhere near as strong. Peglar was skinny, whereas Ragul was thickset and sturdy.

Abruptly Ragul turned nasty. 'You answer me when I talk to you, you ignorant little turd.' He punched Peglar hard on the bicep, a quick jab with one knuckle stuck out for maximum hurt.

Pain shot down Peglar's arm and his eyes watered. He clenched his teeth and swallowed. He was not going to give Ragul the satisfaction of seeing the effect he'd had.

They had been told to attend on their father, Lord Karkis, at the sixth bell. Peglar had got there early, wearing a clean tunic and cloak and with his hair brushed. Ragul arrived much later, sweating and smelling of the stables. They had both been waiting in the lobby outside the study since.

'I don't think he wants to see us about the Sharing,' Peglar said at last.

Ragul's mouth turned down in contempt. 'Course it's about the Sharing, lame brain. He's going to announce how much of the estate we're each going to get. Why else would he want to see us and our mothers all together?' He ostentatiously put his thumbs in his belt and stood with his legs apart in the stance of a warrior. He was wearing a zirca, the stubby hunting blade used by the people of the plains. He was showing off, demonstrating that because he was in the army he was permitted to carry a weapon in the presence of their father.

He moved towards Peglar and put his face very close. The smell of horses was even stronger and the odour of beer soured his breath. 'Oh, I forgot,' he said. 'Under the law you can't inherit anything at all. Because you haven't been initiated, have you, diddums?' He pinched Peglar's cheek between his forefinger and thumb. 'You're not a man, you're still a little boy, and that means you can't take part in a Sharing.'

Peglar wanted to escape but he forced himself to hold Ragul's gaze, and the two stared at each other. Then Ragul shook his head, gave Peglar a half-hearted push and turned away.

Peglar stared at the flagged floor. Two years ago Ragul had gone through Initiation, the ritual which had conferred on him the rights of a citizen of Chamaris. It had been his fifteenth birthday. Peglar was already well past that and had been expecting his own turn, but it hadn't come. Until it did, in the eyes of the law he was still a child.

The lobby was without windows, low ceilinged and dim. Peglar's back was aching but there was nowhere to sit. Ragul unsheathed his zirca and inspected it, eyeing the blade and trying it with his thumb. It looked wickedly sharp.

The door opened and Feldar, their father's Steward, stood framed in the opening. He looked from one of them to the other, nodded to Ragul, straightened Peglar's cloak with a tug and said, 'Your father is ready for you.'

Peglar hung back and allowed Ragul to swagger into the study ahead of him. The room was high and square. It was dark, and the few feeble lamps did little to lift the gloom. The walls were covered in faded tapestries and paintings of old men, long dead. The carpet on the stone flags was so worn its pattern had nearly gone. It had been a warm day, but even so a huge fire burnt in the grate. There were papers on every surface, piles of them, clamouring for attention.

Their father sat at a massive wooden table. The purple cloak of Councillor was draped loosely around his shoulders, and his Master's sash with its golden keys hung from his neck. He was flanked by his two wives. One of them was Chalia, Peglar's mother. She was their father's second wife, half his age, quiet, and kind. Peglar thought she was outstandingly beautiful, and so did many others. On the other side was Ragul's mother, Vancia. She was the first wife and enjoyed her seniority. She was older than Chalia, haughty and domineering. Ragul had inherited her dark hair and complexion, but whereas she was tall and stick-thin, he was stocky and inclined to fat.

Their father did not invite his sons to sit, and they remained standing at the opposite end of the table. He glanced briefly at Ragul, then regarded Peglar, his head on one side as if judging a horse he'd been offered but thought wasn't worth the asking price. He took off his glasses, thick as pebbles, and rubbed his eyes.

Meanwhile Peglar studied him. Although this man was his father they rarely met and he hardly knew him. His face was thin and deeply lined, peppered with brown flecks. He had a long, narrow nose and his hair, grey and wispy, was swept back over his crown to show a broad, sloping forehead. He was Lord Karkis, head of the House of the Leopard and Master of the City of Chamaris. For many years he had been the most powerful man in the land, but now he looked old and tired. Even so there was steel in his gaze and Peglar had to look away. It was as if his father had been waiting for this small sign of submission before he was prepared to speak.

'Peglar, you present me with a problem.'

'Yes, father.' He knew it was a useless response, but some sort of answer seemed to be required and that was what came out. He saw Vancia sneer and his mother looked uncomfortable.

'Yes father,' Karkis mimicked. 'Yes, indeed. So, Peglar, what is my problem?'

There was nothing he could say. He had no idea what his father was talking about. He was nearest the hearth and the fire was hot on his bare calves. He shuffled to put a bit of distance between himself and the flames.

'Well?' said his father.

'I'm afraid I don't know, sir.'

'Don't you now?' Karkis snapped. I thought that when you said, "Yes father," you meant that you did.'

There was a small explosion at his side as Ragul covered his snigger with a cough. Peglar felt his cheeks burning and he knew he was blushing. Vancia was clearly enjoying his embarrassment. His mother was watching him with concern.

'No, I'm sorry father. I don't know what your problem is.'

'Well then,' said Karkis, icily, 'I shall have to enlighten you. My problem is this. I have two sons. The older one is a fine young man. He was initiated into manhood two years ago and now serves with distinction in the army. He is a credit to this family and to his city. The other one is you.'

There was a long silence. Peglar knew he disappointed his father. His skinny frame made him look weak. The way he preferred drawing and reading to the things boys were supposed to like – riding, wrestling and hunting – counted heavily against him. He stared at the floor, listening to the crackling of the fire.

'I am old,' Karkis continued.

'No, no,' Vancia cooed, putting her hand on his arm.

He waved her away. 'I am old. I must look to the future, to the future of my House. I must decide how best to divide my wealth between my sons. I must prepare a Sharing.' He fixed Peglar with another cold stare, then turned to Chalia. 'And there you have it, you see, there is my problem. Until Peglar goes through formal initiation and becomes a citizen he is ineligible, he cannot receive anything. Until he's legally an adult he has no rights, he has no wealth of his own, he cannot own property. But before he can be initiated he has to face the Three Trials.' Karkis's voice was growing louder as he worked himself up and he flapped a bony hand in Peglar's direction. 'I have put off issuing the Call to allow him time to make himself ready to face the trials, time to acquire the necessary qualities and skills, but he does not. Does he train? No. Does he practice with other boys? No, he does not. He spends his time in the schoolroom. He spends his time with books instead of developing and strengthening his body. What's he going to do? Read his way through the trials? Face the challenges with a pen in his hand?' He shook his head.

'Please be patient, my lord,' said Chalia soothingly. 'Peglar is not physically strong but he has many other qualities. Given time I am sure he will succeed in the trials.' She looked at her son with affection, although Peglar could see sadness there too.

'There is - no - more - time,' Karkis said, banging the table to emphasise each word. 'In a few weeks he will be sixteen. If he has not completed the trials by then he will forfeit his right to be initiated altogether, and that will be that.'

Nobody spoke. Peglar shuffled uncomfortably, Chalia looked down at the table, Vancia smirked.

Eventually Karkis made up his mind. 'I decree that your Initiation Ceremony will take place three weeks from today. Before it you must successfully complete the Three Trials. If you can manage to do that the occasion will go ahead as planned. If you do not, if you fail any one of them, it will be abandoned. You know what will happen then.' He left a pause for his meaning to sink in.

'Steward Feldar will be the arbiter. He will see that everything is done properly. Be ready to attend the Calling Ceremony tomorrow morning.' The old man sighed wearily and sank back in his chair. 'I can do no more. It is up to you.'

'Thank you, father,' Peglar said. He tried to speak boldly and with confidence but he felt neither. 'I'll do my best, I'll strive to be worthy of your House.'

'Yes, yes,' his father said, impatiently. 'Just try to be as worthy as your brother, that's all.' He got stiffly to his feet and the Household Guards on the door snapped to attention. He gathered some papers from the desk, wrapped his cloak around him, took his staff and walked through the door that led to his private chambers. Ragul turned towards Peglar. His face wore a sneer and he was going to say something but Vancia took his arm and led him after their father.

Chalia came to the end of the table and took both Peglar's hands. Not so long ago she had been able to look down on him. Now she smiled up at him, but it was a smile laced with anxiety and her eyes were moist. She wrapped her arms around him and for a long time remained with her head on his shoulder. She smelt sweet, a gentle, dusky perfume. Peglar wasn't sure but he thought she might be crying. When she spoke it was no louder than a whisper.

'Well, here it is at last: the Three Trials, Initiation, then manhood.' She looked up into his face. 'You will be the equal of Ragul.' She gave a little laugh, and then almost at once became serious again. 'The trials will not be easy for you, I know that. Trust Feldar. He's a good man and he will see that everything is done fairly.' She stepped away from him and dabbed her eyes with a handkerchief. 'But you must be careful. Until you are initiated Ragul is your father's sole heir and in line to inherit everything. He would like to keep it that way. He will try to stop you.'

Peglar was used to being bullied by Ragul so his mother's warning was not a surprise. However, over the following days he was to remember her words, and to realise how right she had been.

3

CALLING

For many boys the Calling Ceremony was a simple affair held in the family home or a rented room in an inn, but for the son of the Master of the City it had to be formal. Peglar's Calling was held at the Ceremonium, the great domed building in the City Square next to the Assembly.

He got up early and dressed in his best tunic. He was too anxious to eat breakfast, and he killed time while he waited in the Atrium for Feldar, who would accompany him to the Ceremonium. He was not allowed to go inside, that would come later, and they waited on the steps for things to start.

After a few minutes Thornal, the City Marshal, arrived with two uniformed Heralds. Nothing was said, everyone waited for what seemed to Peglar like an age until his father appeared. He was in his Master's robes and using a stick to help him walk. Chalia was with him, looking radiant and happy. They were escorted by four Household Guards.

Thornal read aloud from a book which was held for

him by one of the Heralds. It was in the old tongue but Peglar knew what it said. It was The Call, the formal invitation from a father to a son to take on the rights and responsibilities of a citizen, and to first submit himself for the Three Trials, which he would have to face to become eligible for that. All that was required of Peglar was to kneel and bow his head while two acolytes removed his white tunic and replaced it with a grey one. He would wear this colour from now until he became entitled to the blue of a free citizen. Thornal placed a yellow sash around his shoulders and held out a hand to raise him up.

What happened next was not part of the ceremony. As Peglar got to his feet there was a disturbance in the small crowd that had gathered to watch and he turned in time to see someone running towards his father. The figure was wearing the rust-coloured smock of a churl, with a hood covering its head. It was shouting something in a high voice but the covering over its mouth made it hard to understand. A pair of Guardians were on it straight away and one of them grabbed it. There was a quick struggle, someone in the crowd pushed the Guardian from behind and the prisoner broke free. The crowd parted to let it through and closed up again to stop the Guardians following. By the time more Guardians ran from the other side of the square the figure had vanished.

Peglar turned to Feldar with a puzzled expression. The Steward shook his head. 'It's nothing,' he said. 'Just some crackpot. Take no notice.'

The Household Guards had formed a square around his father and Chalia was fussing over him. She came to Peglar, hugged him and kissed him on the cheek.

'What just happened?' he said.

'I don't know,' Chalia took his hand. 'Some protestor or other, a girl I think. I don't know what it was about.' She let go of his hand. 'Don't let it spoil your day.' She smiled and went back to his father, who gathered his cloak and walked with her into the Assembly.

The onlookers melted away and Peglar was left with Feldar. He felt uncomfortable. Chalia had said that Feldar was a good man but Peglar had always found him strict and distant. He didn't like him, and he was sure that the feeling was mutual. He thought he ought to say something but he didn't know what. Feldar saved him the trouble.

'Well, you have three weeks,' he said. 'That's one trial a week. You get a single shot at each, no retakes. If you fail any one of them, then that's the end of it.' Peglar knew this, he didn't need Feldar to rub it in. 'The first one will be Earth. If you start tomorrow there's time for a couple of day's preparation. Take that one early and it will give you a little more time for the two harder ones, Fire and Water.'

4

A WAGER

The second part of the ritual was the Calling Feast, held in the Great Hall of the Palace. All feasts were for citizens and their partners only, and children were not allowed. That led to the bizarre situation that although the event was in Peglar's honour he could not attend.

The best place to view anything going on in the Great Hall was from the gallery, and that's where Peglar was hidden. It was high up at one end of the huge space. In the past it had been used by musicians who used to play to entertain the diners, but it was a long time since there had been any music in the House of the Leopard and the gallery had become a dump for old furniture. Peglar used it now to watch what was going on below.

Getting onto the gallery was easy. He'd found a secret way just after Ragul had done the last of his trials. His half-brother had come into the schoolroom, strutting and showing off. Peglar had mumbled something insulting under his breath. He hadn't really meant it to be heard but Malina, their sister, heard it, laughed, and repeated it. Ragul snarled and made a lunge for Peglar, but he was by the door and managed to get through it before Ragul grabbed him. Malina squealed with delight and Distul, their tutor, shouted for them to sit down, but all that concerned Peglar was getting away and he fled as fast as he could.

At the end of the corridor was the Atrium. There was a narrow, stone staircase in the corner and Peglar made for it and scrambled up. The stairs led to a dim corridor with five or six doors. The first was locked. So was the second, and the next. They were all locked until the last. That one gave and Peglar burst into the room, yanking the door shut behind him.

It was a bedroom, small and brownly furnished. He cast around for a place to hide but there was nowhere. Under the bed? Too obvious. Behind the door? Useless. He could hear Ragul coming along the corridor, rattling the locked doors and shouting threats.

His only hope was a large cupboard built into the wall. It didn't offer much protection but it was all there was. In a panic he wrenched it open and dived inside. As he tumbled in he felt the back of the cupboard give way and he rolled through the gap into darkness. There was a spasm of fear when he thought he was going to tumble down some dark drop, but he landed on a solid surface only a few inches below. He didn't know where he was but he didn't care so long as he could remain hidden. With trembling hands he pushed the panel back into place and lay still, heart thumping in the dark.

He heard the bedroom door kicked open, and then Ragul. 'Peg-leg, you little bed wetter! I know you're in here. I can smell you. Come out, you reeking runt.'

The cupboard door was tugged open and Peglar held

his breath, afraid to stir in case the slightest movement gave him away. But Ragul didn't notice the loose panel. He hesitated and his search wavered. Where was Peglar? Maybe after all he had dodged into one of the other rooms. Ragul moved away.

The frightened boy listened to the retreating footsteps and to the bedroom door slamming shut, but he kept still in case it was a trick and he would come out only to find Ragul lying in wait for him.

He stayed there a long time until cramp forced him to shift. It was only then that he thought to wonder where he was. He looked around and realised that he was on the gallery overlooking the Great Hall. It was narrow, dark and dingy, laced with cobwebs and thick with dust. However, it gave a wonderful view of the room below. He realised that from there he could see whatever was going on in the Hall without anyone being aware of him. He had always thought it would be great to be invisible, and this was the next best thing.

He looked down now on a scene of opulence and splendour. The room was impressive, its walls hung with tapestries and pierced with tall windows, glorious with the splendour of stained glass. There were candles on the tables, lamps in sconces on the walls, and vapour-jars on metal stands making the air thick with smoke. On the wall opposite him a huge gilded carving of a leopard flickered in the yellow light. It was the family emblem, the crest of the House.

Gathered below were the most important people in Chamaris. The women were like butterflies, in gowns of scarlet, turquoise, saffron, orange, green. The candles threw flickering highlights on elaborately pinned hair, on bare arms and smooth shoulders. The men were more soberly dressed. Many were in the light blue robes of a citizen but some wore the brown of the army, the green of the law or the dark blue of the navy. Others were in the purple of a Councillor.

Almost all the men were decorated with regalia - chains of office, medals, ribbons, sashes. Peglar had seen most of the men before, but only a few of their partners. Vancia was the most prominent of the women, but his mother was without doubt the most beautiful. Her golden hair was elaborately braided and her skin was the colour of honey. She was laughing with Thornal, who was on her far side. She looked so young, no more than a girl.

Next to Thornal was Geraker, reputedly the oldest man in the city, and then Styron, Deputy Master and his father's close ally, with his first wife. Further along the table he could see Uncle Mostani. He wasn't really an uncle, just a close friend of the family, but the three children had always called him that. Then there was Narvil, the family physician and head of the City Sanatorium. He didn't know the man talking to Narvil but he knew who he was, and he was surprised to see him there because he wasn't a friend of the family. In fact he had often spoken out against the rule of Karkis. He was younger than the others and Peglar had heard him called "a rising star", "up and coming". Some said he wanted to be Master of the City himself and was looking for an opportunity to challenge Karkis. His name was Lembick. He was was unpaired and alone.

Near the bottom of the table was Ragul, with another youth. This was Burian, Ragul's "Companion". The custom was that when a boy from one of the wealthy houses was initiated his father would appoint someone of around the same age to be his comrade. Chosen from a respectable, though lesser family, his job was to support his master as he moved into his adult role. Burian had appeared soon after Ragul's initiation and it was easy to see why he'd been picked; the two could have been twins. Both had round faces topped with dark curls, both were sturdy, and both were cruel. Peglar hated them equally. He wondered who his own companion would be. Had his father chosen him yet? Probably not. There was no point until he'd completed the trials, although he must have someone in mind.

On the top table and close to his father was a stranger. Peglar had been watching him throughout the evening because he had never seen anyone so big; the man was enormous. Thick, black hair hung from his huge head and a dense beard flowed onto his chest. His tunic was tight as a drumskin over his vast belly. The size of his stomach made leaning forward an effort, but it had been no barrier to him reaching the dishes and he had coped well, stuffing his mouth with food and washing it down with great gulps of wine from his goblet. He was enjoying himself and from time to time his huge laugh rang out, filling the room. This was Mangal, the Celebrant who, in three weeks time would, all being well, officiate at the Initiation Ceremony.

Peglar was tired and the fumes from the vapour-jars were heady. He lay back on the blankets he had smuggled there for times like this. The voices and laughter receded to a dim hum and he fell into a doze. He was dreaming that he was his imaginary hero, Vandegar, dressed in full armour and riding across the plain on a huge creature like a horned bear. He was in pursuit of Ragul and was drawing close to him when he was suddenly jerked awake. Somebody had called his name! He sat up, alarmed that his hiding place had been discovered, and looked over the parapet expecting to see everyone staring up at him, but no one was. Instead they were all turned towards Thornal, who was on his feet, his goblet raised.

'Gentlemen and ladies, we are gathered here tonight to mark the Calling of Jathan Peglar to the ceremony of Initiation. Tomorrow he will embark on the journey that will take him from childhood to becoming an adult citizen of our glorious city of Chamaris. I ask you to join me in the traditional toast: to the initiation of Jathan Peglar.'

Everyone rose. The ladies sipped daintily from their glasses, the men drained their goblets, banging them down hard on the table when they'd done. All, that is, except Ragul, who remained seated. He looked drunk.

'Come, come, Ragul,' said Uncle Mostani. 'Drink to your brother.'

Ragul stared blearily at him and it seemed an effort to speak. 'Oh, I'll drink all right,' he said. He rose shakily to his feet. His words were slurred and indistinct. 'Anything for a drink,' he sniggered. Burian, who had joined in the toast, looked concerned.

'Either toast your brother or sit down.' This was their father.

Peglar had never heard him speak so sharply to Ragul, and it had the effect of sobering him a little. He gripped the table to steady himself and answered slowly and deliberately. 'Sir, if you order me to join in the toast I will, but I did not because I don't believe Peglar's Initiation will take place.'

A murmur ran round the table. What did this mean?

Karkis looked annoyed. 'Ragul, this is inappropriate. Explain yourself.'

'My lord,' he said, working hard to speak distinctly, 'I mean no disrespect to you or to our great House, but I know Peglar. Although he's over fifteen he is still a little boy, used to running to his nurse or his mother whenever he comes across a problem. He's a weakling. He's got no backbone. He's not up to the Three Trials. I am not the only one who thinks so.' He looked hard at Karkis, and Peglar remembered the previous day's meeting and his father's lack of confidence in him.

There was a hush. A moment ago the guests had been thinking about leaving. Now there was this drama.

Ragul broke the silence. He needed some extravagant gesture to support his outburst and, always the showoff, he found one. He fumbled inside his cloak, pulled out a velvet bag, and with a grand gesture dropped it on the table, where it landed with a dull chink.

'This is my purse. I'll make a wager. Let anyone who thinks I am wrong take it up.' He leant forward and pushed the bag of money further away. 'This purse says that Peglar will fail at least one of the trials.' He looked around the company, smirking and defying anyone to challenge him. There was silence and several of the guests shuffled uncomfortably. 'Come on, it's good money. Will no one pick up my purse?'

Peglar craned forward to see if anyone was going to take his side. Uncle Mostani? Styron? Thornal? His father? His head was now well over the parapet and anyone looking up would surely see him, but there was no chance of that. All eyes were fixed on Ragul and the bag of money on the table. Several of the guests looked uncomfortable. It had been an amusing diversion, but now things had gone too far. Chalia was ashen. Even Vancia appeared concerned. For Ragul to offer a wager on such a matter was vulgar, and the way he had done it was crass.

'What, no one?' Ragul was crowing now. 'That means you all agree with me that Peglar's not up to it. In which case I say his Initiation should be called off.' A smirk spread across his face and he reached out to retrieve his money, but before he could something even more unexpected happened. Feldar, who all evening had been directing the servants, was standing behind Karkis's chair. Now he came quickly to the table and before Ragul could close his hand round the bag he snatched it.

'I'll take your purse,' he said, his face only inches from Ragul's. 'I'll accept your wager.'

Ragul looked murderous and shook his head. 'You can't take the wager,' he snarled. 'You're the arbiter.'

There was a collective intake of breath. This was another insult. Feldar's duty as arbiter was to see that the trials were carried out properly. Ragul was implying that because of the wager Feldar would cheat and make them easier. For a long moment the two men stared at each other, neither backing down. Then a voice came from across the room.

'A moment.'

It was Mangal. Slowly he heaved his bulk from his chair. 'I have no interest here, none. I am sure that Peglar, as a son of The House of the Leopard, is a worthy young man. However, the Three Trials are hard, and it is true that Peglar is not strong. Therefore, although it comes badly from one so close in blood, the wager has some foundation. Moreover, it has been taken up and therefore it must stand. So if both parties agree, I will be stakeholder. I will be present when Peglar takes each of the trials, and together with Steward Feldar I will see to it that all of them are performed to the required standard. Will you agree to this, Ragul? Feldar?'

Feldar accepted at once, Ragul shrugged and sat down. He had to agree, there was no choice, but he was not happy about it and he stuck out his bottom lip like a sulky child. Feldar handed the purse to Mangal.

Karkis rose. He was scowling, his lips a firm line, and he looked angry. 'The Initiation will not be called off. The trials will go ahead. As to whether Peglar is capable of completing them, we shall see.'

5

CITADEL

The Citadel had once been a fortress but it had been abandoned long ago. With its avenues empty, its pillars tumbled and its arches fractured, it had sunk into quiet decay. Ramparts that had defied the attacks of armies yielded now to the onslaughts of nature. In spring the banks were invaded by battalions of blooms. In summer platoons of dry, spiky grass marched through what had once been avenues and squares. Saplings strived towards the light, their roots undermining what was left of the walls. Low, straggling bushes filled the shells of rooms.

Peglar liked the Citadel, its ruin suited him. He was sitting on a raised slab called the Great Stone in the centre of a broad track that bisected the ruins. Known as the Avenue of the Heroes, it had once been lined with statues and carved stones marking the resting places of the champions who in ancient times had created Chamaris and built it up to be the chief of the cities of the plain. The statues had long been removed and re-erected elsewhere but the stones remained, and so did a line of iron gratings that were entrances to the tombs of the dozen or so most important families. Right next to the Great Stone was the vault of the House of the Leopard. Every year on his name day Karkis would visit it to lay flowers. Someday, Peglar reflected, he too would be buried there. Who would then lay flowers?

The view from his perch was magnificent. The outline of the city was a triangle, broadening as it spread down the hill. Roughly in the centre were the public buildings. He could see the Academy, the Gymnasium, the Assembly, and most prominent among them the white dome of the Ceremonium. In three weeks he would enter it for the first time for his Initiation. The thought of what awaited him before that brought a tightness to his chest and a feeling of nausea in his stomach.

These public buildings divided the city. Above them were the houses of the great families, chief among them his father's Palace, the seat of the House of Karkis. It was huge, and in the shape of an E, with a central block and two wings surrounding gardens. He could see servants going about their tasks in the yards, and two women beside the fountain in the women's garden. One looked like Vancia. If so the other was almost certainly his half-sister, Malina, but she was wearing a hood so he couldn't be sure. He looked for his mother but there was no sign of her. She wouldn't be with Vancia and Malina, but she loved flowers and she might have been walking in the gardens, on her own or with one of her women.

Below were the smaller houses. This was where the lesser families lived, the merchants, traders, artisans. These were free men and women, decent and hard-working people loyal to the city and to his father. Lower down still was the city wall. It was tall, with a guarded walkway along its top, and pierced by two gates that gave out onto the plain. Clustered outside the largest, the Great Gate, was a smudge of tumbledown shacks and hovels. This area was known as the River Settlements. It was where the churls lived and, so they said, where the children who came into the city by night to steal came from.

It was hot, too hot even for the cicadas, and the white town below quivered in the afternoon sun. The noises of the city were muffled by the heavy air, and except for the sleepy drone of bees the Citadel was silent. He felt drowsy, lay back on the flat marble, and his eyes closed.

He may have been dozing for what – ten minutes? twenty? – when he was roused by another sound close by. He sat up and craned over the edge of the stone. There was someone there, a figure crouching against one of the collapsed walls. There was a hood over its head and its back was towards him, but the drab, brown smock marked the wearer as female and a churl. She was no more than twenty paces away.

Peglar resented this invasion into what he thought of as his own private space. His impulse was to shout at the intruder and tell her to clear off, but he didn't. Instead he watched. She was busy on something that was clearly absorbing her. She was assembling a small pile of stones against the wall; then she went to a patch of grass where a few spiky flowers grew. She picked some and took them back to the wall, where she crouched and laid them in a semicircle in front of the stones.

Suddenly, as if she knew she was being watched, she

looked up and her hood fell back. She was alarmed and leapt to her feet, hitching up her smock to run.

'Hey,' he shouted, but she ignored him, jumping the low wall in one bound. He called out again but she was gone, leaping down the steep track towards the city, surefooted as a goat. Fifty paces away she stopped and fixed him with a hard, angry stare. Then she spun away and vanished into the scrub.

Peglar slid down from the rock and ran to the wall where she'd been. The flowers she'd picked were already wilting. Wedged on top of the stones was a roll of paper tied with a black ribbon. He loosened the knot and uncurled the sheet. It was a drawing, a child's face. It was a girl, not the one he had just seen, although there was a similarity. This one was younger. The face looked knowing but the features had a child's infirm roundness. Peglar guessed she was probably no more than seven or eight when the drawing was made.

He straightened up and looked at where the runaway had gone. It was obvious what this was. The picture, the black ribbon, the cairn, the flowers suggested some sort of memorial. The girl had been making a shrine. Why? For whom? And why here? Carefully he rolled up the picture, retied the ribbon and put it back where he had found it.

6

RAGUL

Everything about Ragul's wager was staggering. Peglar didn't know how much was in the purse his half-brother had thrown on the table but it had landed with a solid clunk. It would be a tidy sum. He was used to Ragul's jibes and sneers and hadn't given much weight to them, but this was different. When he'd studied the faces of the guests at the feast everyone had looked uncomfortable, even his father. None of the people he had thought might support him had come forward: not Styron, or Uncle Mostani, or any of them. He was as surprised by Feldar's faith in him as he was hurt by the fact that no one else had taken his part.

Every free-born boy in Chamaris grew up with the expectation that one day he would go through the formal process of becoming a citizen. When his voice broke and hair grew on his face and body his father would start the process leading to Initiation. Then he would leave his childhood behind and join the men, starting with a spell in the army. That was what had happened to Ragul.

For girls it was different. There was no formal ceremony, but when a girl started her monthly bleeding she would be removed from the nursery and go to live with the women. That had happened to Malina, and now she was on the market. She was attractive, lively and light hearted and several young men from noble families had been mentioned as potential partners for her, but Karkis knew she was valuable currency and was taking his time to spend her in a way that would bring most advantage to his House.

Crucial to a young man's initiation were the Three Trials, and boys grew up practicing them - well, two of them; you couldn't really practice for the third. Peglar had never been any good at them. His gawky body made him clumsy so that anything physical was awkward, and he treated the practices as a joke. If others were going to laugh at him, and they surely would, he was going to have them laughing on his terms. That meant he had not taken the practices seriously, and now he must.

'Why do I have to do them?' he asked Feldar.

'Why do you have to do what?' the Steward replied.

'Why do I have to take the Three Trials?'

'To show you're ready for Initiation.'

'But why the trials? Why can't I show I'm ready in some other way?'

Feldar was becoming irritated. Surely Peglar knew all this. 'The Three Trials are physical challenges intended to test your skills as a warrior. To show you're ready to join the army.'

'Why do I have to join the army? Why do we need soldiers? Chamaris hasn't been in a war for years.'

34

Feldar sighed. 'Hasn't it occurred to you that it is exactly because we have a strong army that we have not had to fight a war? Anyway, you have to take the trials. Everybody does.'

Feldar had walked out, leaving Peglar to think. All right, he would have to go through this performance but he still thought it stupid. He'd be all right, though, wouldn't he? Surely his father, as Master of the City, wouldn't allow his own son to fail. But he was sure that the appointment of Feldar as arbiter was to make sure that he didn't get an easy ride, and then came Ragul's wager.

The day after the first practice in the Gymnasium Peglar was sitting on the old bench in the schoolroom. He was eating cherries and flicking the stones, trying to hit a box in the middle of the floor, when the door was kicked open and Ragul swaggered in. Burian followed, wearing his usual inane grin. His half-brother stood in front of him and put his hands on his hips.

'Well, little weaner, you're going to be some use to me after all. Instead of just being a pathetic runt you're going to make me some money.'

Peglar said nothing but sat as still as he could, trying to avoid doing anything that might provoke Ragul's temper. If he found an excuse for a fight and Peglar was hurt, as he knew he would be, then he would have no chance at all in the trials.

Ragul studied him carefully. 'I just hope that jumped up cretin Feldar has enough put aside to pay my winnings when you fail.'

'I'm not going to fail,' Peglar muttered, but even to himself he didn't sound convincing.

Ragul threw his head back and snorted with laughter. 'Oh yes, you are. Of course you are. Isn't he, Buri?'

Burian nodded. 'Oh yes, without a doubt.'

'Would you bet on him, Buri? Would you join Feldar and put your money on runt-boy here?'

'No no no, never. Not a chance.' Burian sniggered.

Ragul sat on the bench beside Peglar and put his arm around his shoulder in a caricature of brotherly affection. 'You haven't got a hope, you pathetic little ball of snot. Just think about it, eh?' He leant nearer, his face so close that Peglar could see the pores of his skin, the blackheads on his nose and, what was worse, smell his breath sour with last night's ale.

'First, there's the Trial of Earth, Ragul went on. 'That's completing a circuit within a set time.' He aimed a kick at Peglar's leg. 'You've got long legs but you're clumsy and you've got no wind. Think you can run?'

Peglar looked down at the swirls on the marble tiles to try to force his mind on to something else, to filter out what Ragul was saying. His brother's response was to grip his chin between forefinger and thumb and force his head round so he couldn't avoid looking into his face.

'Then there's the Trial of Water,' he said, relishing Peglar's discomfort. 'Swim a freezing creek full of biting fish. And if you manage that there's still the Fire.' Drops of Ragul's spittle spattered Peglar's face and lips. His half-brother turned to Burian, standing at his side like some grinning ape. 'Will he be able to handle those, do you think, Buri?' Burian shook his head. 'No, I don't think so either,' said Ragul. 'And don't forget, we'll be watching you. Oh yes we will, every step of the way, watching and waiting to see if anything's left after the fishes and the fire.'

Abruptly Ragul let go of Peglar's face and strode to the doorway. He turned, his expression a mixture of spite and glee. 'Just one thing, little brother. Ask yourself why no one else took up my wager. Why didn't our father stop it? The only one on your side is a clapped-out servant who'll soon be out on the street.' He paused and his eyes narrowed. 'You're going to fall on your arse,' he snarled.

'No, I'm not,' Peglar growled, but quietly, and not until Ragul and Burian had slammed the door behind them.

For a long time he sat in the schoolroom while the evening lengthened and the light died. At one point a servant brought in supper but he was too anxious to eat. Failing the trials would mean no money, no property, no rights, nothing. He would have to rely on hand-outs from his half-brother and the rest of the family. He would be forced to work on low and humiliating tasks, things that no-one else would do.

He knew that it would be sensible to turn in early and rest so that he would be fresh for the next day, but he didn't feel like sleeping. He watched the sun sink and heard the bell which signalled the curfew. He watched the moon rise and heard the tramping feet of a patrol of Guardians passing in the distance. At one stage he heard something closer and went to the window in time to see two bulky figures creeping across the yard. Ragul and Burian? Probably, returning from a night's drinking, or whoring, or both. He heard the second bell ring from the distant tower of the Ceremonium, and the third, and still he couldn't sleep. Ragul's visit and the threat that he would do whatever it took to prevent Peglar succeeding tied knots in his stomach that tightened until he could stand it no longer and had to get up.

7

CHURL GIRL

'What are you staring at, arse face?'

Was the girl talking to him? She must be, there was no one else there. Even so, Peglar looked around. No, it must be him, although she wasn't looking at him. He bristled at the insult. This was a low class girl, a churl. How dare she talk to him like that!

It was three days since his Calling and Feldar had drawn up a programme for him. He had also found him a trainer. It was a boy – a young man really, because he must have been around twenty – whose name was Cestris. He was a talented athlete who had been a champion in the last Seven Cities Games. Although Peglar had watched some of his performances in the Arena, to meet him in the flesh, to see him close up was astonishing. He was about Peglar's height but much more impressively built. He was muscled and toned and there was no fat on him anywhere. His oiled, bronzed skin radiated strength and health.

The first session with Cestris had been hard and it

had pushed Peglar to his limit, so that he finished soaked in sweat and with every fibre of his body screaming. Bathed and scrubbed, he had come from the training area feeling exhausted and dragged himself up to the Citadel, looking for peace and quiet.

'Hey, I was talking to you. You spyin' or something?'

She was right in a way. He hadn't been 'spying', but he had been watching her. It was the girl he'd seen making the shrine the last time he'd been to the Citadel, the one who'd run away when she spotted him.

He was behind a pillar and didn't think she'd noticed him this time, and he felt as if he'd been caught doing something underhand. Also he was offended. He had never been spoken to like that by anyone apart from Ragul, and for it to come from someone of her class was unthinkable. Where was her respect? She ought to be whipped. He clambered down from where he'd been sitting, trying to maintain his dignity on the uneven ground and intending to put her in her place.

'I... I... I...,' he stammered. Under the intensity of her gaze he couldn't find the words he needed and he felt himself beginning to redden in embarrassment.

She cut him off. 'Well just look at him. The posh boy's blushing!' Instead of running away, which was what Peglar expected, the girl danced towards him, swinging her arms and chanting an inane, singsong rhyme. 'Blush baby, blush baby, give the pram a push baby.'

She stopped a few feet away and glared, her fists clenched, chin jutting forward, challenging him. His temper rose. This was insufferable. He was the son of the Master of the City and she was a churl. He drew back his hand to slap her when it occurred to him that he was alone and she might have friends nearby, other churls hiding behind other walls. Perhaps that was why she wasn't running away this time, it was because she had reinforcements at hand. He looked around anxiously but could see no one. He turned back to the girl. Her eyes were the most startling blue, bluer even than his mother's. He flinched under her steady stare and had to look away.

'What you got there then? That your spying equipment?'

Her hand shot forward and snatched at what was in his hand. It was a telescope, which he often brought to the Citadel to view the city. Her wrist was bony and her fingers thin, but she was surprisingly strong. He let go rather than risk breaking the instrument in a tussle.

'Be careful! It's fragile!' He moved to seize it back from her but she pulled away and turned her back on him. She obviously knew what it was because she lifted the telescope to her eye. Almost at once she rounded on him, accusing.

'It don't work.' She held it out with an expression of contempt.

Peglar was finding the girl's bluntness hard to handle. At the same time, though, there was a kind of freedom in the way she behaved, a 'don't care' attitude that intrigued him. It was as if she felt no need to please or impress anyone, least of all him. She must know that Peglar was her superior, she might even have recognised him as the son of Lord Karkis, but it didn't seem to matter to her. There was none of the deference that he had been brought up to expect from people of lower birth.

He looked through the telescope. All he could see was a blur.

'It needs focusing,' he said.

He twisted the eyepiece until the image sharpened and the buildings in the distance became clear. Without stopping to think, he handed it back to her. She lifted it to her eye and immediately recoiled, startled by the sudden appearance close to of objects that had been far away. She looked again and this time stood motionless, transfixed by what she saw. After a moment she let the instrument drop.

'It weighs too much.'

He could have taken it from her and walked away. He could have sent her packing. If he had, things might have turned out differently. Instead he said, 'I'll hold it for you,' and found himself taking the telescope and levelling it at a height that was comfortable for her. She regarded him suspiciously for a moment. Then the allure of this new thing overcame her caution and she leant forward to peer through it, steadying the eyepiece with her hand. Mostly she was silent, captivated by the strange toy, but every so often as she panned to some new view she made a little sound of recognition or wonder.

While she studied the view Peglar studied her. She was older than he'd at first thought, probably about the same age as Malina, but she was short and slightly built. In contrast to the rounded smoothness of Malina her body was angular, her shoulders sharp under the coarse fabric of her smock and her arms thin. She looked as though she didn't get a lot to eat. The hand that rested on the telescope was brown and the nails were broken.

Peglar had always understood that churls stank, but this girl didn't; she smelt fresh, a mixture of flowers and open air. Her arms showed some scratches but her skin was smooth and her astonishing, yellow hair was clean. She had a ring through one nostril. And a mark on her cheek. It was a purplish blemish, an irregular oval about the size of a small apple. It made her look vulnerable, in contrast to her aggressive manner. He found it curious, and strangely appealing.

'Thank you,' she said simply, letting go the telescope and stepping back. Peglar looked away quickly, lest she accuse him again of staring. His arms were aching and he was glad to be able to put the instrument down.

'They call me Yalka,' she said.

Again Peglar was taken aback by her boldness. A young woman of his own class, somebody like Malina or one of her friends, would never tell a stranger her name, just like that. She wouldn't even speak, and would wait until someone introduced her. The girl's forwardness disturbed him but it was also fascinating. By rights he should have rebuked her and left, but none of the rules he had been brought up with seemed to apply to her, and before he could think he answered, 'My name's Peglar.'

'I know,' she said. She smirked. 'You're Karkis's son. I saw you when you was called.'

Peglar had a sudden flashback to him standing with his mother and father and Thornal on the steps of the Ceremonium, a movement in the crowd and a slight figure in the russet fustian of a churl running towards his father. It had all been over in a second, but it was this girl, he was sure of it.

'You looked a proper pillock,' she said. 'I thought you was going to piss your pants.'

Peglar squirmed with embarrassment. He'd been nervous but hoped it hadn't shown. Clearly it had. He didn't know where to look or what to say. Then he found himself relaxing and beginning to grin. Her eyes really were the brightest blue. The laugh started there and spread across her face.

Abruptly he was distracted by a rustle in the undergrowth behind her.

'What's that?' he said. 'There's something in the bushes.'

She didn't bother to look. 'Oh that. It's Verit.'

'It's a what?'

'Verit.' Yalka turned towards the disturbance and beckoned. 'Get 'ere, yer young crapper. Come on out.'

There was a rustle in the scrub and a small, scruffy boy emerged. He had a tangled mop of reddish brown hair, a sharp face and a pointed nose. He reminded Peglar of a little fox.

'Who is he? What's he doing in the bushes?'

She looked at Verit and her face softened. She held out her hand to him and tentatively, shyly, he edged closer and took it.

'He comes with me. I look after him. He's me brother.'

The boy's nose was runny and automatically he went to wipe it with the sleeve of his smock. Yalka put out a hand to restrain him but she was too slow.

'I look after him, an' he looks after me,' she said. 'We watch out for each other. Anybody tries anything with me and Verit'll have 'em.'

She said it as if daring Peglar to test its truth. He

doubted that Verit could do much, he was so small. Peglar looked at him and he stared back with the same blue, unblinking gaze as his sister.

'Hello, Verit,' Peglar said, trying to be friendly.

Verit's expression didn't alter.

'He don't talk,' said Yalka. 'He hasn't never talked. He can't. Can't hear neither.'

Peglar looked at Verit again, taking in this knowledge and trying to apply it to the boy he saw. He had a glimpse into a terrifying void of silence, where mouths moved, birds sang and music played with no effect, where the whole world was mime and where even the simplest requests were impossible.

'He won't be no bother.' Yalka swung her arm in a gesture of dismissal and Verit scampered back towards the bushes. There was a brief flurry and he was gone, swallowed by the vegetation.

'Where's he going?'

'He'll be off back to ours. To our granddad.'

Peglar tried to see where the boy had gone but he'd vanished. It seemed that like his sister he could flit around the city and the hill on which it stood like a ghost. Were all the children from the Settlements like them? How many were there?

'Our granddad's a rhymer,' Yalka said. It was a claim, made with pride. 'You know what a rhymer is?'

Peglar shook his head and the girl cast her eyes skywards, unable to comprehend such ignorance.

'A rhymer says what's going to happen. The future. It's done in rhymes. People come to our granddad, or sometimes he goes to them. He chews armanca weed and goes into a trance and then he can see into the future and he tells people what will be. In rhymes.'

Peglar didn't understand. 'What, all the time?'

'No, 'course not. He does it at pairings, birthdays, child namings, anything important where people want to know what's going to happen to 'em.'

Peglar wondered if this girl's grandfather could foretell how he would perform in the trials. He didn't believe that anyone could know the future, but it would be interesting to get his view.

'There's only granddad, Verit and me now.'

There was a silence. The 'now' seemed to be begging another question from Peglar, but he didn't know how to ask it. Instead he said, 'It was you who tried to get to my father at my Calling, wasn't it?' She nodded. 'Why? What did you want?'

'What do you think I wanted?' Peglar shrugged. 'Come here.' Yalka grabbed his hand and before he could snatch it away she pulled him towards the wall. She stopped at the shrine she'd been making when he'd first seen her. She stooped, picked up the picture and unrolled it. She looked at it for a moment before holding it out to Peglar. He pretended that he was seeing it for the first time.

'It's me sister.'

Peglar waited, and again studied the child in the drawing. He tried to see some resemblance to Yalka. It was just a child's face, a girl, short hair, open expression.

Yalka spoke again. 'She were finished off.'

'Finished off? You mean she's dead?'

Yalka nodded.

'When? How?'

'Posh boys killed her. Kids get into the city at night to thieve. Posh boys go round looking for 'em, and when they find 'em they kill 'em. They found her and they killed her. That's what I wanted to say to your old fella. He's supposed to be the boss man. He needs to get it stopped.'

She paused and looked down. She was sad, but not crying. Not then.

8

A BODY

Feldar had said to meet him in the courtyard by the Palace gate at the fifth bell but Peglar was there well before that. When he arrived the sun had not yet risen and a late frost still rimed the yard. He shivered and took a swing at the wall with his sandalled foot. It hurt, but the pain took his mind off his nervousness. This was the first trial. It could all go wrong, right here. He was still kicking the wall when he heard a voice behind him.

'Whoa, you'll have the building down! Don't destroy your father's Palace, save your energy.'

He hadn't heard Feldar approach and he felt silly, but before he could think of a reply a groom appeared leading a horse and a pony. Feldar ran his eye over the beasts, tightened a girth, slapped the horse's neck and swung himself smoothly into the saddle. He didn't wait and started towards the gatehouse without another word. The groom helped Peglar scramble onto the pony and he joined Feldar at the gate. The gateman lifted the bar, pushed open the big, wooden barrier and the two

rode out. Three mounted Household Guards were
waiting in the road outside and fell in behind them.

Peglar followed Feldar, watching his straight back,
his horse's backside and its casually flicking tail, while
the noise of hooves rang hollowly on the cobbles. Peglar
hadn't done much riding and he didn't enjoy it, finding
horses hard to fathom and unpredictable. Feldar, on the
other hand, was an expert horseman. Perhaps it was to
do with being confident, Peglar thought. But how did
you show that to an animal, particularly if you didn't
feel it? How did Feldar make his horse know who was
in charge?

Peglar studied him. He guessed that Feldar was
older than his mother but younger than Vancia, maybe
in his early forties. He was tall, with dark hair and firm
features. His face showed the outline of where a beard
would be if he had one. Peglar had never seen him
anything other than immaculate, his tunic clean and
pressed and his sandals well oiled. He gave no
indication that he was aware of Peglar's presence and
they wound through the empty streets in silence.

At the end of the road that ran along the backs of the
great houses they turned and started down the hill,
leaving the secluded mansions of the wealthy and
descending into the middle city. Peglar's pony was
warm and its breath billowed in the early chill. The
streets were quiet, no one else was about. Peglar had
slept badly and the warmth and rolling movement of his
mount made him feel sleepy.

He was dozing when he was startled by a cry from
one of the guards. Feldar turned his horse and they
looked in the direction the man was pointing. Farther
down the street, against the wall, there was what looked

like a bundle of rags. But there was something wrong. Even from this distance Peglar could see that they were not rags. They hurried forward, and Feldar slid to the ground. He grabbed Peglar's pony, turning it away, but it was too late, he had already seen.

'Who is it?'

Feldar shook his head. 'I don't know. It looks like a child. One of the street children I think.'

'Yes, sir,' said the guard who was squatting over the small bundle. 'It is a child, a little girl. She's been stabbed.'

'Is she dead?' said Peglar.

'Oh yes, she's dead all right.'

Feldar gave up trying to shield Peglar from the sight and went to the body. The child's smock was soaked in blood, the mouth was open and the eyes wide. Her smock was pulled up showing she had no undergarment. Feldar crouched and pulled it down to cover her.

'Her little finger's gone,' he said. 'Just like the others.'

Peglar stared at the girl's hand but it was hard to see the damage through the mess. Feldar went to his horse and took from the saddle bag a large cloth. He stooped and closed the dead child's eyes. Then he opened the cloth and covered her face. Peglar looked down at the small figure, amazed that so much blood could come from such a tiny frame.

Just then there was the sound of tramping feet and a patrol of Guardians came around the corner into the street and halted smartly behind them.

'Typical,' mumbled one of the Household Guards. 'They get here when it's all over.'

The Captain of the Guardians left his men and came towards them. He looked brisk and busy, ready to show these people how important he was, but then he saw the leopard crest on the tunics of the Guards and his manner changed. He nodded to Feldar, bowed to Peglar.

'Good morning, my lords.' He bent and peered under the cloth Feldar had placed over the child's face, taking a long look before replacing it. He stood up. 'It seems we've come too late.'

'Yes,' said Feldar, 'it seems you have.'

The Captain raised one of the child's arms. The whole corpse moved with it, as if she were a doll. 'Mm, she's rigid. Stiffness starts three or four hours after death, a bit sooner when it's cold, quicker still for a child. She's been here some time, though.' He examined the body, turning it so he could see the face. 'She's small, this one. No more than six or seven, I'd say.' He studied the smudgy brown footprints on the paving. 'By the look of it quite a few people were here with her. Another gang job, I should think.'

There followed a round of tedious questioning. Each of them separately – Peglar, Feldar and the three Household Guards – had to describe to the Captain how they had been riding down the street when they'd noticed the body. They explained how they'd thought it was a heap of rags until they'd seen the blood. Sometimes they were asked to repeat their stories, sometimes they were asked the same thing twice.

By now a small group had gathered, people from the houses around who had come out to see what all the fuss was about. A door opened in the wall near where the body lay and a woman pushed her way to the front. She ignored the Captain and curtseyed to Feldar.

'It may be nothing, my lord,…'

'Don't use 'my lord',' Feldar interrupted. 'I'm only the Master's Steward, not family. "Sir" will do.'

The woman curtseyed again. 'Yes, my lord, I mean, sir,' she said, hesitantly. 'It may be nothing really, sir, but I heard something last night. I heard some people in the street.'

'Where do you live?'

'Just here, sir.' The woman indicated the wall behind her. 'That's my window.'

'Did you see anything?'

'Not really, sir. There were some young men, but they weren't making much noise. They just seemed to be in a group, talking. I didn't think anything of it, I just thought they were going home late.'

'How many young men?'

'Four or five, sir.'

'Were they on foot?'

'Yes, sir. But they looked to be high people. You know, from the best families.'

'How could you tell that?'

She frowned. 'It's hard to say, sir. It was just something about them, their clothes and the way they carried themselves. Besides, it was after curfew. Only people from high families would dare to be out after curfew.'

'When did you see these men?'

'Oh late, my lord. Sir. I was in bed and had put the lamps out. But I'm a light sleeper, it doesn't take much to wake me, and I heard them.'

'Would you know them if you saw them again?' the Captain asked.

She shook her head. 'I don't think so. No, I wouldn't.

53

It was too dark and they were all in black and their faces were hidden. They looked young, though, just in the way they moved and acted.' She turned back to Feldar. 'I think they were armed, sir. One of them had a lamp and something glinted in the light. I think it was a blade, a dagger or something.'

'Did anyone else see them?' said the Captain.

The woman snorted. 'I tried to wake my husband but he wouldn't have it. Once he's gone off you could march the whole of the army down the street and he wouldn't hear them.' She looked down at the small body and Peglar saw a tear on her cheek. 'I wish I'd come out, though. I might have been able to save her, poor little mite.'

'Little mite?' The Captain was annoyed. 'Little thief, more like. If she hadn't crawled into the city after dark to steal she wouldn't be lying here now, would she?'

The woman looked at him, her eyes sad. 'No, but she didn't deserve to be murdered, did she?'

'I'm not saying she did,' said the Captain, sounding exasperated. 'What I'm saying is that if these children kept out of the city they wouldn't come to any harm. They should stay in the River Settlements where they belong.' He turned his back on her. 'Hey, you,' he shouted to two of his men. 'Get this mess out of the way,' indicating the girl. The woman watched him stride away, outrage on her face.

'Don't blame him,' Feldar said quietly. 'This is the sixth child murder and the Guardians haven't caught anybody yet. People are grumbling and I think he's feeling frustrated.'

Two Guardians appeared with a handcart and they lifted the body onto it. Another had a bucket of sand and started spreading it over the blood on the pavings. The other Guardian began to disperse the small group that had gathered.

The Captain returned. 'Thank you, gentlemen for helping with my questions. That's all I need from you. Please carry on with your business.'

Feldar remounted. 'Do you have any idea who's doing this?' he said.

The Captain didn't answer immediately. He was clearly weighing up how much to say, then he reflected that Feldar and particularly Peglar were important people.

'We have some evidence that supports the theory that these street murders are not all by the same people. Did you notice the child's forehead? There was the letter R drawn on it in her blood. This is the third one we've found marked with R, but we've found a triangle and a circle on the foreheads of the others.'

'What do you think it means?'

'Well, the R probably means rat, short for street rat. That's what people call these kids. We're not sure what the other symbols mean. We're trying to work that out.'

Feldar nodded. 'Well, good luck with it,' he said. And to Peglar, who was standing by his pony, 'Time to move on. The day is getting away from us and we have a lot to do.'

Feldar and the Household Guards remounted and rode slowly away. Peglar looked at his pony and circled it, trying to work out the best way to get on its back. Eventually he put a foot in one of the stirrups, hugged the animal's neck and clambered onto the patient beast. The Guardians were all busy and he hoped none of them had seen his ungainly exhibition.

A little way on Feldar and the Guards waited for him. No one wanted to say anything and for some time they rode together in silence. Peglar was thinking about Yalka and her dead sister, about the shrine and the flowers and the simple drawing.

'Was that girl from the River Settlements, like the Captain said?' he asked.

'I don't know,' said Feldar. 'That's where people say the street children come from. They must be churls because they're badly clothed and poorly nourished. They come in by night from outside the city and the River Settlements is the nearest place churls live.'

'Hasn't anybody been there to find out?'

Feldar snorted. 'You don't know the River Settlements, do you? The folk there hate city people. Even if you can manage to get in without being knifed no-one will talk to you. No one will say anything, nobody knows anything. Pure as driven snow, they are.' Feldar turned to look at Peglar. 'Hey, are you all right? You look a bit green.'

Peglar was remembering the dead girl. Gruesome images filled his head – her white face, her staring eyes, her gory clothes and her blood-matted hair. Abruptly he slithered from his pony, bent over in the gutter and retched. His stomach heaved but he'd not eaten and there was nothing there to vomit so he could only gag emptily. At first his cramping belly doubled him up and held him there, but after a while the turbulence died down and he could stand. He felt awful.

'I can't do this,' he said to Feldar, wiping his lips, his mouth sour with the taste of bile. 'I can't do the trial, not today.'

The Steward put a hand on his shoulder. His face

showed concern but his words were unwavering. 'I know, and I'm sorry, but you have no choice. Usually the trials take a fortnight each, what with practice and preparation. Six weeks altogether. Your father has allowed you three. The schedule is tight. This trial must be done today. You have to put what you've just seen out of your mind and focus on what you need to do. We're already late starting. We should get on with it.'

9

EARTH

The Trial of Earth was meant to be the easiest of the three; that was why it was always tackled first. Feldar had chosen the location, the sandy track behind the Arena where Peglar had been training with Cestris. Mangal was already there, seated on a stone bench across from the start line. Ragul and Burian were there too, and Peglar could feel their eyes on him as he slipped off his tunic and did the warm up routine Cestris had shown him. The nausea had gone but his stomach felt bruised.

'I thought you'd chickened out,' Ragul called. 'Thought you'd decided to save us all some trouble.'

'I didn't know he was going to be watching,' said Peglar.

'Of course he is,' said Feldar. 'He's desperate to win his bet and he thinks you, we, will try to cheat. Ignore him.'

Feldar took from his pack a sand-filled timer in a brass frame and set it down. This was the measuring device. The challenge was to complete four laps of the track before the sand could drain from its upper to its lower section. Peglar could cover short distances fairly quickly, but he was no good over longer ones. In all his practices he'd never managed to beat the timer. Mind you, he told himself, he hadn't really tried.

It began with Feldar reading from The Chronicles of Chamaris an account of a hero who had demonstrated the quality which was about to be tested. The story was of a warrior called Waldron, a lion of the first Golden Age, who, while on guard on a distant hill, spotted enemies approaching the city. He left his post and ran swiftly to sound the alarm. His speed saved the people from a surprise attack. While Feldar read, Peglar looked around. Farther along the track several athletes were practicing starts. They were bronzed, fit, muscular. They seemed creatures from a different world, Waldron's world, a world of strength, confidence, control.

'Are you ready?' Feldar asked.

He was not, but it didn't matter. He never would be.

'Yes,' he said, and took a couple of deep breaths. Luckily the morning was cooled by a fresh breeze and the heat had not yet built. When it did he would find breathing more difficult. Feldar had probably known that and it was why he'd wanted to start so early. Finding the dead child had delayed them, almost as if Ragul had planned it.

He tried to forget that. He tried to ignore Ragul and Burian watching. He tried to empty his mind of everything and concentrate on the track, his legs, the running. He was sick with dread. This was it. His first challenge, and it could be his last.

Feldar took the timer in one hand and raised the

other. 'Three, two, one, go!' His arm fell. He turned the timer. Peglar ran.

He knew before he'd gone fifty paces that it was not going well. He felt hopelessly awkward as he scrambled round the oval, and he was embarrassed to be so ungainly in front the athletes who were forced to interrupt their practice sprints to make way for him. Four times he circled the track, and when he got to the finish Feldar was looking grim.

Peglar's head was pounding, his chest heaving and he thought he might have pulled a muscle in his right leg.

'How far off was I?' he gasped.

'Count of seven,' the Steward replied, tight lipped. 'Maybe more.'

That was worse than he'd feared. He felt failure gnawing at his guts. He looked up to see Ragul and Burian swaggering towards them. Ragul had a smirk on his face and started braying while he was still some way off.

'Well, well, well. Over already. Who'd have thought that runt-boy would make it so easy for me?' He stopped in front of Feldar, and his tone hardened. 'I'll collect my stake from Mangal. You probably don't have what you owe me here, Steward,' he sneered, 'but you can pay me anytime. Anytime... today.'

Burian at his side sniggered and Ragul made to turn away, but Feldar restrained him with a hand on his arm. 'You are running ahead of yourself, my lord,' he said quietly, 'and of us. The trial is not yet over.'

Ragul looked down at Feldar's hand on his arm as if it was something that had been dead a long time. 'What do you mean, "not yet over"? We've all seen the pathetic little turd try to run the course and he failed.' He swept his arm round to encompass his witnesses — Burian, Mangal, the practicing athletes, everyone. 'What more do you need?'

Feldar shook his head. 'That was not the trial. What you have just seen was Peglar practicing for it, merely a warm up.'

Ragul started to protest but Feldar cut him off. 'The trial must be held today. However, there's no limit to the number of times Peglar may attempt it. So long as he completes it satisfactorily before sundown, he's through.'

Ragul looked incredulous. 'Nobody needs to do this trial more than once. It's the easiest of them all. It's only running!'

'Nevertheless, Steward Feldar is correct.' This was Mangal, who had lumbered across from his bench and come up behind Ragul and Burian. 'The trial may be done any number of times, as long as all the attempts are completed in the same day. So for now I shall retain your stake and we shall see what has transpired by sundown.'

Ragul shook himself free of Feldar's hand. 'Blood and bile!' he fumed. 'If this one's a problem he's got no hope with the others.' He picked up a pebble and Peglar thought for a second he was the target, but he spun away and hurled it in an angry arc towards the trees. Then he seized Burian by the arm and stamped away, back to the bench at the other side of the track where he sat down, legs apart, arms folded, peevish and sullen.

Peglar sat on the ground next to Feldar. There was nothing to be said. He simply had to run faster, that was all. He rubbed some oil into his legs and did some deep breathing, trying to relax.

'Ready for another go?'

Peglar nodded. 'I suppose so.'

This time he did better. He got a good start and hit the first bend well. He was going faster, although each time he passed Ragul and Burian they jeered. Then on the final circuit, just when he thought he was going to make it, he got a stitch, a pain like a spear driven into his side. He couldn't breath. He clenched his teeth and tried to hang on but it was no good. As he finished he saw that the top half of the timer was empty, there was no sand left. From across the track there was a slow handclap.

Peglar clutched his side, fell to his knees and pressed his forehead on the earth, waiting for the spasm to pass. After a minute the agony eased and he rolled onto his back. He felt the sun on his face and the breeze on his body. He felt tears. No matter how many times he scuttled round the track he could never do it fast enough. That was it. He was finding it harder to breath. He might as well chuck it in now. He cursed his bad fortune, his ungainly body.

Suddenly a shadow came between him and the sun. Peglar opened his eyes to see somebody looking down at him. He sat up, raising his hand to ward off the glare. At the same time the watcher squatted, and Peglar found himself looking into the face of Cestris.

'Hello,' he smiled. 'Pity about the stitch. Happens to me sometimes. How are you feeling?'

Peglar shook his head. 'I feel bad,' he said slowly, rubbing his side. 'I don't think I can do it.'

'Oh, I think you can,' said Cestris, standing up. 'I can

63

help you. Here.' He held out his hand and pulled Peglar effortlessly to his feet.

Across the track Ragul was watching keenly but he stayed on his bench.

'All right then,' said Cestris, walking over to the start line. 'To begin with, you should go round the track in the opposite direction from the way you've been running.'

Peglar was puzzled. How would that help?

Cestris put his hand on his shoulder. 'You see that clump of trees over there? They shield that side of the track from the wind, but as you come out from behind them you're running right into it. It's quite strong today. Go the other way and it will be at your back.'

Peglar could see at once what he meant. He had felt the effort of battling against the wind on each circuit. It hadn't occurred to him that he could do anything about it, he just circled as he'd always done, as they'd practiced.

'That's the first thing,' Cestris continued. 'The next is your third lap. I've been watching you, and you slow down. Your first lap is quite good, then towards the end of the second your speed drops. You pick up again on your fourth but you don't make up the time you've lost on the third.'

Peglar shook his head. He thought he'd been running at the same speed all the time. 'I'm sorry. I didn't know I was doing that.'

'You don't need to apologise. The first step in dealing with a problem is to recognise it. The second is to do something about it. Here's what we'll do about this one. I'll be your pacemaker. You have to complete the trial on your own but there's nothing that says you can't have someone to run with you for part of the way. I'll join you on lap one and pick up your stride. Half way through lap two I'll take the lead, keeping the same pace for lap three. You'll have to stay with me. I'll drop out at the start of lap four and leave you to finish on your own. If you like, if you agree.'

If he agreed! Peglar thought that if Cestris suggested he dance backwards across upturned tacks he would agree. His worry was that he wouldn't be able to keep up.

'Yes,' he said. He felt a surge of optimism. Could he do it? Cestris seemed to think so. Perhaps he could. 'Thank you.'

Cestris smiled. 'Good. Then let's go.'

Feldar couldn't be involved in coaching him and he had remained in the background. Now he came forward and Peglar took up position on the start line as before, with the inside of the track to his left. Cestris shook his head, took him firmly by the shoulders and turned him around. 'This way. It will be easier, I promise you.'

Peglar felt stupid. 'Oh, yes. Thank you. I'd forgotten.'

Cestris trotted across to the other side of the track and stopped right in front of the bench where Ragul and Burian sat. The pair stared straight ahead as if he wasn't there, still as stones and about as cheerful.

Peglar found running round the track in the opposite direction easier from the start. As he drew level with Cestris his friend fell in beside him. They came to the last quarter of the circle and left the shelter of the trees. The effect was dramatic. Previously when he'd got to this spot it had been like suddenly picking up a weight. Now it was like a hand in the small of his back, urging him forward, sweeping him on. Why hadn't he thought of it? The effect lasted for less than a quarter of the circuit but it felt fantastic.

Part way through lap two Cestris strode into the lead. He was running easily, not even panting. Peglar was determined to keep up with him and he gritted his teeth, forcing his legs to move, gasping for breath. He knew that he was going faster and he began to feel the strain. He was fearful that his stitch would come back, but just as he was starting to struggle he emerged again from behind the trees and the wind caught him and bore him on.

As he approached the line for lap four Peglar saw the timer and his heart leapt. It looked as though there was plenty of sand left. He was going to do it, he really was. Cestris peeled away, leaving him on his own. 'Now go!' he shouted after him. 'Go, Peglar! Run!'

Peglar's legs raced and his feet pounded. The wind was at his back once more. Each stride thrust him forward. He was on springs, on wings. The finishing line was ahead, closer, at his feet, past. He stopped and bent forward, hands on knees, head thumping, fighting for breath.

Then a hand slapped him on the back. He looked at the timer on the stone. There was sand to spare. Cestris took his hand. 'Well done.'

Peglar shook his head. He didn't know what to say to this hero who had come in such a dramatic way to his aid. 'Brilliant. Wonderful. Thank you for helping me.' He was so overjoyed he could have run through the streets shrieking, naked as he was. Cestris grinned, gave him a thumbs up and jogged back to join the group training on the far side.

Peglar was brought down to earth by a harsh voice

behind him. 'All right,' snarled Ragul. 'You've scraped through this one, runt-boy, but there are two more to go. They're harder, and you won't have your fancy-boy helper for those.' He nodded to Feldar. 'Get your money ready, Steward.'

He walked away, his arm around Burian's shoulders, but Peglar wasn't interested in them.

10

OVERHEARD

Peglar had expected the Trial of Earth to take him all day and when he returned to the Palace he was at a loose end. There was nothing he could do to prepare for the other two. He could practice his swimming for the Trial of Water but he didn't think he needed to do that; it was the one he was most confident about. And there was no preparation anyone could do for the Trial of Fire. It was what it was: a nightmare, and the one he was dreading the most. He had some old books from the Palace Library about the history and constitution of Chamaris – there would be an examination in these immediately before his initiation – but he didn't feel like spending the afternoon with them. Instead he'd go to the Citadel. He needed some peace and quiet. Might the strange churl girl, Yalka, be at the Citadel again? And her ghostly little brother, Verit?

He was approaching the Atrium on his way out of the Palace when he heard his father's angry voice.

'It has to be stopped! The situation is getting out of control.'

Peglar waited at the entrance to the colonnaded space and cautiously peered in. With his father were Thornal, Feldar, Styron and Lembick. Peglar hid behind one of the pillars.

'People are upset,' Karkis was saying. 'They want something done. They're not directing their anger at me, not yet, but they could soon start.'

'Oh hardly, my lord,' said Thornal.

Karkis fixed him with a cold stare. 'Yes, Marshal. Feldar has been telling me that there was another incident this morning. It was near the spot where a body was found last week. And there was that kerfuffle at the Ceremonium at Peglar's Calling when some hooligan ran out from the crowd. The Guardians were quick to stop it but if there'd been more of them it could have been nasty. These things are orchestrated by my enemies and they are increasing. I don't like it.' He looked hard at Lembick.

'That was a petty disturbance, my lord,' Thornal said soothingly. 'The Guardians tell me it was most likely some scum from the River Settlements. She got away but people like that are not very bright and inevitably they're caught. And most of the people I talk to think the street rats get what they deserve.'

'Surely not,' said Styron. 'Nobody in their right mind wants the streets of Chamaris strewn with the bodies of dead children.'

'Children who have no right to be here. Children who have come into the city secretly and illegally, by night, to steal.'

Lembick, who had taken to pacing up and down, stopped in front of Karkis. 'The people who are angry have a point. You, my lord, are Master of the City. It is your duty to find out who is causing this slaughter and stop it. If you are unable to do that, then you should turn to someone who can.'

Karkis scowled. There was a chilly silence while the threat contained in Lembick's words hung in the air.

Thornal spoke again. 'My Guardians have been making enquiries and we now have a pretty good idea of what's going on.'

'Explain,' said Karkis.

'Well, my lord, all the murdered children must be from the slums outside the city. It is hard to say exactly where because the next of kin never come forward to claim the bodies. They seem to be organised. Somehow they get into the city at night, after the gates have been locked, and target the homes of the minor merchants and small tradesmen in the middle city. They are expert thieves. They are small and quick. They are good at dodging the Guardians, and on the few occasions we've managed to nab a live one they've got away.'

Feldar started to speak but Thornal hurried on. 'The murders follow a pattern, my lord. The child is killed with a knife and the body is left in a public place where it's sure to be found. The little finger of the right hand is cut off and a mark is made on the cheek or forehead in the victim's own blood. It could be that the severed finger is used to make this mark.'

'Yes, yes, yes.' Karkis was irritated by the long-winded speech. 'I know all this, but what does it mean?'

'I am not entirely sure, my lord,' Thornal answered. 'There are some pointers, though. For example, the marks on the faces of the bodies. We've noted three: a triangle, a circle and one that looks like the letter 'R'. We think these are the signatures of whoever is claiming, the kill.'

'"Claiming the kill?"' said Styron incredulously. 'What do you mean?'

'My Lord, these marks appear to be the symbols of gangs. We think that there is some sort of contest going on between them to kill the most urchins.'

'A killing competition?'

'That is what it looks like.'

'What evidence do you have for this?'

There was a silence, which Thornal allowed to continue for a moment while he enjoyed his prominence. 'The Captain of the Guardians who attended the scene this morning – I believe Steward Feldar was also present, and your son – interviewed a woman. She reported that during the night she was disturbed by a commotion and saw some men dressed in black. She thinks there were five or six of them. She says she assumed that they were young men on their way home after a night out and she returned to bed. However, it's likely that this group were the perpetrators.'

'I saw the dead girl and I heard this woman,' said Feldar. 'Her account seems believable and the Marshal's theory feasible.'

Karkis looked grave. 'So you are saying that I have in my city some sort of grisly game in which gangs of youths go out after dark looking for stray children, and when they find them they murder them?'

'Yes, my lord. That is exactly what I am saying.'

'Blood and bile!' Karkis fumed.

'What about the fingers?' said Lembick.

'We have not found any of the fingers. We think they must be taken as tokens, souvenirs'

'This is preposterous,' spluttered Karkis. 'The reputation of Chamaris is at stake. The envoy of Semilvarga has had the impertinence to offer help in maintaining law and order in our streets. Help from Semilvarga, would you believe? It's insufferable. We're looking depraved and unable to contain a few churls. Worse than that, we are looking stupid. I want this settled, I want action, Marshal. I shall issue an order. Any Guardian who manages to catch one of these children will receive a handsome reward. There will also be a reward for the capture of a child murderer, and anyone found guilty of such a crime will be punished to the limit of the law.'

'Master, you might not want to be quite so harsh,' said Feldar, quietly.

'What do you mean? Why not?' Karkis was annoyed by his Steward's intervention, but he had a high enough opinion of Feldar to listen to what he had to say.

'If Marshal Thornal is right about the gangs,' Feldar explained, 'it is probable that the young men involved are from high families.'

Karkis didn't like the sound of that. He'd assumed the gangs came from the middle classes, the people who were suffering from the robberies. That was logical; it was also politically convenient. It would not be good if it turned out that the they came from the families of the nobility. 'Why?' he snapped.

'I suggest, my lord,' said Feldar, 'that the sons of merchants or tradesmen would not have the audacity to be out after curfew. Besides, a young man is hardly likely to spend night after night roaming the streets if he

73

has to rise the next day to be at work. Common sense tells me that these young men don't work, they are leisured.'

'Mm. Perhaps,' said Karkis. He was not convinced.

'There's something else,' said Feldar, 'Whoever is doing this must have some influence.'

'Explain.'

'The streets are patrolled throughout the night by Guardians. After the first two murders the Marshal increased the number of patrols.'

'Yes,' Thornal agreed, 'and I've bumped them up again since.'

'Just so,' said Feldar. 'The main streets are now under fairly continuous watch from dusk till dawn. Yet not a single person has been apprehended, not one, let alone a gang. None of the patrols has reported even a sighting.'

'What are you suggesting?' said Thornal, sensing trouble.

'With great respect,' said Feldar, 'I'm suggesting that I don't believe it's possible for several gangs to be out and about at night and not be seen. That is, not unless they are able to persuade the Guardians to look the other way. Only young men with wealth and influence would be in a position to do that.'

Thornal looked as though he was about to explode. 'Are you suggesting that my men are being bought off? That they are taking bribes?'

Before Feldar could reply, Karkis cut in. 'Whether he is or not, he's right that nobody has been caught, Marshal. I shall expect to hear very soon that you have made some arrests. I want this problem done with.'

'Master, it will be.'

'Very good. Leave us.'

Thornal bowed. He was angry, and he glared at Feldar as he went. There was a moment's silence after he'd gone. Then Karkis addressed his Steward.

'I want you to keep an eye on this situation, Feldar. If city officials are being bribed I need to know.'

'Of course, my lord,' said Feldar. Then he added, as if the idea had just come to him, 'There is, of course, something else that could be done.'

Karkis looked interested. 'Yes?'

'My lord, one way to stop the killings is to catch the killers. Another is to remove the killers' prey.'

'Stop the children getting into the city? We've tried that. They find ways in that we don't know about, and some of them could wriggle through the eye of a needle.'

'Indeed, sir, but what I mean is that we remove whatever it is that's forcing them to enter the city in the first place.'

Karkis frowned. 'What do you mean?'

'My lord, how many children have been killed?'

'Six. You know that,' Karkis said crossly. He didn't like question and answer games, not unless he was the one asking the questions.

'Yes, sir. Now if you would, imagine yourself a child living in the River Settlements. You are motivated to come into the city to steal, but you know that six others have been murdered doing exactly that. It must occur to you that if you do the same, the same thing will happen to you. Moreover, the children target the middle city, not the wealthy houses. They take a few coins, some cheap jewellery, an ornament or two. These are hardly things worth risking your life for.'

Karkis was intrigued but couldn't see Feldar's point. 'So what are you saying, Steward?'

'My lord, I think someone is forcing them to do this. They must be frightened of coming into the city, but they must be even more terrified of what will happen to them if they don't. Someone is controlling them and making them behave this way.'

There was a long pause while Karkis thought this over. Then he rapped his staff on the marble floor. 'Find out who this "someone" is.'

'Yes, my lord.'

Karkis turned into the corridor towards his study, his staff tapping on the marble as he went. Feldar followed.

There was a long silence. Styron stood on the other side of Peglar's pillar, so close he could have reached round and touched him. Lembick was a little way off. Finally he spoke.

'What did you think of that?' There was no reply from Styron, and Lembick continued. 'Karkis is not up to the job any more. He gives orders but only when somebody else has told him what they should be. We're in a mess. All this business of the child thieves and the gangs and the murders. It's a complete shambles, and he doesn't seem able to do anything about it.'

'I don't want to hear talk like that,' said Styron. 'Karkis is a great Master of the City. Under the rule of the leopard we have had many years of peace and prosperity.'

'But there are other problems as well as the child murders,' said Lembick. 'The tribute cities are taking liberties. Rasturoth was slow in paying its tithe and the army had to step in as a show of force. Now Semilvarga looks like doing the same, Halish-Karnon too. We depend on the tithes. Without them we're in trouble.' Lembick moved closer. 'I know you are Karkis's friend, but I say this to you.' He was speaking very quietly now, so quietly that Peglar had to strain to hear him. 'There is a growing feeling that the city deserves a leader who will take charge, get things done. It's time for a change.'

11

ARTIST

Peglar would never have admitted it, but all the way up the hill to the Citadel he was thinking about Yalka and hoping she might be there. He didn't understand her and he was actually quite nervous of her, of what she might say, what she might do. She was like no one he had ever come across before. Of course he'd seen lots of churls about in Chamaris. Troops of them flocked through the gates every morning to work in the middle city, and left at curfew to go back to their hovels clustered outside the walls. The high families didn't use many churls. For most things they had their own servants, who were a class above the churls and had been with their masters and mistresses for many years. The few churls they had were slaves, kept to carry out the worst jobs. So he'd often seen churls, but never spoken to one. He'd never even been close to one and had always assumed that they were like everyone said: dirty, smelly, lice-ridden, stupid. Not at all like Yalka.

She was not where she had been before, and Peglar experienced a pang of disappointment. Then he saw her.

She was sitting on a stone a little way off, with her back towards him and her head bent.

She looked to be working on something. He didn't want to disturb her so he moved quietly, and when he got closer he stopped to try to make out what she was doing. She was so engrossed, so still, that she hadn't heard him approach. She looked to be writing something, working with a stubby pencil on a piece of card. He saw that she wasn't wearing her churl smock but instead a short, earth-coloured shift, and there was a scarf of some thin, green material loosely coiled around her neck. The breeze nudged it off her shoulder and she absent-mindedly readjusted it. He moved to the side, better to see what she was doing and something, the crunch of a pebble or simply a change in the light, betrayed him.

She reacted instantly. With a snarl she leapt from the rock, twisting in the air like a cat as she came at him. Peglar had a glimpse of bared teeth, glaring eyes, the glint of a knife blade before she hit him, an explosion of muscle and bone. She struck him with such force the impact knocked him backwards. He felt the knife rake his cheek. He fell hard, jarring his shoulder on the iron earth. She landed on top of him and her knee jerked up, missing his groin but landing painfully on his thigh. He cried out and she jumped back and glared down at him, breathing heavily. Peglar levered himself up, ready to roll away and run if she came at him again. He clutched his shoulder. It hurt. His face stung. Gingerly he felt it, expecting to see his fingers come away covered in blood, but they didn't. He looked for the knife and was relieved to see it on the ground, out of reach. He raised his good arm in a gesture of defence and, he hoped, peace.

Abruptly the tension drained from her. Her shoulders sagged and she sank to the ground in front of him, peering with concern at his face. She put out her hand to touch his cheek but he recoiled.

'It's only a scratch,' she said. She held up her forefinger and showed a single talon standing out from her other, broken nails. 'If it had been the knife your stupid face would've been hanging off by now.'

Peglar was grateful it hadn't been the knife. Nevertheless, the wound was smarting. The tension was ebbing and he was feeling angry. Slowly and painfully he got to his feet and flexed his shoulder. He was relieved he could move it.

'Why did you attack me like that? You could have hurt me.' She had. His face throbbed and his shoulder burned.

She looked at the ground. 'I didn't see it was you,' she said. 'I looked up and the sun was behind you, in me eyes. I couldn't see your face. I thought you was a Guardian.' She pointed at his grey clothing. 'I thought you was one of them, come to get me. I'm sorry.'

Peglar knew that it wasn't easy for her to apologise. He propped himself against the rock. It hadn't occurred to him that the uniform of a candidate for initiation was the same colour the Guardians wore. It seemed to him that she could have taken more trouble to see who he was before attacking, but perhaps the need for immediate reaction was something she'd had to learn from experience. Neither of them spoke. The sting in his cheek was easing, but now his thigh had started to hurt from where her knee struck.

'Anyway,' Peglar said at last, 'what's Verit doing? I thought he was supposed to keep watch for you.'

She looked at him suspiciously, judging whether he was being serious or making fun of her. 'Verit i'n't here. He's with our granddad. He's rhyming at a pairing today and he's taken Verit with him.'

It seemed odd to Peglar, taking a deaf and dumb boy to an event where somebody would be declaring prophecies in verse.

'He takes Verit 'cos people feel sorry for him 'cos he can't talk an' he can't hear,' Yalka explained. 'Then they give granddad more money. Out o' pity.'

Peglar was horrified. Using Verit's disabilities like that was exploiting the boy, and it was taking advantage of people's better feelings.

'Is that how you live?' he asked. 'By trading on people's good nature?' It came out more sharply than he'd meant but Yalka wasn't at all defensive.

'It's how we have to live. We haven't got no choice. We've got nothing, so we take what we can.'

'You mean you take things that aren't yours?'

'Why not? You do.'

Peglar was dumbfounded. 'I do not!' he said, heatedly. 'My family is wealthy, but it's honest.'

Yalka's eyes rounded in incredulity. 'Honest? Honest? Is it honest to take people's land? and their homes? To take their work and pay 'em such a scrappy little bit they can't hardly live on it? To buy stuff for one price and sell it for more, without doing anything to it? To lock food away so there's a shortage and the price goes up, and then sell it to them as is desperate for more than it should be? To fiddle the law so it's always on your side? That's honest, is it? That's fair?'

She stared at him, defiant, challenging. She didn't understand.

'You can't possibly compare what my family does with what you and your friends in the Settlements get up to, with creeping into the city to steal. There's a difference.'

'Yes,' she said, 'there is. We only take from people who have got more than us. You take from people who have got less.'

Peglar's cheeks burned with anger. This girl really was too much. 'No, we don't! Anyway, that doesn't make what you do right.'

'Don't it?'

There was a long pause. Peglar had to admit that it was easy to make moral judgments when you had everything you wanted; probably it was not so easy if you were hungry, when the extra payment that her grandfather might get by parading his deaf, mute grandson could make the difference between being able to eat and going to bed supperless.

'Anyway,' he said at last, and to change the subject, 'what were you writing?'

'Writing?' Yalka snorted. She looked round, picked up the piece of card from where it had fallen and clutched it to her chest. Then she came to a decision and held it out.

Peglar turned it over, and gasped. Nothing had prepared him for what he saw. It was not writing Yalka had been doing; it was the most wonderful drawing. She had created a flower head in intricate and astonishing detail. It was one of the yellow, daisy-like blooms that grew all over the Citadel. The representation was exact. Peglar had seen illustrations in books in the Palace Library that were not nearly as good. Petals, filament, anther, sepal, even the tiny hairs at the top of the stalk, each was beautifully executed, every line perfect, the whole given depth and texture by the skilful use of shading. How could she have done this with a single blunt pencil. He studied it for a long time. Yalka watched him anxiously, and it occurred to him that his judgement might matter to her.

'This is amazing,' he said. 'Where did you learn to draw like this?'

She shrugged. 'Nowhere. Granddad taught me a bit, but I've been drawing since I were a kid. I like to draw when I can, but it's hard to get the stuff.'

Peglar looked at the scruffy, salvaged card, at the pencil almost too short to grip. 'You're very good,' he said.

She shrugged again and dropped her eyes, and for the first time he saw her redden. He wondered if she was aware of the quality of what she'd done.

'You can have it if you want.' Although she said it casually, Peglar could see that this was an important gesture, perhaps a peace offering after her attack and their argument.

'I'd love to have it.' he said. 'I'll buy it from you.'

She looked offended. 'Don't be daft. I'm giving it you. It's only a picture.'

'Thank you,' he said. Verit was virtually begging and the family were desperately poor but Yalka still had her pride. He was chastened. He held the drawing out to her. 'Would you sign it?'

She looked puzzled. 'How d'you mean?'

'That's what artists do when they've finished a picture. They sign it.'

'With their name?'

'Yes.'

She thought for a moment. 'All right.'

She picked up the pencil from the rock. The point had broken. She retrieved the knife and worked on the stub, shortening it still further and shaping the end to a small cone. Then she took the card and squatted down. Slowly and deliberately she incised a letter 'Y' in the corner. She looked at it, blew off the pencil dust and handed it to him.

'What about the rest?'

She frowned. 'What rest?'

'The rest of your name.'

'That is me name. There.' She pointed at the Y. 'That's it.'

Then he realised. She couldn't do any more. She didn't know how to write.

'And I'm sorry about yer face,' she said. Reflexively she touched her own cheek, the purple-pink blotch. She saw him looking. 'It's a whore mark,' she said. Peglar didn't know what she meant. 'This on my face. You know, whores? Women what do it for money?'

Of course Peglar knew what a whore was. Ragul often boasted about going with whores, three in one night he once claimed.

The girl didn't wait for him to reply. 'There's a crazy old man goes about looking for girl babies,' she continued. 'If he finds one that's sleeping and there's nobody about he puts a snake on her face. The snake sucks her blood and leaves a mark. No decent man will pair with a girl who's got that, so all she can do to get by is whoring.' There was a pause. 'That's what they say,' she added, and she wound the green scarf over her head and across her face to hide the mark.

She fell silent and Peglar watched her. She was

striking, but it wasn't the same as the prettiness of Malina and her crowd. They spent a lot of time pampering themselves, curling hair, plucking brows, practicing make-up. Not this girl. Those bright blue eyes and the startling yellow hair needed no adornment. She was quite a bit shorter than Malina and that created the impression of a child, but although thin she clearly had a woman's body under her shift.

'I'm not,' she said, interrupting his thoughts.

Peglar was puzzled. 'Not what?'

'Not a whore. Just in case you was getting any ideas.'

'I wasn't, I mean I hadn't. That is, I didn't think you were,' Peglar stammered.

''Course you did. Everybody does. But it's a birth mark. I was born with it. They run in families. Verit has one on his leg. Our granddad has one over his heart. The one on Verit's leg means he's a good runner, an' he is. He can run quicker than anyone you've ever seen. The one on our granddad's chest is the sign of a rhymer.'

Meeting Yalka again didn't make her any easier to understand, or render some of the things she did and said less shocking. She had no idea of good manners or polite behaviour. Her manners and language were terrible. She refused to be impressed by his father's position, or The House of the Leopard and its wealth. Despite, or perhaps because of this, Peglar found himself fascinated by her and enjoying the time he spent with her. He looked forward to seeing her again, and he knew what he would do; something that would please her, impress her, and help her.

12

WEASEL FISH

Like the other challenges, the test for the Trial of Water was simple. The first test had been to move quickly. This one wasn't a matter of speed, it was endurance.

Peglar was a good swimmer. His slim build and his height meant he was able to move easily through water, and his long arms propelled him effectively. He was more confident about this trial than about either of the other two. That was until he learnt where it was to take place.

The location would be an inlet a little way up the coast. It was called Lovers' Creek, but its romantic name was misplaced. It was fed by mountain streams and was icy cold, even in high summer. There were strong currents and, some said, sudden whirlpools. It was rumoured that there were clumps of seaweed with dark, oily tendrils that would wrap around a swimmer's legs. There were stories of other horrors: jellyfish with lethal stings, lobsters with poisonous claws, nameless creatures with hungry eyes and fearful teeth that lurked beneath rocks to snap at the unwary. Peglar tried to dismiss these tales as so much gossip, but he found himself thinking of them increasingly as the time for the trial drew near.

There hadn't been much preparation for this one. He swam in the sea a few times and he did some work in the gymnasium with Cestris, designed to build his stamina. He felt relaxed and confident, and the afternoon before the appointed day he was in the Palace garden playing compass, a game that involved tossing small hoops over pegs. He was trying for a 'triple', three hoops thrown at once to land on three different pegs. He'd managed it before, but not today. Today the hoops were going everywhere except where they should. He was squaring up for another shot when he heard a shout and saw Ragul swaggering across the grass towards him. As usual Burian was in tow. Peglar's heart sank. What did they want?

'Hey, runt-boy, you need to see this,' Ragul called when he was still some way off. He looked to be holding something in a clenched fist. He stopped in front of him, dropping his voice confidentially as if letting Peglar in on a secret. 'Wha'd'ya think? Buri was fishing this morning and guess what he caught. A weasel fish. Yes, really. And look what he found inside it.'

Weasel fish had a bad reputation and people were wary of them, but Peglar had only ever seen a stuffed one in the City Museum. Cautiously he held out his hand to take what Ragul was wanting to show him. His brother opened his fingers and something dropped onto Peglar's palm. It was cold and slimy. He'd been prepared for it to be nasty, but even so he felt a shudder of revulsion and let whatever it was drop on the ground.

'Go on, have a look,' urged Ragul. 'It won't bite.'

Peglar squatted and examined the thing. It was a small stick, slightly bent, and bleached white. It looked like... but no, it couldn't be.

'Tell him, Buri,' said Ragul, grinning.

Burian edged forward and sniggered. 'I caught this weasel fish, you see, and I cut it open, and I found this, right there, in its belly.' Peglar peered at the object. 'It's a finger,' Burian added.

Peglar looked at the tiny, white stump more closely. Was it a finger? It could be but it was small. A child's finger? He felt a wave of nausea. What had happened to its young owner? Had the finger been bitten off while the infant was playing at the sea's edge? Had it run screaming from the water, waving its bleeding hand? Or had it been swimming? Had a shoal of weasel fish attacked the child when it was away from the shore, pulling it under the surface where its cries were silenced by the waves as it sank in a crimson cloud? Would other fingers, ears, bits of flesh and bone be found if other weasel fish were disembowelled?

Ragul stooped, picked up the object and held it out. Peglar took a step back and Ragul laughed. 'Weasel fish have got wicked teeth,' he said. 'I think that old weasel fish must have just swum up and bitten this kid's finger clean off, don't you?' He took a dirty cloth from his pocket, wrapped the object in it and put it back in his tunic. Then, seemingly struck by another thought, he looked to Burian. 'Hey, Buri. Tell runt-boy here where you were when you caught it.'

'Oh, yes,' said Burian, taking his cue. 'Lovers' Creek. I was fishing in Lovers' Creek.'

'How about that?' said Ragul, with a look of triumph. 'Lovers' Creek, eh. There must be loads of weasel fish there.'

Peglar felt his stomach churn.

13

WATER

The day was dull, the sky leaden and the air cold. It took Peglar and Feldar a good hour to ride to Lovers' Creek from the city, and when they got there he was disheartened to see the water looking dark and forbidding, with grey waves lapping sullenly on the shore.

The story which Feldar read aloud to set the trial in context was in contrast to the bleak setting. It went like this.

In days gone by a poor youth, called Sharaman, loved a beautiful girl from a high family. Because Sharaman was of low birth the girl's father refused to agree to a pairing, so the couple determined to run away. The father discovered their plan, and to thwart them he imprisoned his daughter in a tower far from the city, on the opposite side of a wide creek. He declared that because she had disobeyed him she would spend the rest of her days locked in there, weaving tapestries for his bedchamber. Sharaman discovered where his beloved had been taken and set out to rescue her. However, her father got wind of this too and he hurried in pursuit. Sharaman reached the inlet first, leapt from his horse, plunged into the water and started to swim across to the tower. His pursuers had heard about the perils of the creek – the currents, the weeds, the sea monsters – and they were afraid. They refused to swim and instead galloped on horseback all the way along one shore, around the head of the creek and down the other side. By the time they reached the tower the couple were gone. It was because of this story that the channel had been given the name Lovers' Creek.

Peglar looked across the broken water. The far shore seemed a long way off.

'A thousand paces, give or take,' said Feldar, answering his unspoken question.

'Where's the tower?'

'There, or what's left of it.' Feldar, pointed to a heap of tumbled stones on the far shore. 'The girl's father was so enraged when he found his daughter and her lover gone that he tore it down, they say with his bare hands. That's where you have to swim. From here to there, just like Sharaman.'

'But he had a girl to swim to,' Peglar said, putting on a lightheartedness that he didn't feel.

Feldar laughed. 'Well, you'll just have to imagine her, won't you. Keep you warm in the water.'

A loud voice behind him made Peglar jump. 'A bit rough today, runty one. Weasel fish can hunt better when the sea's choppy. Easier to sneak up on their prey.' Ragul and Burian laughed.

Ragul picked up a flat pebble, crouched and hurled it so that it skimmed the top of a wave. 'Just to get their attention,' he said. 'Let them know that lunch is on its way.' He laughed again.

Peglar slipped off his tunic and handed it to Feldar, who would follow him in a boat. He stood at the water's edge, naked and shivering, and dabbled his foot in the shallows. It was freezing. A greenish grey scum coated the pebbles and there was the smell of something rotting. The forest of weeds that covered the seabed in all directions writhed in the swell. All manner of things could be lurking amongst them. He looked at the remains of the tower that seemed so distant, and he was haunted by fears of what might be waiting for him between here and there.

To his left was a jetty. It looked rotten and derelict, and it creaked loudly as Mangal walked along it. Two small rowing boats were tied there, with servants on the oars. Feldar and Mangal boarded one, the vessel lurching madly as Mangal settled himself at the stern. Ragul and Burian took the other.

Feldar raised his hand for the start and Peglar edged a few more steps into the sea. The pebbles were sharp and bit into his feet. The cold water was like metal braces clasping his legs. His heart was pounding and he felt fear gnawing his insides.

There was a shout from Feldar. 'Are you going to swim this or do we have to to sit here all day?'

'If a weasel fish bites his dick off, can I have it?' Burian cackled.

'A weasel fish wouldn't be able to find it,' Ragul answered. 'It's too small!' They both convulsed with laughter.

Peglar clenched his teeth, gathered his resolve and waded in. He winced and sucked in air when the water reached his stomach. Then he shut his eyes and plunged. The cold smacked into him, taking his breath away. He thrashed in panic, spluttering and swallowing brine before managing to control himself.

The sea was so salty that it was easy to float, but swimming was unpleasant. Fronds of weed brushed his ankles and he gasped as he swam into an even colder current, a finger of one of the streams that fed the creek. He tried to see what was below him and imagined being stalked by terrifying, menacing creatures, brooding just out of sight. He forced them out of his mind and concentrated on finding a rhythm and swimming steadily. He didn't feel as cold now but his shoulders were already starting to ache. He raised his head. The tower seemed no nearer. In fact it looked further away than it had when he started.

'Here, grab this.' Feldar's boat had come up close behind him and the steward was leaning over the prow. He tossed a rope into the water and Peglar seized it. 'The current's pulling you out to sea,' Feldar explained. 'Hold on while we tow you back in.'

The oarsman began to row towards the head of the creek while Peglar gripped the rope, grateful for the chance to rest.

There was an indignant shout from further away. 'Hey! What's going on? You can't do that.' Ragul was standing up in his boat. 'You can't pull him. That's illegal.'

'We're taking him back into the creek,' Feldar called. 'The current's strong today and it's dragging him out. We're allowed to tow him in, so long as we don't take him forward and shorten the distance he has to swim.'

Ragul was not happy. 'Well it looks like a trick to me.

Just make sure you pull him straight in and not towards the tower. I'll be watching.'

'What the Steward is doing is perfectly acceptable,' Mangal answered. 'I have a fix on that large boulder on the shore. That was the point Peglar had reached when the tow began and I'll ensure that's where he starts when he's been drawn back in.'

Ragul wasn't satisfied by this and made their oarsman manoeuvre his boat to seaward and align it so that he would be able to tell if Peglar was pulled any nearer to the tower. The result was that Feldar erred on the side of caution, and Peglar was convinced he was being taken closer to the shore from which he had started.

His shoulders felt easier for the rest, but the break meant he'd got colder and he could scarcely swim for shivering. He gritted his chattering teeth and concentrated on breathing in the way he'd been shown and trying to do the long, steady strokes he had practiced.

'Look, Buri, isn't that a weasel fish?' Ragul's voice came clearly across the water. He was looking over the side of the boat and pointing downwards. Peglar had a vision of sharp, snapping teeth and his stomach heaved.

'Yes,' said Burian. 'I think it is. And that's another, just there among the weeds.'

Peglar swam, and swam, and swam. He didn't watch the tower but he kept his head down and his arms circling mechanically. When he did look up his goal still seemed a long way off. He felt a twinge of cramp in his calf but he swam on. The salt stung his eyes and lips, but he swam on. He thought of the vastness of the sea, his father's vessels with their leopard flags working the coast and striking across the ocean to distant lands, places he had only seen in books and heard of in stories. Would he get any of the ships when his father held the Sharing? Would he sail with them? How long had he been swimming? He had no idea. His head felt light. It was becoming harder and harder to move his legs, but he kept his arms churning. Time, place, motion became distant, his mind a blur. He could hear music, birdsong. Was he becoming delirious? Feldar had warned him about exhaustion. What was it Cestris had told him to remember? Breath deeply, keep calm, keep the rhythm going.

Something brushed his leg and he winced. He tried to look down and thought he saw a shape flash past. A weasel fish! He panicked and flapped his arms, expecting any second to feel razor teeth ripping his foot, tearing at his thigh, his arm, his groin. He took in a mouthful of water and struggled. He could barely open his eyes, but when he did he was astonished to see the remains of the tower close, no more than thirty paces away.

He ducked his head and swam fiercely, desperate to get out of the water, to race away from whatever might be in there. His arms flailed. He couldn't breath, couldn't think, couldn't feel. Then his knee struck something hard and his feet met the seabed. He staggered, slipped, tripped and fell at the water's edge.

Strong hands grabbed him. Feldar helped him up. Mangal gave him a blanket and he clutched it gratefully. His teeth were chattering, and not only from the cold.

'You did it!' said Feldar, raising his hand in salute. 'I knew you could.'

Mangal, too, was smiling.

Peglar shook his head and looked at his limbs, expecting to see raw flesh, a half moon gash on his leg, a crescent torn from his arm. 'Weasel fish,' he murmured.

'What?' said Feldar.

'Weasel fish. I saw one. I thought I'd been bitten.'

'Weasel fish?' said Mangal. 'No, no, there are no weasel fish here. The sea's much too cold for them. I expect what you saw was a sturgeon. They're harmless. You might find weasel fish around the harbour where the water's warmer, but they're quite rare now. I haven't seen one in a long time.'

Ragul came towards them. His face was thunderous. 'That was not fair, Steward. You pulled Peglar towards the tower. Burian's a witness, we both saw it.'

Feldar shook his head. 'You are mistaken, sir. I simply dragged Peglar back into the creek. I was careful not to shorten the distance. Mangal will vouch for it.'

'That is correct,' said Mangal. 'I can assure Lord Karkis that it was all perfectly legal.'

Ragul gave a snort. 'I might have guessed you'd be on his side. How much has he cut you in for?'

Anger flashed in Mangal's eyes. 'You are at risk of losing your wager, sir, and therefore you are perturbed. For that reason I shall overlook your accusation. However, you will be well advised to think carefully about what you say. If you insult me again I will not ignore it.'

Burian took Ragul's arm and pulled him away. 'Never mind,' he said. 'There's still one to go.'

14

A STORY

There was still over a week before Peglar's initiation and he had nothing to do. There was studying for the examination in the law and customs of the city but he knew most of what was needed for that from his time with Distul in the schoolroom. No preparation was possible for the Trial of Fire. It was a single challenge, and the candidate either met it… or they didn't. So he had time on his hands.

Some of it he passed around the Palace. He liked going to the Library but the problem with all the shared spaces was the possibility of running into Ragul and the inseparable Burian, although there was less chance of encountering them in the Library than in many other places. The rooms in the children's wing were dull. The schoolroom was empty, the playroom of no interest to him any more, and his own room little better.

The Citadel had become his favourite place, partly because no one knew that was where he went, partly because it gave such commanding views of the city and the plain beyond, partly because it was quiet and peaceful, and partly – no, mainly – because he might meet Yalka.

Sometimes she was there, sometimes not and he found the times when she was absent dull. He would leave the Palace as quietly as he could and creep back, he hoped unnoticed. One time he returned to find that Feldar had been looking for him to make the arrangements for the examination. He felt he had to give some reason why he couldn't be found and mumbled an excuse about going to look for Cestris. He wasn't sure Feldar believed him.

He knew there was no future in which Yalka might figure. After initiation he would be introduced into a social scene where he would meet suitable girls, some of them Malina's friends, and in consultation with his father and other members of the family he would choose one for his first pairing. He'd heard Ragul boast about what he did with churl girls, but treating Yalka like that was unthinkable. No, there was no future for them, but for now he liked her company and he enjoyed being with her.

Most of the time they talked about anything that came into her head. Rhymings. Why things were the way they were. What the distant cities might be like, whether better or worse than Chamaris. They avoided talk of the child thieves and the killings.

As the day for the final trial drew nearer Peglar found it hard to talk about anything else.

'What do you have to do for this Trial of Fire, then?' Yalka asked.

Peglar told her and she listened carefully. Then she said, 'What's the point of all this?'

'I ask myself that,' said Peglar. 'What does any of it have to do with being a good citizen?'

'There's the history and the law stuff,' said Yalka. 'I suppose that could be useful, and you said you like it.'

'Yes, it's interesting and probably useful, but just because I might pass some sort of test the Marshal will set me doesn't mean that I'll know it all.'

'I thought you knew it all now,' she said. There was a twinkle in her eye but he didn't pick up that he was being teased

'It's all right for you churls,' he said bitterly. 'You don't have to do this.'

'No, we don't,' she said. 'Us churls are nothing.' Her tone was bitter.

He regretted what he'd said and tried to soften it. 'I meant it's all right for girls,' he said. 'Girls don't have to go through this silly performance. Malina didn't. When she started her monthly bleeds she left the children's rooms and went straight to the women's wing. She was immediately treated as an adult. No trials, no tests, no nothing.'

'So you think girls are lucky?'

'Yes, don't you?'

Yalka shook her head. 'For you the trials'll be over in a few days. When a girl begins her bleeding she's starting something that'll go on for ages. Every month she'll feel like crap and have pains. Every month she'll have to wear pads. Every month for the next thirty years, except when she's having a kid. Then she won't have the bleeds but she's got labour to look forward to. That's the price a girl pays to be an adult. I think you men get off pretty lightly, don't you.'

Peglar couldn't argue with what she said, and it

struck him once more that although Yalka's language and speech were poor and she'd never been schooled, she was thoughtful and intelligent.

She liked stories. She loved to hear the traditional tales Peglar had known since childhood, and whenever she could she would get him to tell one and would listen rapt, lying on her back, her face in the sun, spellbound.

'All right. Which story do you want?'

'Tell us a new one. One you've not told us before.'

Peglar thought. There was a story he remembered from the schoolroom. He wondered what Yalka would make of it.

'All right then, here it is. A long time ago Chamaris was not as big or as powerful as it is now. As it grew the other cities of the plain became jealous. Rasturoth, Semilvarga and Halish-Karnon banded together to put Chamaris in its place, and so began the Great War of the Plains.

'The war went on for many years. First one side would gain the upper hand, then it would lose the advantage and the other would be on top. One day a young officer was sent from Chamaris with a raiding party to attack the villages around Semilvarga. He was told to kill all the able bodied men he could find, so that they could not be drafted into the Semilvargan army to fight against Chamaris.'

Yalka gasped and looked up in horror. 'What, kill 'em? All of 'em? Just like that, just for being there, when they'd done nothing?'

'Yes, I'm afraid so.'

'That's, that's - what's that word you said the other day? Barabic.'

'Barbaric.'

'Yes, that's it, barbaric,' she snorted.

'Well, it's interesting you think that, because that's what the young officer thought too. He couldn't bring himself to kill men who had done him no wrong, and who anyway were not soldiers but farmers. Besides, if he did kill them there would only be women and old men left to work the land. They wouldn't be able to manage on their own and the children would starve. But he couldn't spare them either, in case these men arrived in an army to kill his own people. So he decided to do something not as bad as killing them, but that would stop them fighting. What do you think that was?'

'I don't know.' Yalka was sitting up now, wide eyed and engrossed.

'Well, it was this. He ordered his men to cut off their captive's thumbs.'

'Yuk! Why?'

'He reasoned that they could still drive oxen, sow seeds, lift bales, pull ploughs, but without their thumbs they would no longer be able to hold a sword or a spear or handle a bow, and so they wouldn't be able to fight. And that's what he did. He cut their thumbs off and took them back to Am-Sirith to show what he'd done.'

Yalka was riveted. 'And what happened?'

'The Council exiled him for disobeying orders, and one of his own men killed him.'

Yalka shook her head. 'That's not fair.'

'No? They should just have forgiven him for ignoring his orders?'

She thought for a moment. 'If Chamaris was good to the farmers, they could have got 'em on their side. If they could see it was better to be friends with Chamaris instead of enemies they wouldn't have fought for

Semilvarga anyway. Or if they had they wouldn't have done it right.'

Peglar was once again taken aback by the sharpness of Yalka's logic.

'Anyway,' she said, 'tell us another.' Then, when he didn't respond, in a more wheedling tone, 'Please. Except tell this one proper. Like you told me the old bards did.'

She meant he should declaim it in the traditional manner, in rhyme, the way he'd been taught by Distul.

'All right.' He cleared his throat and raised his voice. 'Hear the Chronicles of Chamaris, home of heroes, queen of the plain,' he began in a sing-song. 'Hear now the Tale of the Assassin's Spear. Praise the wisdom of our fathers, and their glorious deeds.'

Then he began to chant.

'Upon a time, in the Age of Gold,
Farumon the hero was a warrior bold.
He ruled his people with wisdom and skill
So that this shining city on the hill
Was the pearl of the plain,
Praised by every mouth,
From the east to the west,
From the north to the south.
Now Farumon was paired with a lady fair,
The loveliest in the land, beyond compare,
And she loved him, so that since time began
There never was a woman more faithful to her man…'

The story went on to tell how Farumon had a rival: Aligar. Aligar was jealous of Farumon's reputation and success. Every time the hero performed some act which received public acclaim, Aligar's envy swelled and his hatred grew.

It came about that the two men were to compete in the Seven Cities Games. Aligar was a great athlete, but not as great as Farumon. In every event Aligar came second: the running, the wrestling, the discus, the weights, the long jump, close to Farumon but always behind. The last competition was throwing the spear. This was Aligar's strongest sport. He had been practicing hard and he was sure that he would win this competition at least.

The contest began and gradually all the other entrants dropped out, leaving only Aligar and Farumon. It came to the final round. Aligar was ahead on the first throw and ahead on the second. At last, he thought, I will win. But on the third throw Farumon made a superhuman effort. His spear soared, hung like a hawk, and dropped to impale itself in the earth, three paces beyond Aligar's best attempt. Farumon had won yet again.

Aligar was beside himself with rage, and when Farumon turned to acknowledge the acclaim of the crowd he could bear it no longer. He snatched the spear from the ground and hurled it at Farumon. The shaft was aimed truly and thrown with deadly force. Farumon had his back to his enemy and would certainly have been killed, but for one thing. His beloved saw Aligar throw and she flung herself into the path of the weapon, taking the point full in her breast. The impact knocked her backwards into Farumon, in whose arms a few minutes later she died.

Yalka was silent, moved by the story. She wiped a sleeve across her eye and sniffed. Then she said, 'What happened to him?'

'Who? Farumon?'

'No, Aligar, the bastard. What happened to him?'

'I don't know. There are no more stories about him that I know.'

'And what about her, the woman?'

'She died.'

'I know she died,' Yalka said, exasperated, 'but who was she?'

'She was Farumon's beloved, his sweetheart, his paired woman.'

'I know that. I'm not stupid! What I mean is, who was she? What was her name?'

Peglar didn't know. He had never known. It was not part of the story.

'None of them have names, do they?' Yalka went on accusingly. 'Not Farumon's woman. That girl in the tower that what's his name swam to…'

'Sharaman.'

'Yes, him. She didn't have no name either. It's like she wasn't important on her own. She had no life of her own. She was only there because of him.'

Peglar looked blank. What was she talking about?

'None of the women are people on their own, are they?' Yalka said. 'The stories aren't about them. Just the men. It should have been her what was the hero. It should have been her that had a statue put up in the square. It should have been her.'

It hadn't occurred to Peglar before, but she was right. All the women in all the old stories were anonymous. If it wasn't for the heroes, nobody would know they'd existed at all. They had no characters of their own, no qualities other than a blind devotion to their partners. They were mere shadows, seen only because of the light thrown on them by their men.

'It's the same in the city. The men own all the stuff and give all the orders. The women are bossed about just like servants.'

Peglar had to admit there was something in what she said, but he felt compelled to offer some defence of his way of life. 'Oh it's not that bad. Anyway, I think we treat our servants pretty well.'

Yalka rounded on him. 'All right then.' She held out her hand, four fingers sticking up. 'Give me the names of four of your servants.'

Peglar felt he was being attacked and he didn't know why. 'No.'

''Cos you can't.'

'I can, of course I can.'

'Go on, then.'

'Well, to start with there's Feldar.'

'He's the Steward, he doesn't count. He's almost one of you.'

'Crestyn, then.'

'Whose he?'

'He's my father's Chamberlain. He manages the household.'

'Hee doesn't count neither. Too important. Somebody else.'

'It's not fair if everybody I name you rule out.'

'I want servants. Not the important ones but the ordinary folk who cook and do your washing and clean up after you and keep the house running so you and your family don't have to get your posh hands dirty.'

'All right,' Peglar said, feeling resentful now. 'There's Halnis.'

'Who's he?'

'A gate guard.'

Yalka grimaced but allowed it. 'All right then. Another.'

'Jelban. He's a gate guard too.'

'That's two. Another.'

Peglar racked his brains. There were no end of servants and he saw them all the time. They mopped the floors, made his bed, washed his clothes, tended the fires, swept the yards, trimmed and filled the lamps, waited at the tables, kept the garden in order. He knew some of them by sight and occasionally acknowledged them with a nod or a word, but he didn't know their names. They were no more than cogs in the great machine of the Palace. They were necessary but expendable. If one cog failed another would straightway replace it.

'It's not fair,' Yalka said, getting up and smoothing down her smock. 'None of it. They're people. You should know them.'

She slid from the rock, jumped the wall and was gone, leaving Peglar to ponder this and wonder what he'd done to make her so angry.

15

SCORPION

It was three days later.

'Ulross is one of the gardeners, Riolla is a waiting woman, Evris is a carpenter. Harlan is a cook. Breda, Cyrolan and Gilat are cleaners.'

Yalka looked amused. 'Very good.' She clapped her hands, slowly. 'How long did it take you to learn their names then?'

'Not long. But I thought what you said was right. I've been talking to the servants and finding out what they do. I agree that if one day I'm going to inherit from my father it's important for me know who our people are.'

'So that's why you've learnt their names. It's 'cos someday you're going to own 'em.'

Peglar was disappointed, and annoyed. He'd worked to get to know some of the servants in order to impress her. He thought he deserved more credit than she was giving him. It seemed that she always had some criticism of him or his family, whatever he did.

Yalka swept her arm over the city below. 'How much

of all this is going to be yours, then? 'How much will you own?'

Peglar shrugged. 'I don't know. Some of it will go to Ragul. That's why it's called a Sharing. My father likes him better than me, so I expect he'll get more than I will, but I think he likes my mother better than his, so I should be all right. So long as I get through the last trial.'

'That's the fire.'

'Yes.' Peglar chilled at the thought. Despite the panic over the weasel fish, this was the one that really frightened him.

'What do you have to do?'

He hesitated. Explaining it made it more terrifying. 'You have to walk barefoot over hot coals.'

'What?' Yalka was incredulous. 'Whatever for?'

'Because that's the trial, that's the challenge.'

'Yes but what use it is? 'How many times in your life are you going to have to do that?'

Despite everything Peglar felt he had to justify it. 'It's not about that. It's about proving you're brave and willing to face anything.'

'Proving you're stupid, more like.'

Peglar couldn't argue with that. He didn't want to talk about it any more. 'Anyway, I expect Ragul will get the good stuff and I'll be left with places like the River Settlements.'

It was out of his mouth before he could stop it, the outcome of years of sniping and prejudice. He wanted to bite off his tongue. 'I'm sorry. I didn't mean…'

'No, you're right. Why would you want them? The place is a shite hole.'

'I'm sure it's not that bad.'

'Are you now? And how would you know?' she

challenged. 'You ever been there?' She answered the question for him. 'No, course you've not. Why would a posh boy go there? If you had been to the Settlements it'd only be to try to find an easy woman. Or to buy hard spirit or armanca weed. But at least if you'd been you'd know what it's like. Look through yer fancy thing.' She meant his telescope. 'Look through that and see how we live, what we have to put up with. Filth. No proper drains. Rats as big as dogs. Flies. Bust walls and roofs that leak like piss. '

Peglar waited. He knew Yalka hadn't finished and expected her to continue sounding off, but when she did speak again her voice was quieter and her tone wistful.

'My granddad says the Settlements wasn't always like that. He says years ago it used to be a good place to live. A great place. The people were free. They could please themselves what they did. There were poets and musicians and artists. They were free and they were happy.'

She looked into the distance, absent-mindedly picking up bits of twig and tossing them along the path. It seemed she wasn't going to say any more, so Peglar asked a question that had been bothering him since he'd first seen the shrine Yalka had made.

'What happened to your sister?'

'You know what. She was killed.'

'I mean why did she come into the city? Why risk her life for the little bit that she might have been able to get?'

At first he thought she hadn't heard him because for a minute she said nothing. Then she told him.

'It was when Scorpion came.'

'Who?'

Yalka sniffed. 'Scorpion's the boss. He runs things.

Your father's Master of Chamaris. Well, Scorpion's master of the Settlements. He tells people what to do and they do it.'

'What does he tell them to do?'

'Everything. Where to go, what to get, how much to pay him. And he runs the children.'

'What do you mean "runs the children"? I don't understand.'

'The kids what come into the city at night to thieve. It's him what makes 'em do it.'

Peglar remembered the conversation he'd overheard when Feldar had suggested that somebody was compelling the street children to do what they did, coercing them through fear. 'You mean he forces them to come into the city and steal?'

''Course.'

'How can he do that?'

'They're scared of him, scared of what he'll do to them if they don't.'

'But why do the adults allow what this man says? Why do they let him control everything?'

Yalka gave him a long, withering look. 'Why do people do what your father tells 'em?'

Peglar bristled. There was no comparison. 'My father was elected as Master of the City.'

Yalka nodded patronisingly. 'Yes, elected by his rich pals on the Council and there for life.' She didn't give Peglar chance to reply. 'People do what your father says because they're afraid of him. He has a bunch of guards who'll beat the shit out of 'em if they don't obey him. So folks are too scared not to. Same with Scorpion. When he gives an order everybody bricks themselves.'

There was a lot that Peglar wanted to challenge but

he needed to find out more about the child thieves. 'Where did this man you call Scorpion come from?'

Yalka shrugged. 'Dunno. He turned up one day with a few men and took over one of the empty houses. He was nice at first, but then he started to give orders and tell us what to do. Just a bit to begin with, and easy stuff, then some more, then a lot. He told people they'd have to give him money so he could protect them, and if they didn't pay they got beaten up or their houses was wrecked. But Scorpion kept wanting more, and it got so people didn't have no more money to pay him, so a few families had the idea of sending their kids into the city at night to thieve. When Scorpion saw what they were doing he thought he'd do it his self and cut out the parents, so he rounded up all the kids and started sending them in.'

'And their families put up with this?'

'They didn't have no choice. We was better off than most, though, me and granddad and Lila and Verit. He used to give us special treatment because granddad's a rhymer. Scorpion would send for him to know what was going to happen and what to do and that. Granddad didn't have to pay for the protection, and me, Verit and Lila didn't have to go thieving. We was all right but other people wasn't. Granddad wanted to help 'em and he told Scorpion that if he didn't treat people right things would turn out bad for him. Scorpion asked what he meant and granddad gave him an augury and said that he'd seen a time when there wouldn't be no River Settlements any more. Scorpion didn't like the augury and told granddad to change it, but granddad said he couldn't. He said the only person who could change the augury was Scorpion himself by behaving different.

Scorpion got angry then. He said if granddad was going to be trouble we'd lose the special treatment we'd had. He took Lila and sent her into the city to thieve with the others. One night she never come back.'

'He didn't send you? Or Verit?'

She shook her head. 'Verit wouldn't be no good 'cos he can't hear, so he couldn't hear the Guardians coming. And I'm too old. He only wants kids because they're small and can squeeze through the tunnels.'

'What tunnels?'

'The secret ones. Back in the old times most of the city was built by slaves from the Settlements. They made tunnels to carry water, and for drainage, and to keep the air moving in hot weather. Lots and lots of 'em. When the buildings was finished they left the tunnels. City folk forgot about 'em but we remembered.'

'And they're still there?'

'Yes. A few have collapsed but most are still there. They go all over. How do you think me and Verit get in and out of the city without being stopped by the Guardians?'

'And Scorpion makes the children go through them?' The idea horrified Peglar. Years ago when they were both in the nursery one of Ragul's favourite tricks was to shut him in the store cupboard. The memory of that brought him out in a cold sweat; he hated small enclosed spaces.

'Yes. It has to be kids because some of the tunnels are really tight. But Scorpion's got a problem because all the kids from the Settlements are gone now.'

'Gone where?'

Yalka looked at him accusingly. 'Well some have been killed, haven't they. But most have disappeared, sent away to the villages where Scorpion can't find 'em. He brings kids in from outside now, orphans and that, kids from Rasturoth, Halish-Karnon, other places. He starves 'em and beats 'em and makes 'em do what he wants.'

Peglar was struggling to understand. Why did the Settlement people put up with it? Surely there were enough of them with the will and determination to resist. 'Why don't you join together to get rid of him, refuse to co-operate.'

Yalka sounded weary. 'We can't. The people don't have the spirit no more.' She wasn't looking at Peglar but he could see that her eyes were moist. 'Your father could help us, though. The River Settlements belong to him. He could get rid of Scorpion. Then the kids would stop being sent into the city and the killings would stop.'

Peglar had a sudden insight. 'That's what you were shouting at my father about, the day I was called.'

'Yes, and much good it did, too.'

There was a silence. Yalka stared moodily in the direction of the Settlements, biting a nail.

Peglar tried again. 'Why live there, then? Why not leave, just move out?'

Yalka looked bewildered. 'Where? Where could we go? To another shite hole, that's all. Why move from one shite hole to another?'

Peglar wished she'd stop using that term. It disturbed him, coming from a girl.

'You could live in the city.'

She suddenly seemed weary, all her fight gone. She lifted herself onto the wall, hoisted her smock above her scarred knees and crossed her ankles. It was not a ladylike posture, Malina and her friends would never sit like that, but it seemed natural in Yalka.

'None of us have any money. Anyway, only citizens can live in the city,' she said, 'and we're not citizens. Stupid, init? You can't live in the city if you're not a citizen, and you can't get to be a citizen without living in the city.'

Put like that it did sound crazy. 'But there are ways to become a citizen, surely,' Peglar said.

'Three.' She had obviously studied it. 'Three ways.' She held up three fingers and counted them off. 'One: you work your arse off all your life for a rich family and get given it, just before you die. Two: you get it as a reward for a lifetime in the Army, if you've not got killed first. Three: you do something very very very very special, and the Council's so impressed they make you one.'

There was a pause.

'So you see,' she said simply, 'we can't go nowhere else. We're stuck.'

Peglar couldn't accept that. There must be some way to change things.

16

A CHALLENGE

Karkis was never alone. In the Palace he would always have people in attendance – Feldar, one of his secretaries, Crestyn, an adviser from the Council. Occasionally Vancia or Chalia would be with him. When he was moving around there would always be a servant in attendance and when he went out, say to the Assembly, he would be accompanied by several Household Guards. So Peglar was surprised to come upon his father on his own, in the Atrium.

He didn't see Peglar at first. He was peering at a sheaf of papers, holding them close to his face and screwing up his eyes. He tilted them towards the windows to catch the light, his lank, white hair falling forward and hiding his face. One of the stained glass panels splashed red and blue blotches on his head and robe. It gave him a gaudy, festive look, like a clown. The thought was in such contrast to his father's usual grim demeanour that it dispelled some of the anxiety Peglar felt at running into him.

The old man looked up when he heard the footsteps

and he peered in Peglar's direction, sweeping his hair back with one hand and frowning. He made a gesture, a sort of haphazard hand-flapping, which Peglar interpreted as a summons to approach, and he realised that his father was unable to see him properly until he was much closer.

'Ah, Peglar, it's you. Good, good. Come here, read this to me.' He wagged the papers. 'I don't have my lens.' His father lowered himself stiffly onto one of the benches and pointed for Peglar to sit beside him.

For the next twenty minutes Peglar read aloud from the papers his father had handed to him. It was a single document, some sort of legal matter, marked 'Confidential' in big red letters at the top of every page. Peglar couldn't take in most of the meaning, all his attention was focused on not making any mistakes with the reading, so he sounded very wooden. It was hard going, too. There were several words that were unfamiliar because they were legal or technical, and in one or two places he stumbled. His father didn't seem to mind, or even to notice. He sat still, with his head cocked on one side and his eyes closed. Occasionally he raised his hand to stop the reading and pondered for a moment, head back, eyes half shut, before making a circular motion with his finger, which he took as a sign to carry on. A couple of times he asked for a passage to be read again, but mostly he listened in silence.

When Peglar had got to the end his father looked at him with unaccustomed warmth, and smiled. A smile from Karkis was rare indeed.

'Thank you, thank you,' he murmured. 'It's my eyes, you understand. I don't see as well as I used to.' He paused. Then he seemed to gather himself, as if what came next was hard to say. 'You read well.'

'Thank you, sir.' Peglar flushed with pleasure. He couldn't remember ever being thanked by his father for anything. Come to think of it, he had never had an opportunity to do anything to be thanked for.

They sat together on the bench in silence for a moment. Then Karkis turned to Peglar and peered into his face. 'Tell me,' he said, 'how are you finding things?'

It seemed to Peglar an odd question. What "things" did he mean? He supposed the trials.

'The trials are going very well, thank you, sir,' he said.

'On track to complete them in time, are you?'

'Yes, father. The last one is the day after tomorrow.' Surely he must know this. Surely Feldar must have told him.

'Mmm. Good. And what are you doing now?'

Peglar wasn't sure what he was being asked. Did his father mean this instant? Or did he mean how was he spending his time in general? He thought he'd better say something his father would approve. 'I've been studying some of the books from the Library to prepare for the examination in the law and constitution of the city.'

Karkis nodded. 'Good, good. I expect you'll find that easy. Distul always used to tell me that you were a fast learner, quicker than Ragul or even Malina.'

Peglar felt a glow of pleasure. He'd never known that Distul discussed with his father what they did in the schoolroom, and he would not have expected the reports from their tutor to be so warm.

'I've been thinking about your companion. Your

stepmother tells me she has someone in mind. He's a noted scholar, doing important work at the Academy.'

'Yes, sir.' A scholar at the Academy? How old must he be? Ancient! A companion should be someone his own age, like Burian is to Ragul. Was his father serious?

'That is always assuming,' the old man continued, 'that you successfully complete the Trial of Fire.' He paused, while Peglar once again felt the dread he always experienced at the thought of what he must do. 'Your brother is a fine young man,' he continued. 'I believe you could be, too.'

'Yes, father.'

'"Yes father, yes father",' Karkis mimicked in a sudden burst of irritation. 'Anybody can say, "Yes father." What I'd like to see from you is something that will prove me right.'

Peglar managed to restrain himself from saying 'Yes, father' again. He knew that anything he said would be badly received so he waited silently for Karkis to say more.

'What I need from you is a contribution to solving some of the problems I face. There is one in particular which is causing considerable distress in the city and is losing me support. People are dissatisfied and some are becoming openly critical. I have enemies who see it as an opportunity to undermine me. It's a problem which doesn't originate in the city, but the citizens are looking to me, their Master, to solve it. So solve it I must.'

He got stiffly up from the bench and retrieved his staff. Peglar rose too.

'Do you understand to what I am referring?'

Peglar thought he did. 'Yes, sir, I do.'

'Good.' He started to leave, then looked back. 'The

son who is able to provide a solution to this matter will deserve my extreme gratitude. Gratitude I will be sure to remember.'

He turned and hobbled away, the clatter of his staff receding down the corridor.

Peglar was left to reflect on what he'd just heard. His father had talked about an issue which was causing trouble in the city, a problem that affected the city but didn't originate there. He'd said that it was causing unrest. Peglar knew that only that morning there had been a protest about the child thieves in the street outside the Palace. It had been a small affair, just a few people shouting, and the Guardians had swiftly cleared them away, but demonstrations of any kind were almost unheard of. This must be the unrest his father meant. He was setting him a test, perhaps Ragul too: which of them could stop the killings? It was typical of the old man to be so obtuse, to veil what he wanted. On a matter like this he would never come out openly and simply say what he had in mind. Understanding that was part of the challenge.

Peglar needed to think. Ragul already had an advantage because a lot of the young men from the high families were in the army with him. Probably some of them knew about the gangs. On the other hand, Peglar had a direct route into the River Settlements through Yalka, and she knew about Scorpion. Would she help him?

Of course there was a further possibility, one which would certainly give Ragul an advantage. It was that he might himself be one of the killers.

17

A GIFT

The idea came to Peglar the next day. He had placed the drawing Yalka had given him on one of the shelves in his room. The card it was on had been used before; it was an irregular shape and creased. He remembered the pencil scarcely long enough to hold. He remembered her saying that she couldn't draw as much as she wanted because she couldn't get the materials. Then it occurred to him. Why had he not thought of it before? It was simple: she had talent, he had money, or rather his father had. He could get her whatever she needed.

It was raining, a sharp midsummer shower, as he hurried down the hill. He was heading for the part of the city beyond the Academy where the artists and craft workers lived. The district was unfamiliar to him and it took a little time to locate what he was looking for, but in the end he found a merchant who had exactly what he needed. He selected a large pad of drawing paper in a scarlet, canvas cover, and a polished wooden box full of shiny pencils.

'I am Jathan Peglar, son of Lord Karkis,' Peglar said to the Merchant, as importantly as he could manage. 'Please send your account for these items to my father.'

The merchant was a plump, smiling man with glasses. 'I know who you are, sir,' he replied, and made a slight bow. 'It is my honour to serve you. Would you like me to arrange for your purchases to be delivered to the Palace?'

'No, I'll take them now.'

'As you wish, sir. Thank you for your patronage.'

It was as easy as that. He would have bought more, but Yalka was proud and he was worried she might think he was showing off if he gave her too much. This would be a start, and he could always get her other things later.

When he came out of the shop the rain had stopped but the thoroughfares were still wet. He was hurrying along a back street behind the Gymnasium, purchases clutched under his cloak, and he didn't see the young men until he was nearly on top of them. They were spread out and he had to step aside to pass. He was negotiating a puddle when he heard his name, not called to get his attention but muttered, one to another, talking about him, not to him.

Then without warning somebody stamped in the puddle and muddy water splattered his legs and cloak. One of the youths bumped him and he lost his balance, staggering into the road. There was a yell and Peglar jumped aside, narrowly avoiding a cart as it splashed past, the driver cursing. He lost his grip on the drawing pad and it fell. He picked it up quickly and wiped it on his cloak. The youths were walking away, laughing. One of them turned to raise his fingers and

Peglar recognised him as someone he'd seen with Ragul.

He was shaken, and he kept an eye open for further trouble as he hurried home. When he got back to his quarters he examined the pad. The paper was all right but the lovely scarlet cover was wrinkled and there was a brownish smudge from the muddy water. He dabbed it with a towel and managed to remove most of the mark, but in doing so he took off some of the red dye too. It didn't look too bad but it was not perfect, it was not what he had wanted to give her.

By the time he'd changed and cleaned himself up the rain clouds had cleared, and he climbed the hill to the Citadel in bright sunshine.

He wondered whether Yalka would be there because of the rain, and he felt a rush of pleasure when she called to him and smiled, and he realised she'd been looking out for him. She dropped lightly from the wall she'd been on and ran to him. He caught a glimpse of Verit as he flitted out of sight behind the wall.

'I've been waiting ages. I thought you wasn't coming.' She stopped in front of him and extended her hand to touch his cheek, where she'd scratched it. Then, to his surprise, she reached up and planted a firm kiss on it. It wasn't an invitation, it was a kiss-it-better peck of the sort that his nurse or his mother would give him when he'd hurt himself as a child. He felt a warm rush of pleasure.

'I've got a present for you,' he said.

'A present?' She jumped with excitement, her blue eyes shining. 'Why? What is it? Give it me.'

'Here.' Proudly Peglar held out the drawing pad and the shiny box.

Yalka took the pad and peered at it closely. She flicked back the cover and ran her fingers over the rough, creamy paper, feeling the grain. Then she opened the box and gave a little gasp when she saw the neat row of glossy, new pencils.

'I dropped the pad and the cover got wet. I'll get you a new one, but you might want this one for now.'

She shook her head. 'It's beautiful,' she said quietly. She took out one of the pencils and held it firmly in her left hand, very close to the point. She made a few exploratory sweeps and stabs at the paper and tilted the pad, squinting at the weight and texture of the marks she'd made. Reverently she placed the pencil back in the box and tried another.

She looked up at him and her eyes were moist. She stroked the box lid and ran her fingers along the row of pencils. 'They're lovely.' She picked one up and held it out to him. 'Can you teach me to write me name?'

'Of course.'

He took the pencil from her, rested the pad on the rock, and in firm, clear stokes wrote Y - A - L - K - A in large letters at the top of the first sheet of paper. She looked on in admiration at this display of skill. Peglar gave her the pad and she examined what he'd done, frowning at the lines. Then she nodded, as if confirming that yes, that was her name.

'Now you try,' he said, holding out the pencil. She took it from him and gripped it like she did the short stump. 'No, like this,' he said, and adjusted her fingers, moving them into a more relaxed hold, better for writing.

She was used to directing a pencil and getting it to

make marks where she wanted, so it was not too hard for her. She managed to copy the letters reasonably well, hair falling either side of her face, her tongue between her lips as she concentrated, but she got the K and the L wrong way round. When she'd finished she looked critically at what she'd done. She could see that there was a problem.

'It's wrong.'

'Yes. Look at it again.'

She studied her writing and his, and then copied her name again. This time she got the letters the right way round. They were better formed, too, more nearly the same size and in line. She knew it was an improvement and looked pleased.

'How does it say Yalka?'

'Every letter makes a sound,' he explained, and pointed to each one as he voiced it. 'Yuh - A - Le - Kuh - A. Yalka.'

She traced the letters with her finger, repeating the sounds slowly as she did so.

'You need to practise copying it until you can write it easily. When you can do that I'll teach you to write your family name. And some other things.'

She turned her back to the rock and hoisted herself up to where she was sitting when he arrived. She considered for a minute, looked down at him and then quite casually said, 'Do you want me to do it for you now?'

Peglar had no idea what she meant.

'Do it,' she said. 'You know, what boys like.'

Peglar was thunderstruck. She couldn't possibly mean what he thought, surely.

'That's what rich boys do with a churl girl, init? They give her a present and then they expect something back. Some girls go all the way but I don't give no more than a hand job.'

Peglar was horrified. This was the sort of thing that he'd heard other boys snigger about, and Ragul often boasted about what he got up to, but to hear a female talking like this was appalling. His embarrassment found an outlet in anger.

'No! How can you think that? Those things were a present for you. A gift. So you can do more pictures.' He was shouting and his face felt hot, he was probably blushing.

Her gaze didn't waver but it hardened. 'All right, suit yourself,' she said.

Abruptly, she grabbed the pencils and the pad, slid down from the rock and dashed away. Peglar watched in silence as Verit scampered after her, over the wall and into the trees. She didn't look back.

Peglar's emotions were in turmoil. Had he misunderstood what she meant? He was sure he hadn't. Although she did enjoy teasing him, so perhaps it was meant as a joke. He hadn't wanted her to say what she did. He didn't think of her in that way. Was that denying her as a person? Ignoring her womanhood? Was it simply another 'posh boy' attitude, just of a different sort?

It seemed from what she said that she'd done this before. Who with? Please not Ragul. Or Burian. Or any of their slimy friends. Did it change what he thought of her? Was the seedy reputation of the River Settlements because of people like Yalka? He pictured her yellow hair, her bright blue eyes flashing with mischief and laughter, her clear skin and her fresh smell. He thought of her sense of fairness, her concern for the unfortunate. No, he couldn't think of her like that. He wished she hadn't gone. He needed to talk to her. He wanted to be with her.

18

MANGAL

The final trial was the one that everyone feared. Like the other two, the challenge itself was straightforward. However, in this case the actuality was terrifying. It was supposed to be a test of courage and of the capacity to withstand pain. To succeed the initiate must walk barefoot across a pit of burning coals. Then he must walk back again. It sounded simple, but when you thought about it, it was unimaginable. Visualising it made Peglar feel sick. Tales of horror abounded, stories of burns that never healed, of boys fainting and falling into the fire to be scarred for life. As the time for the ordeal drew nearer Peglar found it increasingly hard to settle.

The day before it was due he was in his room, thinking about what he could do to calm his nerves, when he heard a noise outside. He expected Ragul, come to torment him again, but to his surprise it was Mangal who came through the door.

'Well, no need to ask how you are,' Mangal said. 'You look terrible. It strikes me it's a good job I came.'

Without being invited he lowered himself into a chair. It creaked in protest. 'Why am I here? you want to know. Well, there are no prizes for guessing that it's about tomorrow and the Trial of Fire.'

The huge man adjusted his bulk and the chair complained some more.

'How much help have you been given to prepare yourself?'

Peglar looked blank. 'None. Felder's not allowed to help me and Cestris has gone back to his own city. Anyway, what's to be done? How can you prepare yourself for walking through a fire?'

'Some people do,' said Mangal. 'Have you never seen Ibram the Fire Walker at the fair?'

'Yes.'

Peglar knew the man, who once a day for the five days of the fair not only walked but danced across a tray of burning embers. Like all the boys, he watched fascinated, and even at an early age was filled with dread about what he would himself one day have to do.

'But everyone says he cheats,' said Peglar, 'and besides, the soles of his feet are like leather. It must have taken him years to get them like that.'

'Well, no and yes,' said Mangal. 'No to the cheating. He really does walk on the fire. And yes, his feet are probably now as tough as a horse's hooves, but they weren't like that when he started. When he began his feet were as tender as yours, and I'm going to teach you to do what he did.'

Peglar leant forward. He had no idea what Mangal had in mind but he felt his spirits rise.

'The mystery behind walking on hot coals and how it is done can be understood by considering how materials behave,' Mangal said. 'Different substances carry heat in different ways. Let me give you an example. If you were to put a poker in the fire and then touch the end of it, what would happen?'

'I'd get burnt,' said Peglar.

'Yes, you would. Now have you ever reached into the oven and touched the top of a cake? No? Well, if you did you wouldn't burn yourself. The top of the cake would feel hot, but it wouldn't hurt you, at least not if you took your finger away reasonably quickly. That is because the metal of the poker and the mixture from which the cake is made retain heat differently: the metal well and the cake poorly.'

Peglar had never baked a cake and wondered where this was going and how it could possibly help him. He waited for Mangal to explain.

'For the Trial of Fire coal is used, not wood. That's because whereas wood holds on to the heat like metal, coal is more like cake.'

That sounded crazy to Peglar. Coal like cake? He almost laughed, but he listened.

'Although coal burns and we use it to heat ovens and to warm places, it's actually pretty terrible at conducting heat. Add to that the fact that when it's been burning for a while it gets covered in a layer of ash, and ash doesn't retain heat at all well. So what you have is something bad at transferring heat to your skin encased in something that's even worse.'

Peglar understood the logic, but what Mangal was talking about didn't sound convincing. He could remember standing near Ibram's fire tray and feeling the heat from it. He told Mangal so.

'What you were experiencing was the excellent way

the metal of Ibram's tray conveyed the heat from the coal. Your feet are not the same. They too are poor at transferring heat.'

'So you mean I won't feel anything?' Peglar asked in amazement.

Mangal laughed and shook his head. He stirred in the chair and it groaned. 'Oh no, you will feel it, but not as much as you might have thought, provided you approach it properly. The technique is in the speed you go. We call it pacing. If you're not spending time on the coals but walking briskly across them there's a lower risk of being burnt. You have to get it just right, so each foot is out of contact with the coals for the same amount of time as it's touching them. Go too slowly and the fire has more time to burn your feet. Go too fast and you'll sink into the coals through the layer of ash and be burnt. People like Ibram, who master fire walking, go quickly but without rushing. And you must take smallish steps. The temptation will be to stride out to get it over with, but doing that will force your feet down into the embers.'

'How will I know how fast to go?'

'You will know. This will help too.' Mangal took from the folds of his cloak a twist of paper. He opened it on his palm to show a small collection of what looked like short pieces of brown string.

'What is it?'

'Armanca weed.'

Peglar looked at it with interest. This was what Yalka said her grandfather took when he did his rhymings.

'You chew it. Too much and it would put you into a trance, knock you out. This is just the right amount to help you. There is one more thing, and it's up here.'

Mangal tapped his forehead. 'It's common for troubles to be made worse by thinking about them too much. If you dwell on a problem it becomes more intense. If you rise above it, it recedes. So as you stand on the edge of the pit and prepare yourself, pay no attention to what you are about to do. Ignore the coals, forget the heat, empty your mind. Then begin. Don't look down at the fire, look straight ahead way beyond the end of the pit. Like many other things you will encounter in your life, if you think you can do it, you can do it. Stand tall and walk with pride.'

'And at the right pace.'

'Of course.'

'Which I will know.'

'Yes.'

Peglar had so many questions. 'Why are you helping me like this. You're the stakeholder for Ragul's wager, you're supposed to be impartial.'

'Now whoever told you that?' said Mangal. 'Just because I am the stakeholder doesn't mean I can't have a view about who I would like to win. And while I am not allowed to assist you when you take the trial, there is nothing to prevent me advising you beforehand.'

'But why has no one else told me this?'

'Feldar is the arbiter so he can't. You are a solitary boy and have no older friends. In a normal family your brother would help you, but obviously not here. Cestris might have come to your aid but he's spending some time at his home in Rashturoth. So I concluded it was appropriate for me to be the one to tell you what all the men who have been through initiation know.' He smiled at Peglar's expression. 'Yes, even me. I was not always the size I am now. Once I was as slim as you, and once I too was taught how to walk across the coals.'

'And the armanca weed?'

'Ah, yes, well that could be construed as illegal. But am I to blame if a small packet that was for my own personal use accidentally fell from my pocket while I was with you?

19

FIRE

Despite Mangal's intervention Peglar was afraid when the time for the trial came, and he was shaking as he stood with Feldar and a few others beside the fire pit. He'd chewed the armanca weed about half an hour before, as instructed, and it had made him feel calmer but had it done anything more? He'd thought the drug might make everything numb but it hadn't and he could feel plenty of heat coming from the coals.

It was after sunset, and the circle of faces – Feldar, Mangal, Ragul, Burian – was lit from beneath by the glow from the coals. It made them look unreal, like masks in a pageant. There were a few others there too, standing in clumps a little further back. This trial always drew morbid onlookers, eager to see the initiate failing, falling in the fire, running screaming from the pit. A man in a leather apron moved to stir the coals but Mangal stopped him. Ragul didn't look pleased.

A couple of minutes ago Peglar would have done anything to put off the trial. Now all he wanted was to finish it. In a few minutes it would be ended, one way or another.

'Are you ready?' said Feldar.

'Yes.'

'Very well. Take up your position and begin in your own time.'

Peglar moved to the the very edge of the pit and tried to remember everything Mangal had told him. He stood straight and looked over and beyond the pit, focussing his eyes on a clump of trees a hundred paces away. He closed his mind to thoughts of the burning coals and their potential to hurt him. He rose over the noisy chatter of the onlookers, the jeers of Ragul and Burian. He let go of the present, pulled his shoulders back, filled his lungs, and stepped forward.

Mangal began a rhythmic clapping. Peglar assumed that it was the rhythm he was supposed to follow and he fell into step. To say he didn't feel the fire would be wrong, but it was like touching something hot from a stove or a skewer from the fire and letting go. He placed one foot forward and just as he removed it from the embers in time to Mangal's beat he felt the heat. Then he did the same with the other one. He kept his eyes on the trees, his body in tune with Mangal's clapping, and stepped out of the pit at its far end.

There was a shallow tub of cold water waiting for him and he stepped gratefully into it. He stood for a moment, relishing the ease that the chill bath brought. Feldar had a timer, not the same one used for the Trial of Earth but a shorter measure. Peglar had until the sand ran out to recover, then he must go back into the fire again to cross back the way he had come.

The return was easier at the start because his feet were wet, but then the pain insisted and he lost concentration. Mangal's beat was too slow. He had to get out. He leaped from one leg to the other, and as Mangal had predicted it had the effect of thrusting each foot further into the fire. He reached the far side of the pit and collapsed. He was in agony. He felt someone wrap his feet in wet cloths and the pain eased a little. He raised his head to see who it was. It was one of the servants. His name was Gilat. He would not have known that but for Yalka. He thanked him, and let his head fall back. Then he heard a commotion. It was Ragul, and he was enraged.

'What in the name of all the powers do you think you were doing?'

He was shouting at Mangal but the big man appeared unconcerned.

'That was a bare faced swindle!' And then when Mangal still ignored him, 'The clapping! Blatant cheating! The whole business is a cheat. First the help he got with his running, then being towed half way across the creek, and now this!'

At last Mangal responded. 'This? This? What would "this" be?'

'You know perfectly well, you fat fraud. The clapping. You clapped so the little shit could time his steps.'

Mangal looked at Ragul as if he was something he ought to scrape off his sandal. 'Yes, I clapped. I clapped to encourage the candidate, as I would do with any young man facing any trial. I am surprised that as his brother you did not do the same.'

'But it was the beat.' Ragul clapped his hands in the

rhythm Mangal had set. 'You set the beat so he'd know how quickly to walk.'

Mangal turned away, leaving Ragul yelling at his broad back. He scuttled around to the other side where could again see Mangal's face.

'There is no way that little turd has completed the trials, no way he can be initiated. You and Feldar are in this together. You planned the whole thing so you can split my purse between you.'

Peglar was still on the ground, looking up at all this and momentarily forgetting his injured feet. Ragul was becoming more agitated all the time, and Mangal's refusal to react was making him even worse. Burian was trying to calm him and pull him away but Ragul wouldn't have it.

'I'm going to my father.' Ragul was almost whining now. 'When I tell him what's happened he'll declare this whole business null and void. Peglar will slink off, you will be thrown out of the city, and Feldar will be given the boot.'

Mangal put his hands on his hips. He looked as though he had had enough, and Peglar would not have been surprised to see one of those great, hammy fists swing in the direction of his half-brother.

'I am here.' It was a voice from the darkness and everyone turned to see Karkis come forward into the light. How long had he been there? He advanced towards the group around the pit. There was a stir among the onlookers. Peglar climbed to his feet.

'I have been fully informed of the progress of all the trials,' said Karkis, 'and I have watched this one. Not only has Feldar, who has my total confidence, reported to me regularly, but independent witnesses placed by me have corroborated everything he has told me. I have no doubt that Peglar has satisfactorily completed the Three Trials. Perhaps he has not managed them with the ease and self-assurance that you showed when you undertook them, Ragul, but completed them he has. Tomorrow the Marshal will examine him in the law and practices of Chamaris, and assuming he is satisfied the following day he will be initiated as a free man of our glorious city.'

There was complete silence. In the fire pit one of the coals sputtered and flared. Ragul dropped to his haunches and put his hands over his face. Peglar didn't know whether he was choking back sobs, or cries of rage.

20

INITIATION

The white rotunda of the Ceremonium was dazzling in the sunlight, and its intense glare made Peglar's eyes water. Furtively he wiped the tears away. He didn't want anybody to think he was crying.

Around the outside of the building was a circle of smooth pillars, about half topped by carved stone heads. These were effigies of leaders of the past, great men who had served the city. One day his father's likeness would join them. Peglar followed Feldar between the two tallest pillars and up the steps to an enormous door. It was faced with burnished copper worked in an elaborate relief. Muscled men fought with serpents, and bare breasted women with the tails of fishes sat on rocks while savage seas churned below them. Fantastic animals, some half human, paraded across the centre in a frenzied procession.

Feldar raised his staff and beat heavily on the door, three times. He swung his staff so fiercely that Peglar thought he might damage the fabric. Then he saw that what he had taken to be stones in the road at the feet of the animal pageant were the marks of numberless previous strikes. The blows made a deep, booming noise that Peglar thought must be heard all over the city.

There was a moment's silence before the door swung back to reveal Mangal in his formal robes of green and gold. He stood in the centre of the doorway, staff in hand. His long hair poured onto his shoulders and his black beard had been brushed till it shone. He looked stately and impressive.

'Who seeks admittance to the Ceremonium of Chamaris?' he bellowed in his deep, rich voice.

Feldar gave Peglar a dig in the ribs. 'I, Jathan Peglar,' he said as loudly as he could.

'For what purpose do you seek admittance?'

'To answer my father's call to Initiation.'

'Enter, Jathan Peglar.' Mangal turned and began a slow march into the building.

Inside was cool. Above Peglar's head sunlight streamed in narrow beams through a row of round windows below the dome, but despite this the interior was dark and after the brilliance of the square it took a moment to get used to the change.

People were standing around the walls. Peglar saw his mother, who was radiant, her smile wonderful. She gave him a little wave, just a fluttering of the fingers. There was Vancia a little way from her, looking grim, and Malina at her side. There was Styron, and Geriker, and Lembick. He looked for Ragul and Burian but couldn't locate them.

The floor of the Ceremonium was made of black and white tiles in a series of tiered circles, each higher than the one before. Mangal led the way to the top, where Karkis was waiting, and took up a position facing the people below. Two acolytes stood behind him, and beside them was a tall rack made of gilded metal. It held three scrolls, each tied with a scarlet ribbon.

Mangal began in a voice that resonated in the vast space. 'My Lord Karkis, members of your noble House, honoured representatives of the Council, citizens of Chamaris, we are gathered here today to witness the Initiation of a youth of this city, a son of The House of the Leopard. Initiation is a solemn rite which marks the passage of a boy child into manhood with the privileges, rights, duties and responsibilities of a citizen.'

Mangal paused, allowing time for the echo to die and his words to sink in. Then he spoke again. 'Who calls Jathan Peglar?'

Karkis took a pace forward and raised his right hand. 'I do.'

Mangal indicated for Peglar to move to his father's side. 'Has Jathan Peglar been instructed in the duties and responsibilities of a citizen?'

'He has,' said his father.

'Has Jathan Peglar completed the first trial, the Trial of Earth?'

'He has.'

One of the acolytes took a scroll from the rack, untied the ribbon and handed it to Feldar, who began to read from it a description of what Peglar had done to succeed, completing four circuits of the designated course within the time allowed. He did not say that it had taken him three tries and the help of Cestris to manage it. When Feldar had finished he handed the scroll to Mangal, who cried in a loud voice, 'It is completed.' The other acolyte struck a gong and there was applause from the gathering at the foot of the steps.

Mangal placed the scroll in a long box covered in crimson leather. Peglar saw that his name was embossed on the lid in letters of gold, together with the leopard crest.

Mangal moved on. 'Has Jathan Peglar completed the second trial, the Trial of Water?' Feldar took the second scroll and read from it, and that too was placed in the box. The same with the third. When that had been added Mangal held the box up, tipping it forward so that everyone could see the scrolls nestling within. Then he closed the lid and, with a slight bow, presented it to Peglar. This was now his, evidence that he had answered his father's call and completed the trials. It would join similar boxes in the Library, piled on the top shelves, one for each male adult in the family going back over the years. The oldest boxes had faded to pale pink.

Mangal beamed and held out his hands in a gesture of welcome. 'Whereasmuch as it has pleased his father to call Jathan Peglar to manhood and he has answered that call, I present him to you as a citizen.

There was clapping and cheering from the crowd at the foot of the stairs. Except for Ragul. He'd now appeared and was at the back of the group, glaring. Peglar stood his ground and scowled back. He was Ragul's equal now. There was nothing he could do to him.

Peglar's vision was blurred and he was light headed as he received the congratulations. Styron shook his hand, and Uncle Mostani. Then it was Feldar's turn.

'Well done,' he murmured, 'I knew you could make it.' He smiled and stepped away, and there was Cestris.

'You're back,' said Peglar.

'I am.' Cestris hugged him. 'You did it,' he said,

releasing his hold but leaving one hand on Peglar's shoulder. 'I always knew you would.'

Peglar shook his head. 'I couldn't have managed it without you. That first trial was the worst. If you hadn't helped me I would have failed right there and then.'

Cestris smiled. 'You say so, but I think you would have been all right. You just needed a bit of confidence, that's all. That half-brother of yours didn't help, though, did he?'

Peglar pulled a face. 'Ragul? No, he never does.'

Cestris leaned closer. 'You need to watch out for him. Until you were initiated he was in line to inherit everything. Now you have been, there'll be a Sharing and he won't get as much. Watch him.' He glanced across the space to where a group of women were gathered. 'His mother too. And your half-sister. Don't trust any of them.

Peglar scarcely registered the faces of the others queueing to shake his hand, and he smiled and thanked them mechanically, his mind far away.

Last in the line was Ragul. There were no congratulations from him. He snatched Peglar's hand, crushed it briefly and painfully, and dropped it. Burian followed. As Ragul turned away he muttered something. It sounded like, 'Have your fun,' and Peglar thought it was an olive branch. Later, though, he realised that what Ragul probably said was, 'I'm not done'.

The men stood back for Peglar to lead them out of the Ceremonium into the square. Light and heat beat off the paving and he had to screw up his eyes. For a moment he could see nothing, then he became aware of the women, fluttering like a flock of festive birds.

His mother was first. She gave a cry, broke from the throng and came over. She hugged him, kissed his cheeks, and pressed something into his hand. It was a small box.

'Here,' she said. 'Keep this with you. It will remind you of today and bring you good luck.'

She started to weep, and she held him tight for so long that he thought he would never get free. At last two of her women gently pulled her away. Her carefully coiled hair had come loose and hung down in a wayward, golden tumble. Her tears had left a damp patch on his shoulder. She gave him a smile and dabbed her eyes. Peglar smiled back and put the box into his pocket. He would open it later.

Vancia stepped impatiently round Chalia, giving her a contemptuous look. There was no preamble, no embrace. She leaned forward and gave him a perfunctory kiss on each cheek, while her waiting woman held her garments out of the dust. The air was static with the heavy perfume she always wore.

'I suppose I must congratulate you,' she said, silkily. She looked him up and down. 'We shall be seeing much more of each other now. For the time being, anyway.'

Her expression hardened. She was looking at him in the way someone would regard another over whom they had power and who was to be disciplined. Peglar had seen his father look at a clumsy servant in the same way. He felt uncomfortable, but before he could find the words to respond she tossed her head dismissively and walked quickly away, her women scuttling after her.

Then Malina was before him. She was tall, as tall as Peglar. Her hair tumbled from a silver circlet in an avalanche of curls. Her robe was without decoration, a soft, salmon pink, of silk so fine that it clung to her like another skin. She smiled, leaned towards him, put her arms around his neck and hugged him. She smelt wonderful. 'Congratulations,' she whispered, 'Now you are a man.'

Her breath brushed his face as she kissed his cheek. Then, abruptly, she let go and turned away, laughing softly. Peglar stood with his arms dangling at his side, watching her go and feeling ungainly and deficient.

21

MEN'S TALK

Eventually the congratulations were over and the procession back to the Palace formed in the square. A noisy crowd of people had assembled, many blowing the tuneless horns that were traditionally used to greet an initiate. In front of him was an ornate chair, blue and gold, painted with moons and stars. It had a scarlet awning on carved supports and the seat was covered in velvet of the same colour. Peglar climbed onto it, but the seat had no back and when the six servants lifted it onto their shoulders the whole contraption lurched alarmingly. Peglar grabbed at the arms in panic. Some of the onlookers laughed and blew raspberries on their horns.

As the procession left the square and turned into the Grand Parade, Peglar was surprised to see the number of people who had turned out. He was used to crowds gathering for his father, but these people were there for him. They shouted and clapped and some threw flowers, and Peglar sat in his chair with a foolish grin on his face.

The procession rolled on, turning uphill towards the high city and the Palace. The gradient was steep and the horses puffed and heaved. Half way up Peglar's six bearers were relieved by six more. When they reached the residence there was a gathering of servants outside the gate, watching, bowing and applauding.

The carriages rumbled into the yard, iron-rimmed wheels crunching on the gravel, and drew up beside the main entrance. Everybody hung back, waiting for Peglar to enter first. The bearers lowered his chair and he stepped off, a little shakily.

Suddenly there was an explosion of noise from behind and a riot of strangely adorned people bounded through the gate. There were about half a dozen of them, garishly dressed with hair died in lurid colours. They cartwheeled and whooped and eventually ended up in a knot around the entrance. They barred Peglar's path. He had no choice but to push through them towards the doorway. As he passed between them they pulled faces, made baying noises and performed exaggerated, mocking bows. Some of them tugged at his cloak and blew whistles. He'd been told to expect this. It was the traditional greeting for an initiate after the ceremony. It was meant to bring him back down to earth. You may have been the centre of attention today, the revellers' antics were saying, but really you've not done much yet.

He was glad to get away from them and into the Atrium, which was cool, and quiet after the racket. Peglar paused to clear his head. A servant waited patiently at the way into the men's wing, where his quarters would now be. He followed the man – somebody new, I must learn his name, he told himself – past a row of imposing doors. One of these, he knew, was Ragul's suite. He had been in there once and it was impressive. Would his own rooms be as grand? He needed to be left alone for a while. The morning had been hectic and he wanted some time away from people. He wanted to think. He wanted to attend to his feet, which were sore after the fire pit.

The servant directed him into a small, narrow hallway, with a door at the far end. It was dark and still, and the walls were bare. It seemed forbidding and gloomy, very different from the brightly coloured nursery room he'd left only a few hours before. He approached the far door, stepped through into what the servant said was his day room, and stopped in astonishment. It was huge: high, bright and airy, with a line of windows down one side and a painted ceiling and walls. One mural was of a ship fighting through a storm, with land in the background and, in the distance, the unmistakable pyramid shape of the city. Greenish waves broke over the bow and the flag, scarlet with with his father's leopard crest in gold, streamed in the wind. On the ceiling was painted a blue sky with a few small clouds. A flock of exotic, brazenly coloured birds flew across it, so lifelike you could almost feel the beat of their wings and hear their squawking.

'Impressive, isn't it?'

It was a voice from behind him. He turned to see Feldar smiling as he too looked up at the ceiling.

'It was Karkis the elder, your father's father who had this done. These were the rooms used by your father before he took over as Master.'

Peglar was surprised. Presumably, then, this suite was the best. He would have expected it to be given to Ragul.

Feldar answered his thought. 'Your half-brother was offered these rooms but declined. He said that as he would some of the time be away with the army he didn't need anything so grand. I think the real reason was that he wanted somewhere he could slip in and out of without being seen. To leave here you have to go through the Atrium. Your brother's suite has its own door which leads directly to the rear courtyard.' Feldar came further into the room. 'How are your feet?'

'All right.' They were, just. Immediately after the trial they'd been bathed. Then, back at the Palace, Narvil, the family physician, had applied a cream. The costume for the initiation ceremony included long, white tights, and he had padded the feet with soft cloths, which had given some protection, so he'd got through the ritual better than he'd expected.

'They'll be sore for a day or two,' said Feldar. 'The water they were bathed in was from a special well which is said to have healing powers.'

Peglar needed to find out how much Feldar knew of the help he'd been given by Mangal. 'Congratulations on winning your wager,' he said. 'And thank you for being on my side.'

Feldar smiled. 'I wasn't really. As arbiter I had to be neutral. But naturally I am pleased at your success. I would have been pleased even without the wager.'

Peglar believed that, although if he'd been told it a few weeks before he would have dismissed it as nonsense. He'd always found Feldar distant and rather severe, and assumed this came from personal dislike. It seemed not. Or perhaps it was just that he disliked Ragul more.

'Thank you,' he said. 'Thank you for what you did.

And I would never have got through the trials without Cestris, and Mangal.'

'Mangal, yes. He intervened because he thought you were being treated unfairly. What he told you before the final trial, how to manage the walk across the fire and minimise the damage, is something that's told to every young initiate beforehand. Normally it would be the job of an older sibling, or if there wasn't one a family friend. Ragul certainly wasn't going to help you, and because of the wager your father's friends were reluctant to get involved. So Mangal decided he would do it, wager or not.'

Peglar was grateful that he had, but there was still something that baffled him. 'But why leave it to the last minute?' he said. 'If somebody had told me about the fire right at the beginning, before any of the trials started, it would have been easier.'

'No one is let into these secrets until the night before,' said Feldar. Then, responding to Peglar's puzzlement, he went on, 'Think about it. The object of the trial is for the candidate to demonstrate his courage. It would be less of a test if it were known well ahead that it wouldn't be as hard as it at first might seem. There's an unwritten code of silence amongst those who have gone through initiation and no one ever speaks of it, not even to each other. You must honour that code, the only exception being if you are ever in a position like Mangal you may instruct one other person, as he did you.'

'What about my mother?'

'No, I'm afraid not. Particularly not her, but not any woman. Not your mother, or your girlfriend, or your paired women. This is a secret shared only amongst men.'

Peglar was surprised. 'Don't any women know about it?' Surely someone like Vancia must. There didn't seem to be anything she wasn't informed about.

'It's likely that women do, but they keep up the pretence because they know how important the Trial of Fire it is to the ritual of citizenship.'

Peglar wondered what Yalka would make of it. She already had a scathing view of the honesty of people in the city and this would confirm everything she thought.

'Now, to business,' Feldar said briskly. 'Tomorrow I'll assign one of my people to handle your affairs, but for the rest of today you have two further commitments. First there is an audience with your father. He has set it for the fifth bell. Then this evening there is your celebration feast. You will be expected to make a short speech. Oh, and your mother has asked for you. There is time for you to see her before the audience.'

22

AN AUDIENCE

Peglar should have gone to see his mother as soon as Feldar left, but he didn't realise that until much later. In any case, he assumed she would be at the audience and he would see her there. If she wanted to speak with him they could talk after the meeting.

The problem was that he was exhausted. Three trials in three weeks, when most people are allowed six and don't have a hated half-brother and his slimy friend trying to upset them, the Initiation Ceremony, the incident on the Citadel with Yalka all piled in on him and he felt more weary than he could remember ever feeling before. And besides all that, his feet were hurting.

He went to his bed chamber at the far end of the day room, and removed the heavy robes and the citizen's sash he was now entitled to wear. He stripped off his tights and peeled the pads from the soles of his feet. One foot looked to be okay but the other was weeping. He picked up the jar of ointment that Narvil had provided and applied it liberally to both feet. Then he lay back naked on the bed. A kind breeze came through the open window and soothed him, and within seconds he was asleep. He slept until a servant woke him soon before the fifth bell. That was why he didn't go to see his mother.

The audience was to take place in the Library, not in his father's study. That was something of a relief. Peglar had been dreading the idea of spending time in the stuffy oven that Karkis inhabited. Although termed an audience, it was in fact a family meeting, although it was clear who was in charge and who would do almost all the talking. For Peglar the immediate difference from previous meetings with his father was that he was invited to sit, and he took a place at the foot of the table.

Karkis was in a mood Peglar hadn't seen before, almost jovial. Vancia at his side was the opposite. She was erect and severe, her eyes cold and her mouth a firm line. The chair the other side of Karkis, where his mother should have been, was unoccupied. Opposite Peglar was Ragul, and next to him, Malina. Looking elsewhere, Ragul swung a kick at Peglar under the table as he settled, but he was expecting something like that and he kept his feet out of the way.

'Well, Peglar, you have made my Steward very happy,' said his father. He turned in his chair to where Feldar was in his usual place behind him. 'I understand from Ragul that you have won a tidy sum, Feldar.'

Feldar bowed. 'Yes, my lord.'

'Nigh on a year's wages, Ragul said grumpily.'

'Yes, my lord.'

Peglar was surprised. He hadn't asked Feldar about the money and had no idea Ragul had staked so much. If Feldar had lost he would have been in trouble.'

'Well, don't let it go to your head,' said Karkis. 'It was a strange business. You took a wager against my son, which is not good. On the other hand, you were supporting my other son, which is admirable. I think the punishment you deserve for one and the reward for the other cancel each other out, don't you?'

'Yes, my lord.'

'So you will return his purse to Ragul.' The smirk on Ragul's face would have lit the city. It soon faded. 'However, Karkis continued, fixing Ragul with a steady look, 'you made a bet against your brother, which is a hostile act and against the unity I expect amongst the members of this House. So you will receive your purse back from Feldar and give it immediately to Crestyn, who will deposit it in your name as a donation to city funds.'

Ragul's head sank. He gazed at the table top and picked at a knot with his forefinger. Malina's face was expressionless, although Peglar thought he discerned a hardness in her eye. She had always been close to Ragul and there was no doubt she would be on his side.

'The matter is closed,' Karkis leant forward and spoke to Peglar.

'Your mother would normally be present but she is indisposed.'

'Indisposed?' Peglar heard himself echo.

'Yes. According to her women she was feeling unwell before going to the Ceremonium but of course she was keen to attend. She took to her bed as soon as she returned.'

'Oh.' Peglar was concerned. Now he came to think of it Chalia had not seemed her usual self after the ceremony. He wished he'd gone to see her as Feldar had suggested.

'Woman's trouble, I shouldn't wonder,' said his father, turning to Feldar with a prodigious wink. Vancia and Malina were detached and clearly not amused.

'Very well.' Karkis became immediately businesslike. He looked hard at Peglar. 'I now have to decide what's to be done with you, my boy. It's customary for a newly initiated young man to spend some time in the army.'

Vancia snorted. 'What possible use could Peglar be to the army? He's hardly warrior material.'

Peglar winced at the abruptness and cruelty of this remark. He had assumed he would join the army. That's what all boys did after their initiation. They would serve for a couple of years before starting on whatever they would turn to next. He had not been looking forward to being in the army because it would mean contact with Ragul again, but he hated the idea of not joining and being different,.

Karkis broke in on his thoughts. 'You are right, my dear,' he said to Vancia. 'The normal course would be for Peglar to enrol in the army, and it could be argued that by completing the Three Trials he has shown himself capable of that. However, they were not easy for him and an alternative might be preferable. What do you suggest?'

Peglar squirmed. They were talking about him as if he wasn't there. His father didn't seem to think it worth asking Peglar himself what should happen to him. He looked across the table at Ragul, who appeared to have recovered from his disappointment over his wager and was enjoying this.

Vancia gave a thin smile and paused, seeming to

consider. 'Peglar means well, but he is immature. Had he been as strong as your other son, my lord, the army would have been ideal for him. He needs a sense of purpose, something on which to focus, otherwise he will simply drift. He must grow up. His body is underdeveloped. He needs a routine that will strengthen him both physically and mentally.'

Peglar wished he could become invisible. It was excruciating. He didn't expect any kindness from Vancia, but this was awful.

'So I repeat, what do you suggest?' said Karkis.

'My lord, I suggest we consider the next stage in Peglar's development alongside the appointment of a Companion. I believe under your instructions Feldar has been looking at families in the middle city who have sons who are Peglar's contemporaries. However, I believe that it would not be to Peglar's advantage to spend a lot of time in the company of another person of his own age. Instead he needs someone from whom he will learn. I suggest you choose for him a Companion who will be a tutor, a mature person who can advance his education.'

Peglar was appalled. Throughout the whole of the run up to his Initiation he had been looking forward to meeting his Companion, hoping that it might be someone who would stand up for him in the way Burian supported Ragul. The last thing he wanted was a tutor. He was horrified to see that his father was nodding.

'Where might we find such a person?' Karkis said.

Vancia's smile was pure syrup. 'As it happens, my lord, I have just the man in mind. His name is Abriul Sainter. You may know of him. He is a noted scholar and lectures sometimes at the Academy. I have taken the liberty of asking him to be here this evening. He would be honoured to take Peglar under his wing. I am sure that a man like Sainter can teach Peglar a great deal.'

'I think I have heard the name,' said Karkis. 'Where is he now?'

'He is waiting in the Atrium. With your permission Feldar will see that he is summoned.'

Karkis nodded and Feldar left the room.

Peglar was speechless. The plan was appalling, and so was the fact that Vancia had already spoken to this Sainter behind his back, behind his father's back. He would have expected Karkis to be angry, but he seemed pleased with Vancia's interference. 'There remains Peglar's physical development.'

Peglar didn't know if he was allowed to speak but he had to. 'May I speak, sir?' he said.

Karkis looked surprised, as if he'd forgotten he was there. 'Very well,' he said.

'I had some help preparing for the first trial from Cestris.'

Karkis didn't know who he meant, but Vancia did. Ragul, who had been looking very cheerful, frowned.

'Cestris?' said Vancia. 'You mean the athlete who was a champion in the Seven Cities Games? Why on earth would a young man like Cestris want to help you?'

'Actually they got on rather well, my lord,' said Feldar, who had re-entered the room. 'I know Cestris and I am sure he would be willing to assist Peglar. He would see it as a way of serving you and your House, sir.'

Karkis beamed. Peglar had never seen him smile so much.

The door opened and a servant entered. He was

followed by an extremely fat man. Peglar guessed he must weigh as much as Mangal but he lacked Mangal's height. He waddled towards Karkis and bowed, first to him, then to Vancia.

'Abriul Sainter, at your service,' he said.

'Lady Vancia has discussed with you the possibility of being my son, Peglar's, Companion.'

'She has, my lord.'

'And you are willing to take on this role?'

'Oh certainly, my lord. I am honoured to have been chosen.' He turned towards Peglar. 'Congratulations on your initiation into The House of the Leopard.' He made a stiff bow. Peglar had never before thought that a voice could sound fat, but Sainter's did.

'Excellent,' said Karkis. 'You, Sainter, for my son's academic development and Cestris for the physical.' He stood up. 'A sound mind in a sound body, eh? Well, we'll see if Peglar can manage either of those things.' He went out, laughing at his own joke.

Back in his quarters Peglar thought about what had just happened. The idea of training under the guidance of Cestris was appealing; the idea of being 'tutored' by Sainter was not. He had taken an immediate dislike to the man. Peglar didn't need a tutor. There'd been a tutor in the schoolroom, Distul, who'd been boring in the extreme and who, as they all grew up, couldn't keep Ragul in order and couldn't keep his eyes off Malina.

He stood in front of a mirror, pulled back his cloak and flexed his arm. Nothing. When Cestris bent his arm his biceps bulged. When Peglar did the same and there was hardly any change. He could use some help. If he was ever going to be able to take on Ragul, as he knew some day he must, he needed to build himself up.

He sat down and put his hand in the pocket of his tunic. His fingers closed around the little leopard that his mother had given him, and he stood it on the arm of his chair. He was worried about his mother. He must go to the women's wing and see how she was.

He was on the point of getting up when there was a loud bang as the door was kicked open. In the doorway was Ragul and behind him, of course, Burian. Ragul sauntered over and stood in front of Peglar's chair. He sneered and bent forward. 'Well, well, well, runt-boy, ' he intoned. 'How are you finding manhood, eh?'

'I'm not a runt,' Peglar said, as calmly as he could. 'I'm as tall as you.'

'Are you, now?' Ragul leered. 'I supposed your dick's as big as mine, too.' Burian snorted and Ragul guffawed. 'Let's see if it is.'

He made to grab the hem of Peglar's tunic. Reflexively his knees came together and his hand went to hold the fabric in place. Ragul pounced on what he interpreted as a feminine gesture. 'Oh my, will you look at this? She's scared we're going to look up her skirts!'

Burian could hardly control himself. Ragul moved round behind Peglar and rested his hands on his half-brother's shoulders. His laughter abruptly ceased. He placed a hand each side of Peglar's neck and drove his fingers into the gap between muscle and collarbone. Peglar winced. Ragul knew exactly where to squeeze to hurt most and it was excruciatingly painful. Peglar swallowed hard, determined to stay silent.

'I've got some news, and as it concerns you I thought I'd come to tell you first.' Ragul kneaded with his fingers to emphasise each word. 'Tell him, Buri,' Ragul said.

Burian came over and squatted down in front of

Peglar's chair. His skin was greasy and there were spots on his chin.

'Ragul's decided not to go back to the army.' Burian had a whining voice that sounded even more nasal when he was taunting. 'You see, he'd volunteered to stay on after his two years so he could be there when you joined, to help you settle in.' He sniggered. 'But it seems that now you're not going to be in the army after all, so he's going to stay here. He's not going back.'

'No,' said Ragul, taking up the refrain. 'I'm going to stay just so I can be near you. Now isn't that kind? Isn't that what a good brother should do?'

Peglar said nothing and the pincers drove into his shoulders again. He gasped.

'Say thank you, then,' growled Ragul.

Despite himself Peglar had to get the words out, just to stop the pain. 'Thank you.'

'Say thank you kind brother.'

'Thank you, kind brother.'

Ragul eased his grip. 'It's not going to get any better than this, runt-boy. Not ever. I'll see to that. Trust me.' He let go of Peglar's shoulders and peered closely at his cheek. 'Well now, will you look at this?' he said, turning to Burian. 'I do believe it has started shaving! Well, isn't it just the complete man.' He pinched Peglar's cheek where he had that morning nicked himself with his razor. He frowned at the smear of blood on his thumb and wiped it on Peglar's chest, poking him hard. 'Come on, Bury,' he said. 'Let's leave this little runt to play with himself.'

He was turning away when he caught sight of the leopard, which had fallen off the arm of the chair and was on the floor. He picked it up and looked closely at it.

'Nice,' he said. 'Very nice. I think this must have been meant for me.' He tossed the carving in his hand and dropped it into the purse at his waist. Without looking back he walked out, Burian behind him. They didn't close the door.

Peglar stayed in the chair, his eyes following them. He rubbed his shoulders, aching from Ragul's torture. His head throbbed. He ground his teeth, and for a moment tears of impotent rage pricked his eyes. He made a vow to himself, one that would be the first real test of what he knew was going to be a long struggle with his half-brother; he would get his leopard back.

23

PALACE ILLS

Peglar hadn't been looking forward to the feast and he didn't enjoy it. He would rather have wrapped his feet in cold cloths and gone to bed with a book. There seemed to be an endless number of people wanting to shake his hand, and each of them required welcoming with a sentence or two thanking them for thanking him.

Everyone took their places at the tables and the meal began. Peglar sat to the right of his father on the top table. His mother should have been on his other side but she wasn't there. Instead he found himself beside Geriker, who insisted on tedious small talk. At least Ragul and Burian were too far along the table to speak to him, or to hear what he said.

There were toasts to the city, to the House of Karkis, and of course to Peglar himself. He remembered being in the gallery what felt like many months ago and viewing another feast and other toasts, and wondered at how different things seemed now. His father spoke, and then it was his own turn. He wished he didn't have to stand because his feet were painful but he supposed that was all part of what he was expected to endure. Feldar had given him some tips on what to say and he thought he followed them, but afterwards he couldn't be sure; it had all passed in a blur and he couldn't remember what he'd said.

At last the ordeal was over and the guests began to drift away. Peglar was required to wait until they had all gone before he could himself leave, but eventually there was just his father and Vancia left. Karkis was engaged in a discussion with Feldar and Peglar took the opportunity to ask Vancia about his mother. Her reply was noncommittal, but the message Peglar got was that her condition was women's business and none of his.

Despite the wear and tear on his feet Peglar slept soundly and woke late. He bathed, dressed and went through the door to his day room. On the table were figs, yoghurt, oatmeal, berries, dried fish, eggs, sweet rolls, flatbread, cheese, butter, preserves. There were fruit cordials and cold mint tea. There was enough to feed a dozen and Peglar wondered if he was supposed to be expecting visitors, but there was only one place set; all this food was for him. He thought of Yalka, of her underfed body and the poverty she and others endured in the River Settlements. It shamed him to think what she would say if she could see this, his breakfast table.

He ate well. His feet were improving and he was feeling cheerful about the day. He'd had a note from Feldar to say that one of his staff would attend later to go through his duties and appointments. He was about to leave the table when there was a noise in the antechamber, the door opened and everything took a turn for the worse. Sainter shuffled through.

'Excellent news, excellent news,' he announced from the doorway. 'I thought I would be unable to join you yet because I had some business to complete. However, I was able to settle my affairs more quickly than I anticipated and I am available now. I can start my duties as your Companion this very day.'

He ambled towards the table, took a chair opposite Peglar, picked up a roll and took a large bite.

'I have put all my other commitments on hold,' he said grandly, 'all of them, in order to answer the call of the House of Karkis.' He somehow managed to convey that he was doing Peglar a great favour by being there. 'I think we will begin in the Library,' he said, reaching for a peach. 'I understand I might find there some works which will assist me in my research, and familiarity with the contents of the book collection will be useful for you.'

Peglar had spent a great deal of time in the Library. It was one of his favourite places. He knew its contents very well.

'Then perhaps a short walk in the garden,' he took another roll, 'a little light luncheon, and this afternoon we will devise a programme for our work together. It will be best to concentrate initially on Philosophy, Literature, and Mathematics. You do, of course, have to give some attention to this man Cestris. I don't think what you are to do with him deserves much of your time but we can allocate him a little.' Most of this accompanied Sainter consuming the roll, and was delivered with a full mouth. He was now eyeing up a banana.

'Allow me to tell you a little about myself.' Sainter leant back in the chair. He had clearly resisted the banana and as a reward for restraint cut himself some cheese. 'My family is from Halish-Karnon, where we are well known. I came to Chamaris as a boy when my father accepted a post at the Academy. Shortly after this I myself came to prominence when I...'

Peglar's attention drifted away. It seemed that Sainter was happy to go on talking and required nothing from him, not even the odd phatic grunt. He looked at the mural of the ships to distract himself from the droning little man. His voice had an irritating squeaky quality and he wheezed when he breathed. Peglar thought it would do him good to join in some of the sessions with Cestris and laughed inwardly at the idea. Or rather he thought the laughter was inward, but he was aware that Sainter had stopped talking and was regarding him.

'I must see my mother,' Peglar said to explain the interruption. 'She is ill. I must go to her now. I don't know how long I will be.' He rose from his chair.

'Ah,' said Sainter. 'Yes. Of course. I see. Well if you must, you must. I'll wait here for your return, then we can begin.' The banana won and Sainter reached for it.

As he walked to the women's wing Peglar tried to absorb what had just happened and what he could do about it. The situation was impossible. The idea of Sainter as his Companion was preposterous. He was old. He was probably older even than Vancia, although it was hard to tell because the chubby, round face was largely free from wrinkles. What could he possibly have to say to someone so much younger? And did he ever listen, or did he talk all the time? He seemed to think that he was Peglar's teacher. Nothing could possibly persuade him that there was anything worth learning from this man. And what right did he have to organise his time, which in any case would not all be his own. Feldar had referred to 'duties' and 'appointments', and he had other plans for what he would do as well as these. Important among them were visits to the Citadel.

He was so wrapped up in these thoughts that he didn't see Narvil and as he turned into the corridor towards his mother's quarters he almost collided with him. The physician took his arm and steered him into an alcove.

'You are on the way to see your mother?'

'Yes.'

'She is not well.'

'Oh.' Peglar knew that and was hoping for some information. Whatever was wrong with Chalia must have happened quickly. He felt guilty that he'd not gone straight to see her when Feldar had mentioned it yesterday.

'Her condition is puzzling. I have given her a tonic and I prescribe fasting and rest. Plenty of rest. Do not tire her.'

'No.'

'Lady Vancia has kindly offered to care for her and has made one of her own waiting women available.' Narvil had been holding on to Peglar's arm all this time. He abruptly released it. 'How are your feet? Improving?'

'Oh. Yes, thank you, they are much better.'

'The balm is proving effective?'

'Yes.' It wasn't. Peglar didn't think it made any difference and had stopped using it.

'Good. Continue to apply it, twice a day, and in between times if needed.'

Narvil walked away, leaving Peglar troubled. Vancia

didn't get on with his mother. Why would she volunteer her help? And why the loan of a waiting woman? Chalia had waiting women of her own.

What Narvil said prepared him for what he found when he reached his mother's rooms, but only in part. He knew her day room well and had spent many hours there. When he was little his nurse would bring him to play, and he would sit on a rug on the floor and watch his mother sewing, drawing, studying a book. When he grew older she would read to him or tell him stories – some of the ones he passed on to Yalka – and if she was busy one of her women might stand in. The room had always been bright, airy, cheerful. Today it was different. The windows were closed and shutters blocked out the light. The colourful fabrics that his mother liked to scatter had gone and a scented lamp burned on the table, producing a heavy odour.

A large woman in servant's livery occupied a chair in the middle of the doorway to his mother's bedroom. Peglar approached her but she didn't move. He stood before her and folded his arms. She looked up from her chair.

'Lady Chalia is ill, sir, and is not to be disturbed.' She folded her arms across an ample bosom.

'I know she is ill. That's why I have come to visit her.'

The woman didn't move. 'Physician Narvil said she is to have complete rest.'

'I have just now talked with Narvil and he encouraged me to see my mother.'

The woman reflected, then said, 'Lady Vancia placed me here and said I was to admit no one.'

Peglar fought to control the anger he felt rising within him. 'What is your name?' he said.

'Forta, sir.'

'Well, Forta, I am sure that Lady Vancia did not intend her instruction to apply to me. I will see my mother. Now kindly remove yourself.'

The woman moved, but not willingly. She got up slowly from the chair and took two steps to the side. The chair remained in the doorway. Peglar's impulse was to kick it out of the way but he didn't want to prolong the confrontation so he seized it with one hand and pushed it aside.

What he saw in the room was a shock. His mother had always been smiling, carefree, beautifully dressed and made up. The thought of her being anything else was inconceivable. Now she lay on her bed with her hair tangled and spread untidily over the crumpled pillows. Her face was the colour of a cheap candle, her lips mauve. She looked a different person from the one who had hugged him only the day before. She opened her eyes, gave him a weak smile, and held out her hand. He took it. It was clammy.

'Mother, what's happened? When did this start?'

It took her time to answer and her breathing was laboured. 'It came on during the evening before your Initiation Ceremony. I took some fruit tea and soon after I began to feel ill.'

Peglar sat on the chair beside the bed and stroked his mother's hand. 'Ill in what way?'

'A headache. I have it still. And nausea. Cramps in my stomach.'

'Was there something wrong with the tea?'

There was another pause. His mother was finding it

hard to speak and her voice was weak. 'Narvil says it's probably an infection and I should fast.' She withdrew her hand. 'You should be careful, it might be something you could catch.'

Peglar took her hand back. He doubted it was an infection. It was more likely something in the tea, perhaps a fruit that had started to decay. If that was so, a period of fasting and rest while she got it out of her system would see her well again.

He sat with her while her eyes closed, her breathing settled and she fell asleep. Then he kissed her forehead and returned to his own rooms. He would visit her again tomorrow and he confidently expected that by then she would be back to her usual self.

24

THE APOTHECARY

He was pleased and relieved that when he got back to his rooms there was no sign of Sainter. There as no sign of the breakfast either and he had the mischievous thought that Sainter might have eaten everything, the whole lot.

'When did Sainter leave?' he asked a servant. He told himself that he really must learn the man's name, and not just the name of this one but of all of them. He would write them down, but later.

'He didn't stay long after you had gone, sir,' said the man.

'Is he coming back?'

'He didn't say, sir.'

To Peglar it seemed that the best way to deal with Sainter was to avoid him. Perhaps his "companion" would tire of coming to his rooms and finding him not there, and his visits – and his interfering, irritating "programme" – would fade away. He sank into a chair and closed his eyes. There was nothing he could do for Chalia other than wait for her to get over her illness. He would have got her some sweetmeats but Narvil said she was to fast. She had the tonic and that ought to help. He would get her some flowers to brighten up the dark, airless room. He called for a servant.

'Please take a message to Steward Feldar that I would be grateful if he would organise some flowers for Lady Chalia. Tell him too that I have a headache and won't be at dinner, and to convey my apologies to my father.' The latter was an afterthought but he couldn't face company. He needed peace.

'Of course, sir. I'm sorry to hear of your mother's illness and of your headache. Would you like me to arrange for dinner to be brought here for you?'

'Thank you. Perhaps later.' He studied the servant for a moment. He was dark haired and looked strong. How old? Younger than Feldar, certainly. 'What's your name?' he said.

'Travis, sir.'

'Well, Travis, thank you. It's a pleasure to meet you.'

'It's my pleasure to serve you, sir.' Travis bowed and withdrew.

In his sleeping chamber there was a robe neatly laid out on his bed for him to change into for the evening meal. He pushed it aside. The decision to skip dinner was a relief. It meant not only that he would not see Sainter but also that he would avoid Ragul. Although Ragul's rooms were only a few doors along the corridor and there was always the chance that he might take it into his head to call. And of course, Sainter could return. It would be as well to go out. Was this to be the pattern of his life now? Being driven from his own territory in order to avoid the possibility of unwanted visitors?

He thought about where he could go. The west court

beyond the women's wing would be a good place. It was not overlooked by any of the other parts of the Palace and it was unlikely that anyone would look for him there.

It had been a hot, sticky day and the air felt tight as a bowstring. A thunder storm was brewing and huge columns of cloud were building in the eastern sky. Daylight was fading, and that was why they didn't see him. He had stopped close to a flight of shallow steps down to the cellars when he heard something moving. He dropped back behind a cypress and peered around its trunk. Two figures were walking along a narrow path between the shrubs. They were identically dressed in charcoal grey gowns with hoods, the uniform of female servants. Peglar thought at first that they actually were servants, leaving the Palace at the end of their day's work. However, they were heading away from the gate.

He was struck by something about the way one of them walked. Her bearing seemed too lofty for a servant, and as the pair came out from the shadows he saw her face. It was Vancia! Her raven hair, usually piled in imperious coils, was hidden under her hood, but there was no mistaking who it was. He recognised her plump companion as the woman who had been outside his mother's room, Forta.

The two women stayed close to the bushes until they were only a few paces from Peglar, then they stopped. He thought they might be going to turn around and go back but they didn't. To his surprise they scanned the garden, then furtively hurried down the cellar steps.

Peglar was astonished. Why on earth was Vancia going down there, and why was Forta with her? And why was Vancia dressed like a servant?

He left the shelter of the tree and crept closer. The door at the bottom of the steps was open and he could see that the stairway continued on the other side, turning at a landing a few feet in. A flickering, yellow light came from beyond the bend. There was no sign of the two women.

He hesitated. He desperately wanted to know what they were doing down there, but what would he say if he suddenly came face to face with Vancia? What possible reason could he give for being there?

It was risky, but curiosity overcame caution and he started warily down the steps. He half expected to see the two of them just past the bend, but all was clear. He reached the bottom step and peered round the edge of the wall.

Peglar had never been in the cellars, although he knew they were there. He had expected them to be damp, but the passage he was in was dry and dusty. The floor was level, of beaten earth, and the walls were dressed stone. At some stage they had been covered in whitewash but the surface was patchy and flaking. There were spiders, plenty of them, and big ones judging by the webs. There was also a faint smell of drains.

After a few steps the passage widened enough for two people to walk side by side. It ran straight, not under the house but away from it, beneath the rear garden. Part way along there was a burning torch fitted in a sconce, the source of the stuttering light. It was smoking slightly, filling the top of the passage with a haze. At the far end, about fifty paces away, he could see Vancia and Forta. They were at the foot of more stairs and were too busy adjusting their cloaks and hoods to look back and see him. He stayed still until they began to climb the steps and disappeared from view. Then he hurried after them.

It was a gamble. There was nowhere to hide, and if they came back they would be sure to see him. His heart was beating fast as he reached the end of the passage and looked up the stone steps. There was no one there but he could see a small door at the top. He crept up, pushed the door open, and emerged into the open air.

At first he had no idea where he was. Then he realised he was in the small memorial garden on the other side of the lane behind the Palace. The door he'd used was at the rear of a stumpy, marble obelisk. He'd seen the garden and the obelisk many times, in fact he passed it every time he went up the hill to the Citadel, but he'd never known the door was there. Anyone who did see it would have thought that it was something to do with the monument. They would never guess that it concealed a secret entrance to the Master's Palace. Some people would give a lot of money for that information. Peglar was surprised it had never been sealed up.

Vancia and Forta were some way off and walking briskly, cloaks fussing in the dust. Peglar followed, keeping to the shadows. What could they be doing? Usually when Vancia went out everybody knew about it. She used the main gate and rode in one of the best carriages, with a clutch of waiting women and servants and several Household Guards. Yet here she was, slinking out on foot by a secret exit, with only Forta to attend her. If she had left by one of the gates it would have been recorded in the gate log. She could only be acting in this way because she didn't want anyone to know she was going out.

The lane backing the great houses was level until it met the city wall. Here there were two choices: left and up the hill, following the wall until it butted against the Citadel rock, or right, where the way widened as it descended towards the lower streets. Peglar couldn't risk being spotted, so he hid in an archway to see which way they would go. It was right, downhill.

He jogged to the corner, fearful of losing the pair but ready to dodge if they looked back. When he got there they were a little way down the road, maintaining a good speed and keeping their heads down so that their faces were hidden. As the street descended there was more cover and Peglar was able to slip from opening to opening, hiding in the mouths of alleyways and yards, the passageways and paths that were the veins of the City. It was close to curfew and there were few people about.

They left the upper district and reached the point where the road widens as it crosses the end of the Grand Parade. Peglar thought they might stop here but they carried on, skirting the middle city and plunging more steeply towards the lower, less wholesome quarter. The street names there were at odds with the murky surroundings: Honeypot Lane, Rose Avenue, Spice Yard, just discernible amongst the muck that grimed the buildings. The road twisted and turned and there was a prevailing smell of sewage.

Peglar had never ventured into this area before and would not have chosen to visit it now. The daylight had almost gone and torches were rare. The atmosphere was threatening. The women were running a risk. It was astonishing that Vancia should venture into such a run-down neighbourhood at all, but incomprehensible that she should choose to do so at that time of the day, and with only one other person. Peglar closed the gap between them. A few heavy drops of rain begin to fall, landing with a fizz on the dusty roadway.

Just when Peglar thought Vancia and Forta must be going all the way down the hill to the Port Gate they slipped into an alley. It wasn't actually an alley, just a small yard. There was a single door, with yellow lamplight spilling through a cracked glass panel. Forta waited beside it. She was facing away from the mouth of the alley and Peglar pulled back quickly in case she turned around. He carried on down the hill until he came to a niche where he could watch the yard entrance, and he stood amongst rubbish and weeds, waiting. Why had the women come to this dingy spot?

They were not long, but when they did reappear Peglar almost missed them. They looked around as if to check they were not being watched before emerging into the street and starting quickly up the hill. They hurried, heads bowed, two serving women out a little later than they should have been and hastening to be home before the curfew.

He needed to know what they had been doing, what it was that had drawn Vancia to this place. He waited until the pair were out of sight around the first bend, then returned to the smelly little yard. A hand-painted sign on the corner identified it as Blossom Court, although it must have been many years since anything but weeds had flowered there. The ground was rough and uneven, with missing cobbles and upended pavings. Dilapidated buildings were on three sides. Slabs of plaster and masonry had fallen from the walls, adding to the rubbish in the yard. In one corner a slimy excrescence glistened in the feeble light. There was a pile of debris in another, and something moved amongst it. A rat? The place was infected with the smell of decay.

It was now quite dark, the only illumination the light from the door. Peglar picked his way towards it, taking care where he trod. There was a name on the glass door-panel, and a sign saying enter. As he pushed the door a bell jangled and he stepped into a low, square room. Everything was dark brown – walls, ceiling, floor, a table, a chest and a chair. In the middle of the room a single, stout post supported a boarded ceiling. An oil lamp cast a pale glow over the scene. Beside it on the table was a glass jar half full of a brownish powder, and next to that a pair of scales.

There was another door, facing the entrance, and from somewhere beyond it came a scraping noise and a wheezy cough. A moment later a tiny, ancient man shuffled into the room. He was wizened and bent and had a hump back, and he was so small he scarcely came to Peglar's waist. His face was deeply lined and a pair of gold-rimmed spectacles perched on his nose. He wore a coat of purple silk, embroidered with the black outlines of geometric shapes. It must once have been a fine garment, but like its owner it appeared past its best. It was patched and darned, and some of the needlework had pulled so that the threads hung in inky trickles. In one of his mottled hands the man carried a stick with a heavy brass ball on the end. He twisted his head to the side to look up into Peglar's face, his expression part enquiry, part challenge.

'I am seeking Nortus Feldar,' Peglar said. 'Is he here?' He had to give some reason for being there and this was the first thing that came into his head, although even as he mouthed the words they sounded absurd. The man looked at him sharply. His eyes were rat black and piercing.

'I know no one of that name,' he said in a reedy voice.

The door behind him opened and a woman came in. She was easily as aged as the man and just as crooked.

'What is it?' she croaked.

'Nothing, nothing. A stranger. He's leaving.'

The old man waved his stick to shoo the woman away. She reversed through the door, letting it slam behind her, but before the door swung back Peglar saw enough to know what this place was. He glimpsed shelves of coloured jars and bottles, racks of potions and powders which left him in no doubt about what went on here. Vancia had been visiting the premises of an apothecary. And before the old man moved in front of it, Peglar read the label on the jar on the table: *Arnica Montana (Leopard's Bane)*.

25

OVERHEARD

By the time Peglar started back up the hill towards the Memorial Garden it was raining hard, with sullen drops slapping the road. Within a minute there were streams running down the gulleys. He pulled his cloak over his head. His sandals were soon soaked and his tunic drenched.

He assumed that Vancia and Forta were well ahead of him and was worried they might lock the door at the rear of the obelisk. He was relieved when it opened easily on well-oiled hinges. He was glad to get out of the downpour, and stood for a moment dripping on the steps. The torch was still burning and that was a relief too. He'd been imagining having to grope his way through the passage in the dark and he'd not been looking forward to disturbing the spiders, but he couldn't re-enter the house by the gate. It would raise questions about how he'd managed to leave unnoticed, and about where he'd been.

He went down the steps and walked quickly along the passage. He was about half way when he noticed a small door he'd not spotted before. It was low, waist height, narrow, and in the darkest part of the tunnel. That was why he'd not seen it before. He hesitated; what might be on the other side? He eased it open and cautiously peered into… nothing. Blackness. But it must go somewhere because he could feel a draught on his face.

He lifted the torch from its sconce on the wall. It wouldn't last much longer because the flame was dying and it had started to smoke, so he'd have to hurry. He got down on his knees and held the torch out into the space. It looked to be another passage, smaller than the first one and twisting into darkness. His fear of enclosed spaces plucked at him. What would happen if he got stuck in here? Nobody knew where he was. He'd be lost. He'd starve to death in the dark. He took a deep breath, told himself not to be soft, and squeezed through the opening.

This new tunnel was much narrower, and too low for him to stand up. The roof was uneven and protruding lumps of rock had to be dodged. He didn't duck low enough for one of them and the result was a painful blow on the top of his head. There was an opening directly ahead where this tunnel met another, even lower and even more cramped.

He could make out a dim glow coming from the roof a little way along. He moved a few paces towards it, and became aware of a noise. It was scarcely there, just a faint, insubstantial murmur. He felt a sudden shiver. Ghosts? Invaders from the River Settlements threading their way under the Palace? As he moved the sound grew louder and he thought it seemed like someone talking but he couldn't make out what was being said.

His heartbeat increased. Were there other people down here in the dark?

He stood still, trying to work out where the noises were coming from. He edged further along the passage and found himself standing at the bottom of a brick well. It was like a chimney, except it was sealed at the top. There were metal rungs set into the wall and, at about a man's height above him, what looked like a grille. That was where the light was coming from, and the sounds too. The rungs felt firm, and cautiously he climbed until he reached the grille and was able to look through.

At first he couldn't understand what he saw. Then he realised that he was looking into the Library. The aperture was at floor level and it gave an odd view of the room, but he could see chairs and book-lined shelves. And he could see three men, or at least he could see their lower halves. He knew that one of them was his father, another looked like Styron, and he thought that the third was Uncle Mostani. He could hear what they were saying clearly enough now, although it at first made no sense.

'I don't know. I came here straight from the Council,' Uncle Mostani was saying.

'Where are they being held?' That was his father.

'The Guardians have them.'

'Just the two of them?' said Styron.

'The others got away.'

His father sounded angry. 'Got away! Pah. Bribed the Guardians, you mean. Anyway, don't they know who they've got there? Don't they understand that Ragul is my son, my preferred son?'

Styron tried to calm things down. 'We can soon get this settled. I'll see the Marshal. Oil a few wheels.'

Uncle Mostani wasn't convinced. 'I don't think you'll be able to get them out of it that easily. Lembick's handling it. He's vowed that everyone gets the same treatment, however high-ranking they may be. He's making a big thing of it to get support from the middle city.'

'It sounds like it's all rolled up in his plan for the House of Lembick to take over from the House of Karkis,' said Styron.

'House of Lembick?' my father shouted. 'There is no House of Lembick! The man doesn't even have a pairing, let alone an heir. Blood and bile, I ought to have him arrested!'

He heard movement and it seemed as though Karkis had walked out. Peglar's arms were aching from hanging on to the rungs and his rain-soaked cloak was sticking to him. His legs wobbled as he climbed down. He wasn't sure what the three men had been talking about, but his father had referred to Ragul as his "preferred son", and that hurt. It sounded like he'd been arrested by the Guardians. Whatever for? The idea of his half-brother or anyone else in the family being apprehended by Guardians was unthinkable.

26

LEOPARD'S BANE

Peglar made his way towards the main passage and up the steps into the courtyard. The rain had stopped but the ground was soaked and it was pitch dark. He was thankful to be out in the fresh air again. The torches had almost burnt out and some of them were smoking badly, making it hard to breath in there and stinging his eyes. He slipped off his sodden cloak and his wet sandals, and leaving puddles on the floor made his way to his room.

The cold supper he'd asked for was on the table in his day room but he didn't want it. Beside it was a note from Sainter saying that he'd called, he regretted Peglar had not been there, and he would return the following morning. Peglar didn't want that either. He needed to think. He went to his bed chamber and towelled himself dry. Then he lay on the bed and closed his eyes.

Nothing made sense. His mother, who had always been in fine health, was ill. His step-mother, who had never been friendly, had volunteered to take over her care. Now she had visited an apothecary, apparently to obtain a preparation of some sort. Finally her son, his half-brother, was in custody.

He assumed that Vancia had been buying what was written on the label of the jar he'd seen on the apothecary's table: *Arnica Montana (Leopard's Bane)*. What was it? Some sort of medicine? If it was a treatment for Chalia, why didn't Narvil provide it? Why did Vancia have to slink out by night dressed like a servant to get it? And then there were the tunnels. How many of them were there? Did they run under the whole Palace? Were these the secret ways that Yalka had talked about? Lots of the rooms had low level grilles like the one he'd looked through into the Library; in fact there were a couple in his own day room. He'd always thought they were for ventilation. Well, maybe they were, but it seemed they had other uses too.

He got up from his bed and went back to his day room. He couldn't help peering into the grilles, half expecting to see a pair of eyes looking out at him, but there were none.

He scanned the shelves until he found what he was looking for. It was a work on botany, an alphabetical compendium of plants that he'd been made to study in the schoolroom. He'd not paid much attention to it at the time but was glad he'd kept it. He thumbed through the pages until he found the entry he was looking for.

Arnica Montana (Leopard's Bane)

Arnica montana is a tall plant with yellow, aromatic flowers. Despite having some clinical properties it is toxic and no part of it should be swallowed or applied to broken skin. If taken it is likely to cause stomach pain, diarrhoea, and vomiting. Occasional mild doses are unlikely to be seriously harmful, but larger quantities will result in internal bleeding, liver damage, nervousness, accelerated heart rate, muscular weakness, and, if enough is ingested, death.

He picked another book but it didn't tell him anything more. What were the plant's "clinical properties"? Did Vancia know that it could also cause harm? How much was needed for it to do that? How quickly did it act?

He felt a sudden chill, the cold embrace of a growing fear. Perhaps Vancia *did* know that it was a poison. Perhaps that was the reason she'd gone out in secret to get it. Then he had another thought. What would Vancia gain from poisoning his mother? She was the senior wife and Chalia was no threat to her. So who else might be the target? His father? Certainly he'd not looked well recently. But what possible reason could Vancia have for that either? If his father were to die before the Sharing his wealth would be divided equally between his two sons. Surely that would be to Ragul's disadvantage because Peglar had no doubt that in the Sharing his father's "preferred son" would get more. Better for Vancia and Ragul, then, if their father lived.

Peglar felt as if the world was coming to an end. He started to tremble and nausea gripped him. He felt faint and clutched the back of a chair. The room spun. He was going to throw up. He staggered to his bathroom and bent over the bowl. He hung there as the room revolved around him. Then he made his way unsteadily to his bed, clutching walls, the doorframe, the furniture for support before flopping onto the mattress. He was sweating and he felt disconnected. Had he himself been poisoned? It would make much more sense for Vancia to be going after him rather than his father or mother. He was the one whose existence was preventing Ragul inheriting the whole of the family fortune. But how could he be poisoned? He hadn't eaten anything since breakfast and that was a long time ago.

Stress, confusion, weariness and unease bore down on him. He lapsed into a fitful sleep, where he heard the Ceremonium bell every hour and the time between was filled with troublesome dreams.

27

ARREST

'Ah,' Feldar said as Peglar opened the door of his office. 'I thought I might see you.'

If Peglar had expected some show of deference from his father's Steward now that he was an adult male member of the powerful House of Karkis he was disappointed. Feldar behaved towards him just as he always had. Obviously his initiation didn't make much difference.

Feldar gestured towards a chair. Gratefully Peglar sat down. He'd got out of bed at the fifth bell. He felt that he hadn't slept at all but he couldn't bear to stay in bed any longer. Physically he was better, but mentally the sensation remained of being locked in a tunnel as black as the one he'd seen the night before.

He'd been hungry and gone through to his day room. The supper which had been put out for him the night before was still there. He took some bread and examined it. It was dry and hard but it looked all right. He sniffed it. It smelt as he expected. There was nothing unusual about it, but if it had been tampered with would it smell? It was the same with the cheese and the meat. It all appeared to be fine, but how could you tell? There was a dish of hard boiled eggs. He thought that it would be difficult to interfere with these so he'd broken the shell on one and taken a bite. It had tasted good, and it went down in a couple of mouthfuls. He'd eaten another. There were some oranges, and apples, and figs. He'd thought it might be possible to smear the skin of an apple with poison, and the same with the figs, but he was confident that an orange in its protective sheath would be fine, so he'd eaten two.

He'd always found it easier to get things straight in his head if he wrote them down, so he took a sheet of paper and a pencil.

- <u>Mother</u>: Is she being poisoned? By Vancia? Why?
- <u>Action</u>: Talk to Narvil (but is he in on it?). Visit her more. Get her own women back to keep watch on her.

- <u>Yalka</u>: Did I misunderstand her? If not, do I mind what she said?
- <u>Action</u>: Go to Citadel and find her. She might be able to help with the Ragul issue.

- <u>Ragul</u>: Wants to do me harm.
- <u>Action</u>: Avoid him. All I can do but I don't like hiding. Face him?

- <u>The Sharing</u>: When will it be? How will my father divide the estate.

- Action: Do something to impress my father.
  Ideas??

- Sainter: !!!!
- Action: Avoid him. Am I just running away?

All that seemed to do was make things worse. He put his elbows on the table and his head in his hands. He was tired but if he returned to bed there would be no chance of sleep. The seventh bell rang, and that was when he decided to seek out Feldar.

The Steward leant back in his chair. 'You're here because you've heard about Ragul.'

'Yes,' said Peglar.

'How much do you know?'

'Not much. I overheard Uncle Mostani saying that he and Burian had been arrested and the Guardians had them in custody but he didn't say why.'

'Very well. The "why" is easy. A Guardian patrol was in the lower city, near where the stream ducks under the wall just the other side of the River Settlements. They heard a commotion and found a group of young men. They were holding on to a child, a small girl, and as they approached she bit the hand of one of them and ran off. Most of the gang followed her, except for the one with the bitten hand and another. The bitten one was Ragul, the other Burian.'

'If the child ran away what are they supposed to have done wrong? Why are they being held?'

'Well for one thing they were out after curfew. For another the Guardians appear to have been tipped off that your brother and his pal belong to one of the gangs that have been killing the feral children. This one calls itself the Rat Catchers.'

'But that's just gossip, isn't it? There's no proof.' Or was there? Peglar had a sudden vision of the "finger" Ragul had shown him before the Trial of Water. He'd not examined it up close and had assumed it was a piece of meat, but it was just possible it might have been a real one, a finger cut from a dead child.

'It's more than gossip. Ragul admitted it. He tried to blag his way out of trouble, saying he was cleaning up the streets, clearing away vermin, doing his civic duty, that sort of thing. It might have worked too because the Guardians were minded to let them go, but the duty councillor is Lembick and he's decided to make an example of them.'

'Oh.'

'Yes, oh indeed. Lembick's going by the book. He sees this as an opportunity to undermine your father and to challenge him. It's a gift, your father's eldest son in trouble. He points out that your father declared that anyone caught in a gang would be severely punished, and that's what he wants.'

'So what's he going to do?'

'There'll be a hearing before a magistrate later this morning and Ragul and Burian will be found guilty.'

'What will happen then?'

'Well, at one time your father was threatening that anyone caught doing this would be exiled, but that was never part of the final edict, so they'll be flogged.'

Flogged? Ragul, Karkis's "preferred son" flogged? He couldn't believe it. 'Can't our father stop it?'

'Your father is a wily old fox. He says the two of them should be punished. He says no one is above the law, not even a son of the first family. It's his duty to set an example and any punishment given by the magistrate must be applied. It will be hard for Ragul and Burian, but it will soon be over, and it means that Lord Karkis has upstaged Lembick.'

Peglar got up to go. He'd found out what he came for and he needed some time alone to work out what it all meant. There was one more thing.

'You said somebody tipped off the Guardians about Ragul and Burian, what they were doing and where they'd be.'

'Yes,' said Feldar.

'Do you know who it was?'

'I do. It was your friend.'

'My friend?'

'Yes. The girl you've been meeting up on the Citadel.'

28

THE SENTENCE

The flogging was to take place in the public square outside the Ceremonium. Although the event was public it wasn't staged as a show. There was no platform, and anyone in the crowd more than a couple of rows back wouldn't see much.

As the hour for the punishment approached a nervous silence fell on the household. Servants went about their business with their faces down, there was whispering in corners and meaningful looks from behind hands. Peglar left the Palace by the main gate with a couple of Household Guards and walked down the hill to the square. Much as he hated Ragul he didn't want to watch him being flogged, but Feldar said he should go because it was important for all the family to be there.

The crowd was substantial – how did people hear so quickly about these things? The Household Guards forced a way through to where some chairs had been placed on the steps outside the Ceremonium. Peglar was no sooner settled than his father arrived, with Styron and Vancia. Karkis looked ashen. Styron, beside him, was grave. Vancia had a face as black as thunder. 'The son of the Master being flogged like a common thief. How can you allow this?' she muttered. Karkis ignored her.

The punishment was to be carried out by the City Corrections Officer and his assistant. Peglar watched them arrive, both cloaked in black and masked. They took up positions beside a timber 'A' frame that had been erected at the base of the steps. They were soon joined by two Councillors, who were there to see that the sentence was carried out properly. Two bells rang from the great clock, and almost immediately the door to the Ceremonium opened and Ragul and Burian appeared, led in by a pair of Guardians.

Peglar was shocked. His half-brother was hobbled at the ankles and he had a rope around his neck, like an animal. Apart from a small and dirty loincloth he was naked. His face was white, except for his eyes, which were red and puffy. There was a large weal on his arm and a raw-looking graze all down one leg. One hand was roughly bandaged. That must be from the bite. The sad creature Peglar saw now was so different from the strutting bully he was used to that he found himself feeling sorry for him. Burian looked no better. There were a couple of jeers and a few shouts of encouragement from people Peglar recognised as Ragul's friends, but for the most part the crowd was silent.

Immediately following this dismal procession were Lembick and Thornal. The Marshal stood on the steps to address the crowd.

'Be it known that this day in the City Court of

Chamaris the two individuals presented here were found guilty on two counts. Count one, that they did knowingly and willingly contravene city regulations in that they were on the streets after the curfew. Count two, that they did conspire with others to commit violence in a public place by seizing a child with the intent to cause the said child grievous harm. The sentence is that they are to receive twenty lashes each.'

'Twenty,' Vancia murmured. 'Oh my god.'

'Twenty is lenient,' said Styron. 'Fifty would be usual, and in any case the punishment for murder is exile.'

'That's for murder of a citizen,' said Vancia. 'Anyway, they didn't kill the child and there's no proof that they would have.'

'No,' Styron said, 'but Ragul has confessed to other child killings. Lembick tricked him by promising leniency if he made a full confession, and besides it's said that he's been bragging about them in the city taverns.' There was a hostile silence from Vancia. Styron continued quietly, 'Thornal has told the correctors to carry out the sentence quickly. Normally they pause between strokes so that the pain builds, but he's instructed them to get the floggings over with as fast as they can.'

'I'm grateful to the Marshal,' muttered Karkis. 'My son will appreciate that.'

The two Corrections Officers strapped Ragul's wrists to the top of the wooden frame, pulling the leather bindings tight. When they were satisfied with the fastenings each chose a long, thin cane from among an armful carried by an assistant, and made a few practice swishes. Then they began their work. The older

Corrections Officer went first. There was a hiss and a sickening crack as the first stroke landed on Ragul's bare back. Without pause his assistant followed, then a third and a fourth as the two men got into a rhythm, swinging in turn. Ragul was silent for the first few blows but as they continued he started to cry out.

Peglar watched for a few moments more, then had to turn away. The sickening crack of the canes and Ragul's cries followed him into the Ceremonium, where he slumped on a bench just inside the door.

There was a cheer from the crowd and noise from outside. Then the door opened and Ragul came through. This time he wasn't tied up. His sentence paid, he was now a free man. His face was twisted in pain and streaked with tears, but when he saw Peglar he fought to control it and straightened his back. He stopped before him.

'You're next, runt boy,' he said. 'I'm going to see that you are.' He stared at Peglar, then turned and walked on. His back was covered in red weals and bleeding.

Outside there was the hiss and the thwack of the canes again as Burian received his beating.

29

LEAVING

Throughout the rest of the afternoon the Palace was hushed. Peglar found it hard to get what he had seen and heard out of his mind. He saw no one and nobody came to see him. He had expected Sainter to come and was thankful he didn't. He went to visit his mother but she was sleeping. He was surprised to find Malina there, but she said that their father had asked her to spend some time keeping Chalia company. He told her that he would return later, and went back to his rooms wondering if Malina was in on whatever it was that Vancia was doing, always assuming she was doing anything. He could do with some answers. Were there tunnels like the one under the Library beneath the women's wing? Yalka would know if there were? Would she show him how to keep watch on whatever was going on in there? Would she even do it for him?

Yalka was a problem. She'd obviously misunderstood the motive behind his gift of the drawing things, and her offer had been what she thought he would expect. Was is something she'd done before?

She'd run off. Was that because she was offended by how he'd reacted? Did she resent him judging her? What should he have done? He needed to talk to her. He needed to see her.

As the afternoon heat waned he went to the courtyard, down the steps to the cellar and along the corridor. He thought the door out through the obelisk might be locked but it wasn't. As he climbed the hill to the Citadel he reflected on what an advantage it was to have this secret way of getting in and out of the Palace. It must have been the gate guards who'd been telling Feldar about his comings and goings. But how did Feldar know that he'd been heading for the Citadel? And how did he know who he'd been meeting there? He must have been followed. Spied on, as Yalka would have said. If he didn't know before he knew now that there were no secrets in the House of Karkis, and that everything he did could be seen, noted, and reported.

The Citadel was deserted. The stones were warm and the scrubby grasses baked by the day's sunshine. There was no sign of Yalka, or of Verit. Peglar waited, and watched the evening draw in and the city settle. In the streets below torches were kindled and windows lit. It would soon be time for the curfew. Were gangs of young men getting themselves ready for a night's hunting? Or had what happened to Ragul and Burian made them think again.

It was dark before he returned to the Palace. In his day room he found another note from Sainter. This one didn't hide the little man's irritation. He had written that he had called "yet again" to find that Peglar was absent. He would return at the ninth bell tomorrow, the note said, "and would be obliged if you could see your way to being present". Peglar screwed the paper into a ball and flung it into the basket. Perhaps, he said to himself.

There was no family meal tonight and another cold supper had been laid for him. Peglar investigated it, sniffing suspiciously at anything he thought could have been doctored. He suddenly thought of Ragul, and wondered where he was and how he was. He might be in his rooms, just along the corridor. For one mad moment Peglar thought about going to see him, to offer an olive branch. But what was it he'd said? "You're next." What did that mean? Was he saying that Peglar would be flogged too? What for? He wasn't in a gang and there was nothing he'd done wrong, or could think that he might do.

He wanted an update on his mother's condition. Going in person would probably mean another confrontation with Forta or one of the other women whose job, he'd decided, was to obstruct him when he tried to see her, so he sent Travis to the women's wing to find out what he could, and waited. It was some time before Travis returned.

'What news?'

'I was unable to see your mother, my lord, because I was told she was sleeping.'

'Who told you that?'

'One of the waiting women. I don't know her name.'

'Did you ask how my mother is?'

'Yes, sir, I did, as you instructed. I was told that there has been some improvement in her condition.'

If Chalia was asleep he didn't want to disturb her. He'd visit her in the morning. It would be a good reason to dodge Sainter.

He read for a time, but his restless night caught up

with him and his eyes drooped. He fell asleep with the whistle of the swinging cane, the crack as it struck flesh, and his brother's cries resounding in his head.

Very early the next morning he was disturbed by a commotion outside. There was the sound of horses, and men's voices. It was still dark, and he got out of bed and went through to his day room. A servant was tidying.

'What's going on?'

'It's Lord Ragul, sir, and Master Burian,' said the man. 'They're leaving.'

'Leaving?'

'Yes, sir.'

'Why? Where are they going?'

'They're going back to rejoin the army, sir. By order of Lord Karkis, your father, sir.'

'Bring me a cloak.'

The servant hurried off to fetch one while Peglar waited. If Ragul and Burian were leaving he wanted to see them go.

Wrapping the cloak around him he slipped out by a side door and walked quickly to the front terrace. In the space beside the main gate a groom was harnessing a pony to a cart, which a couple of servants were loading with several large boxes. Another groom was preparing two horses, checking their harnesses and bridles. Peglar kept to the shadows.

After a moment or two Ragul and Burian appeared. They were walking slowly, as though every step was painful. Vancia was with them, shrouded in black. She held a handkerchief to her face. There was no sign of their father.

Ragul said something to his mother and hugged her

gingerly. Burian bowed stiffly. As Ragul turned away he saw Peglar in the shadows.

'What are you doing here, runt-boy?' he called. 'Come to crow?'

'No. I've nothing to say to a child killer.'

Ragul's face contorted with rage. 'You've picked your time to insult me, you little pervert. You can be thankful I'm in no state to knock you into that wall, else you'd be the one killed. I've got to leave now but I've not finished with you, Jathan Peglar.' He turned away, leaving Burian standing alone.

Peglar sneered at him. 'Where's your stupid laugh now, "Buri"? Not sniggering today, are you?' Burian clenched his fists and moved forward.

Despite everything it might have come to blows, except that Vancia intervened. She was distressed but her voice still carried the authority of a consort of The Master. 'Enough. This is not appropriate at this time. Peglar, your half-brother and his Companion are suffering. Show some sensitivity, please.'

Peglar wanted to say that he'd show them the same sensitivity they'd always shown him, but he bit his tongue and stepped back. Burian turned away.

There were a couple of Household Guards at the gate. One of them took a key from his belt and undid the huge lock. As the chain rattled to the ground he lifted the metal bar and swung the gates open. The groom led the horses out into the street and the cart followed. Ragul and Burian limped behind.

Peglar watched them go through the gateway. He watched a servant climb onto the pony, and his half-brother and his Companion climb the mounting blocks and get onto their beasts. He watched the pitiful procession turn into the broad street, watched until the gates closed and the guard refastened the chain. Vancia let out a sob, controlled herself, glared at Peglar and went into the house.

Peglar knew he had not behaved well. It had been spineless to attack Ragul when he knew he couldn't do anything about it. But, he told himself, it was no different from what Ragul had been doing to him all their lives.

He felt a heady lightness. Ragul was gone. He had been dismissed in disgrace. The relief was indescribable. There was the Sharing, too. Peglar knew that he had not been their father's favourite, but nothing he had ever done matched this crime of Ragul's. If the Sharing were to be held now, how would Karkis divide his wealth? The estate was huge. There was money, obviously, but it went beyond that. There were the ships. There were farms and lands on the plain. There was property within and outside the city. There were commodities and businesses of all types. All these would be shared according to their father's estimation of his sons' worth. What was not so simple was what would happen to this building, this mansion, the gem of the estate. That could not be split. Peglar had assumed that it would go to Ragul, but surely not now. Not after what he had done. Vancia would be desperately disappointed; she would be furious.

Peglar returned to his day room and sat at the window, watching the dawn turn the sky from indigo through azure to aquamarine as the brand new sun gilded the pinnacles and towers of the Palace and the civic buildings beyond. The residence had returned to its customary early morning torpor. Soon it would come to life as the attendants and waiting women prepared for the emergence of their masters and mistresses.

He was still thinking about Ragul when an idea struck him.

He passed no one on the way to his brother's quarters. He was afraid the door might be locked, but he pushed it and it gave. He'd half expected to find some of Ragul's people cleaning and had already worked out what he would say to explain his visit, but the day room was empty and dark. So, too, was the bedchamber. Peglar groped his way through the gloom towards the window, pulled back the heavy curtain, and was appalled by what the light revealed.

The place was in chaos. Clothes and belongings were strewn across the floor, furniture was askew, cupboards open, drawers leaning drunkenly and spewing their contents. However, that was not what horrified him; it was the state of Ragul's bed. The pillows were in a crushed heap, the sheets creased and crumpled. All over them were terra cotta blobs and smears, the soilings of blood. Peglar had left the scene of the beating before the end, but already the canes had split Ragul's skin. The bloody bedding brought home the horror of what had happened to him.

Peglar shuddered. There was a gruesome fascination in this confirmation of Ragul's pain, but he hadn't come there to gloat. He had come to find something, although amongst such a shambles he had no idea where to look.

He began with the cupboards and drawers, sure that the object he was seeking would be there. It was possible Ragul had taken it with him, but unlikely. Personal possessions were discouraged in the Army, so he would have left it behind. But where? He combed the shelves, opening boxes, pushing things aside, looking under them, all without success.

He was on the verge of giving up when he noticed something hanging at the back of the clothes closet. It was a blue velvet purse, a money pouch. It looked like the one Ragul had been wearing the last time he and Burian had burst into Peglar's room. He unhooked it, slackened the cord, and there it was: the little, marble leopard. It had probably been there ever since Ragul took it. He hadn't wanted it, Peglar thought bitterly, he'd just wanted to deprive him of it. He fondled its smooth back, its head, its ears. The carver had laboured over his work so that the tiny stone creature seemed alive. It sat on the palm of Peglar's hand, its yellow eyes staring back at him.

'You're all right now,' Peglar whispered. 'You can come home.'

Suddenly there was a sound next door, footsteps in Ragul's day room. There was no time to get out, not even to hide in the bath chamber. All Peglar could do was squeeze behind the open door. It was a hopeless hiding place, he would easily be seen. But why should it matter? he thought. Why should he worry about being found by a servant?

It was not a servant, though. It was Malina. She was on her own. She didn't notice Peglar, but gasped when she saw the bed. She picked up one of the bloody sheets and held it to her face, her dark curls tumbling forward. Then she turned, and looked straight at him.

She didn't cry out. She didn't even seem very surprised, she just gave the slightest start when she realised she was not alone. Her face was strained, her cheeks wet with tears.

'His poor back,' she said simply, shaking her head. 'How they must have hurt him.'

She took two paces towards Peglar and stood close, still holding the sheet. Then her head came forward and rested on his chest and she began to cry, softly, quietly, her shoulders shaking gently. For a moment he did nothing. Then, tentatively, he put one arm round her, then the other. He held her awkwardly, partly because he felt self-conscious but also because one hand was a tight fist around the leopard. Malina didn't make any sound beyond a subdued whimper. Her hands dropped to her sides and he felt her closeness, the warmth of her breath on his neck, her body leaning against his. She smelt intoxicating, and Peglar was embarrassed that he had not yet bathed and the odour of sleep must be on him. He eased away from her and she stepped back, dropped the sheet and fumbled for a handkerchief. She dabbed her eyes, gave him a wan smile, sniffed.

'Peg,' she said. 'You're sweet.'

Then she was gone, leaving behind the troubling ghost of her perfume.

For a long time Peglar stood in Ragul's bedchamber, feeling the echo of Malina's body against his and wondering what had happened. This girl, technically his half-sister, who had often in their childhood conspired with Ragul to make him miserable, had turned to him for comfort. She had said he was 'sweet'.

He left Ragul's quarters and wandered back to his own rooms. His head was so filled with what had just happened that he overlooked the significance of what he had really seen. It was not an indication of Malina's feelings for him: it was a demonstration of how much she loved Ragul. He should have realised that.

30

WARNING

There was a woman sitting in the ante-chamber outside Chalia's rooms. Like before, her chair was bang in front of the door, blocking the entrance, but this time it wasn't Forta, it was someone he'd not seen before.

'Who are you?'

'I am Qila, sir.' The woman stood up, but didn't step aside.

'Are you new?'

'In a manner of speaking, sir. I am one of Physician Narvil's staff. He told me to attend your mother.'

'Why? Where are her own women?'

'Gone, sir.'

'Gone? What do you mean "gone"?'

'Your mother has been taken worse, sir. Physician Narvil has diagnosed a severe infection. He has ordered complete isolation to prevent it spreading, and installed myself and a colleague to nurse her. There have been several cases of this infection in the city. It's extremely contagious and very serious. Lady Vancia dismissed your mother's own women and withdrew her own servant, for their safety.'

'What, you mean all of them?'

Yes, sir.'

Peglar made to pass but Qila didn't move.

'I am sorry, sir, but no one is to enter,' she said firmly. 'Physician Narvil was most insistent that until Lady Chalia's condition improves she must remain in complete isolation.'

Peglar felt frustrated but clearly he couldn't just push past this woman. 'How is she? How long will she be like this?'

'Physician Narvil was here earlier and pronounced that the infection is progressing as expected and is no worse. Your mother may be allowed visitors in a day or so. Until then I must ask you to respect Physician Narvil's wishes and not enter.'

'Is my father aware of the situation?'

'Oh yes, sir.'

'Has he been to see her?'

'No, sir, even he has not entered. But he ordered a large bunch of flowers from the gardens to be brought to her this morning.'

'Very well, I'll come back tomorrow. If there's any change in her please inform me at once.'

'Of course, sir.'

'And when Physician Narvil returns tell him I wish to see him.'

'Yes, sir.'

The exchange made Peglar uneasy. He wanted to go into his mother's room to see her for himself, but it would be wrong to disregard Narvil's orders. One of Styron's servants had contracted an infection last year and within days it had spread through the entire household; he could understand the need to be careful. What really disturbed him, however, was the news of his mother's waiting women. Why had Vancia dismissed them? They could have been found temporary work in other parts of the household while their mistress recovered. What would happen when his mother was better and Qila and the other one went back to Narvil? She would require attendance. Who would provide it? He needed to talk to somebody and there was only one person he could think of.

Peglar had thought Feldar might be on his father's business and was relieved the find him at his desk.

'I'm sorry your mother is ill,' Feldar said. 'I thought you'd been told. Narvil examined her yesterday and then saw your father. He said she was very infectious and needed special treatment.'

'But I sent one of my men last night to enquire after her and he came back with the message that she was improving.'

Feldar shook his head. 'He was misinformed.'

'Vancia has dismissed all my mother's women. Every one of them, and some have been with her for ages, for as long as I can remember.'

Feldar rose from his desk, closed the door and returned to his seat. When he spoke again it was quietly, even though he'd looked up and down the corridor to check that no one was eavesdropping.

'I think Vancia has done that for a purpose.'

'What purpose?'

'To isolate your mother.'

'Isolate her? Why?'

Feldar put his elbows on the desk and cradled his

chin in his hands. He regarded Peglar for a long time before he spoke. Then he said, 'There's trouble brewing.'

'Trouble? What? How?'

'Let's start with your father. You know his eyesight is getting worse.'

Peglar did. The meeting in the Atrium was just one illustration of what had been going on for some time. His lenses were thicker, yet he still needed to get very close to something to see it properly. He was no longer able to recognise people by sight and had to rely on the sounds of their voices. This lessened his authority. The piercing eyes, which at one time could have put fear into any opponent, were now lustreless, pale as milk, and they watered all the time so that he was constantly dabbing them. Out of his study he navigated by tapping his staff in front of him. When he left the Palace he needed someone to guide him.

Feldar continued. 'Last week he saw another physician, an expert on eyesight. He is going blind.'

Peglar was shocked. This was awful. 'What, completely? Is there no cure?'

'Yes, completely, and no, there is no cure. Soon he'll be unable to see anything at all.'

Peglar was appalled. He closed his eyes and for a second imagined what it might be like to never open them again, to be condemned to a world of perpetual darkness, to never again look on the blue of the sky, the green of a tree, the cobalt sea, a friendly face.

Feldar took a deep breath. 'Vancia,' he said her name with a sort of hiss that made Peglar think of a snake – it seemed appropriate, 'has already started to turn your father's misfortune to her advantage. She's always poked her nose into his affairs and now she has the excuse to go even further. She reads his papers to him. At first it was only the ones to do with household matters, but now she has access to everything, even confidential city business that I don't see. Lately she's gone beyond simply reading the papers aloud and has started pushing her own ideas. She tells your father what to think and what to say. She writes his letters and his edicts for him, and he's not in a position to know whether what she has actually written is what he told her to write.'

'How can we stop her?'

'We can't, not easily, but that's not all. There's Ragul.'

'How can he be a problem? He's in disgrace. Besides, he's gone away.'

'He has, and sending him back to the army was a master stroke on your father's part. If he'd stayed around the scandal would have rumbled on and on. Every time he was seen outside the Palace people would have been reminded. Now he's gone they'll quickly forget it all and find something else to gossip about. But even though Ragul's away he has a very effective presence here: Malina. As you know, your father has always been particularly fond of her. Of late she's taken to coming to his chamber every night to read to him. While she's with him she doesn't only read. She talks to him about Ragul. She tells him about Ragul's achievements, what great things his commanders are saying of him. Some of it is made up but your father believes it all, wants to believe it. After the shame of the flogging he's already feeling warmer towards Ragul.

'What I'm trying to tell you is that Vancia is aiming to make herself and her own children indispensable to your father, and as long as your mother is ill she's in no position to prevent it.'

Peglar shrugged. 'I understand what you're saying, but it doesn't matter. If Ragul gets a bit more out of the Sharing and I get a bit less, so what? There's plenty for both of us, and to be honest I don't want much. I don't need a quarter of the things I already have.'

Feldar thought for a moment. 'That's very admirable, but how do you feel about being completely disinherited and having nothing?'

Peglar shook his head. 'Can't be. I've been initiated. That means I've been accepted as one of my father's heirs and I have the right to a share. It can't happen.'

'Oh yes it can, and very easily too. If you were to do anything that could be seen as damaging the interests of your father or the House you'd be out.'

'Yes, but I'm hardly likely to do that, am I?'

'Of course not,' said Feldar. 'But Vancia's got herself into a position where she could write a denunciation accusing you of something and have your father sign it without him even knowing what it was. The first you'd hear would be the declaration dispossessing you, and that would be it.'

Peglar was horrified. Is this what Ragul had meant when he'd threatened him?

'What can I do?' Feldar didn't reply and Peglar thought for a moment or two. 'I ran into my father the other day in the Atrium. He had a paper that he wanted me to read to him. Afterwards he said something I didn't properly understand. I think it was a sort of challenge. I think he wants Ragul and me to find a way to stop the child murders, and he hinted that whichever of us does will be rewarded in the Sharing.'

'Did he say how he wanted you to do that?'

'No,' said Peglar ruefully. 'He didn't say anything directly at all. It was just hints. Everybody says the children come from the River Settlements, so I think the key must be there somewhere.'

Feldar leant back. 'I'm sure you're right. I don't think all the children come directly from the River Settlements, there are too many of them, but I think they may well be lodged there. I think whoever's organising them has a base there. You would have thought that the killings would put the child thieves off but they don't, they keep on coming. It follows that whoever's sending them in is scaring them so much they're prepared to take the risk. If you can find out who's doing this, and how, you're half way there.'

Peglar was thinking about what Yalka had told him of the man they called Scorpion, but he wasn't ready to share that yet. Instead he said, 'Easier said than done. Anyway, why doesn't my father just send some men into the Settlements to sort it out?'

'He has. Or rather, he's tried. The Guardians carried out a raid only the other day.'

'What did they find?'

'Nothing. They did door to door searches and asked questions but nobody admits to knowing anything. The commander thought it was a wild goose chase so he ordered a punishment burning and left.'

'What's a punishment burning?'

'They turned three families out on the street and set fire to their shacks.'

Peglar was horrified. 'But that's terrible. What had those people done?'

Feldar shrugged. 'Nothing. It was a threat, a warning

219

to the others, just to show how easy it would be to destroy the whole place.'

'And what do you think?'

'I believe that whoever's behind the child raiders is getting the wind up. One of the captains of the Guardians told me he's convinced something's going on and that some of the settlers want to talk, but either they're too scared or they can't bring themselves to co-operate with the authorities.'

Peglar was silent. 'What do you suggest I do?'

'Well, you have your little friend.' Feldar held up his hand to ward off questions. 'Don't ask me how I know about her; it's my business to keep up with things like that. Why don't you see what you can find out from her?'

Peglar was silent for a moment, pondering how much to reveal. 'I seem to have lost touch with her,' he said. 'She doesn't come to the Citadel any more.'

'So why don't you go down there? Go to the Settlements and take a look for yourself. See if you can work out what's going on. Just a quiet visit. Go in daylight and keep it low key. Wear something scruffy and don't go alone, take a couple of Household Guards with you. Talk to her and to the others. See what you can find out. When you've done that, let's meet again. We may be able to work something out. But you need to move fast. Your father's tossed out this challenge and you can be sure Ragul is already making plans.'

'Ragul's in the army and miles away.'

'You'd be surprised how quickly he could get back here if he wanted to. And don't forget that he's not alone, he has friends in the army. Whatever answer he comes up with will be violent.'

'Feldar,' Peglar said as he moved towards the door. 'Why are you talking to me like this? Why are you on my side rather than Ragul's?'

The steward seemed about to make a lighthearted reply, then changed his mind.

'I've watched you for a long time now. You've always been honest. Now you need to get tough, too. I think that for a long time your father has underestimated you. I think Vancia and Ragul still do, and that's to your advantage. Ragul is shallow, a liar and a bully. It would be a disaster if he were to get control of the House. He would be Vancia's puppet. She would be the one really in charge.' He smiled. 'That enough for you?'

Peglar was touched by his confidence and trust. 'It'll do for now,' he said. 'I'll try my best. Thank you.'

31

THE SETTLEMENTS

The source of the River Maris is just below the Citadel. When it springs from the rock it's clear and fresh and its waters are sweet. On its way through the city it gathers tributaries but it also becomes defiled. By the time it's half way down the hill it carries so much of the city's filth that it's no longer fit for drinking, and when it leaves through a tunnel under the east wall it's a sluggish, loathsome mess. From there it seeps down a narrow channel to the bottom of the hill, where it opens out onto the plain and crawls towards the harbour.

The River Settlements were built on its banks. At the time it must have been a pleasant area, before the water turned foul, life became hard for those who lived there, and their shacks rotted. Now it took a huge effort to imagine the sparkling waters and scented shade that drew the first settlers there.

'Shacks' was a fair description, although it didn't fit the buildings at the very top, close by the city wall. These must have once had gardens, because the plots showed in their rampant growth traces of a grander past. Rusty balconies, uneven terraces and rotting balustrades were further signs of a previous, gracious ownership. The buildings themselves had long ago been ransacked: roofs stripped, doors and windows breached, the fabric fleeced of anything of value.

Lower down the hill, nearer the harbour road, the homes that still stood were cramped and insanitary. For several years it had been Karkis's plan to demolish the River Settlements and rebuild better in order to house the growing population of the city. To further this he'd ordered that when an occupier died or was driven out their place was to be torn down to prevent others from moving in. The gaps left by these haphazard clearances had become rubbish tips, strewn with waste and junk. Gulls jostled and bickered, rats, big and bold as house dogs, made nests and runs. The whole place stank.

It was a week since Peglar's conversation with Feldar. He had been every day to the Citadel in the hope of seeing Yalka, but she had not appeared. Something was wrong; with her, with him, with the relationship between them, or with all three. She was on his mind most of the time. Thinking about her was the only thing that kept him sane during the tedious conversations with Sainter that he was no longer able to avoid. She interrupted his work when he was at his desk in his day room. She was with him whether he was alone or in company, when he rose and when, at the end of a day, he settled to rest. The only time she was absent was during the strenuous physical training bouts with Cestris. Contrary to what he'd expected he enjoyed these, and he gained huge satisfaction from the sensation of his growing strength. But as soon as the session was over his mind would revert to thoughts of her.

At the close of day six he addressed his reflection in the polished mirror in his bathing chamber. Yalka is unpredictable, he told himself, and she can sometimes be difficult. She is disrespectful and rude. She won't take orders and she thinks herself above the customs and rules that apply to other people. She may or may not be morally loose. She appears to do no work. And she's a churl. On the other hand, she's intelligent, cunning, and quick. She has a sense of humour. She's afraid of nobody, and nothing intimidates her. She has a strong sense of what's right and what's wrong. She has amazing eyes, astonishing hair, and she's pretty. Despite – or perhaps in a way because of – the birthmark.

At the end of this inventory he concluded that the only way he could find any peace was to see her again. If she would not come to the place where she must know he would look for her, his only hope was to seek her in her own lair. He resolved to take Feldar's advice.

He hadn't, as the Steward recommended, come to the Settlements with some of the Household Guards. He'd brought just one of the gatemen, a giant called Halnis. Peglar reckoned that this man's muscular bulk would be enough to deter most people, and if not and they ran into trouble his fighting skills would prove useful. As added insurance he wore a zirca, which hung conspicuously from his belt. He had told Halnis not to dress in the Palace livery. They both wore scruffy tunics and old cloaks, and they'd rubbed their faces with damp earth. The dressing down worked, because the few people who were about paid them scant attention. They were strangers, but not particularly interesting ones.

Peglar needed to find Yalka but he also had another plan which, if he could pull it off, would stand him well in the yet to be announced Sharing. He had given a lot of thought to this.

On the face of it the situation was simple. His father had tasked him, albeit obliquely, with removing the problem of the feral children. Yalka had told him that they were sent into the city by this Scorpion creature, who exploited the Settlements as a staging post. Although there were no children apparent now, there must be a place where they were kept while they were prepared for their raids. If he could find that and close it down the problem would be solved. But how could he do that? His father not only wanted to clear the slum, he wanted to provide something better. Peglar had a plan that would deal with both these things. It was no more than the glimmer of an idea and it required help, which had to come from someone who lived in the River Settlements and was trusted by the settlers. It needed Yalka. If he could find her.

The Settlements seemed to be almost deserted. It was hard to tell, but it looked to Peglar as though no more than than half the dwellings were lived in. He couldn't believe that they contained enough people to organise the felonies and abominations that city people attributed to them. Besides, he'd always understood that the crimes the settlers were accused of would be very profitable, but what he was seeing were the homes of people who appeared to have nothing. He couldn't imagine Yalka, with her golden hair, her fresh face and her bright eyes, living here.

He and Halnis moved from one reeking alley to another. The part they had just reached was the worst yet, and the stench, a combination of rotting food and human waste, was overpowering. Peglar trod gingerly through the mess. He was on the verge of retching, and wondered if he'd ever rid himself of the stink. Swarms of flies erupted in resentful clouds as he passed, and dogs, starving and dejected, slouched and skulked.

Halnis was becoming uneasy. 'I think we should be careful, sir. One or two people are giving us funny looks.'

Peglar glanced around. There was a man standing in a doorway with his arms folded. He looked lean and mean, but when Peglar stared back and rested a hand on his zirca he turned away and disappeared indoors.

'Just a bit longer,' he whispered. 'There's someone I have to find. She must be here somewhere.'

As Halnis took in the feminine reference his expression changed and there was an almost imperceptible arch of a knowing eyebrow. Peglar frowned and shook his head. He didn't want the guard misinterpreting the reason for his visit. Halnis looked away.

They continued through the ruins. Ragged clothing, shattered pots, broken furniture, the exhausted debris of lives suffered at the limit of endurance, were scattered haphazardly. Everything of use had been taken, recycled by poverty and theft. It was hopeless.

He was on the point of giving up and going back to the city when he saw her. She was on the other side of the river and hadn't noticed them.

'Yalka,' he called.

She saw him, hesitated for a second, then ran.

Peglar gave chase, but by the time he'd wobbled across the plank bridge over the river she'd gone.

'Yalka, come back. I need to talk to you.' He scrambled up the muddy bank, thinking he'd lost her, but then he glimpsed her again in the gap between two ruins. He ran after her and found himself in a narrow passage. The path branched into two. Which way had she gone? He guessed left, but soon saw it was blocked. He turned back, rounded a corner and there she was. She'd blundered into another dead end and was crouched against a tall, wooden fence. She was in the same animal squat Peglar had seen before on the Citadel, and he looked warily for the knife.

He held up his hand, palm out, a gesture of peace. 'Don't run. Please. I need to talk to you.'

She remained still, glaring at him. Peglar took a step towards her and she at once twisted and sprang for the top of the fence. It was high but she was agile and it was a good jump. Her fingers hooked over the lip and she pulled herself up. Peglar leapt forward and grabbed her legs. She kicked him and her heel struck his cheek so that he almost let go, but he held on and she fell back. She was strong but Peglar was stronger and he gripped her tightly while she wriggled and squirmed. He managed to twist behind her and pull her arms tight across her chest. She jerked her head to the side to bite him but he thrust his forearm under her chin, forcing her mouth shut and her head back. She tried one last kick and her heel connected painfully with his shin, but he didn't release his grip.

'What are you going to do?' Peglar hissed in her ear. 'Get your knife out? Scratch me again?'

Then she buckled, like a marionette whose strings had been cut. She became dead weight in his arms, and unbalanced they both collapsed to the ground.

'Yalka, please. I won't hurt you.' She writhed again and Peglar shook her. 'Why are you being like this. I'm your friend. I want to talk to you. I need your help.' She stopped struggling and they were both still for a moment. 'Will you listen to me? Please?'

'What do you want?' It was sullen and suspicious, but at least she was answering.

'Keep still and I'll explain. Will you?'

There was a slight nod.

'Promise?'

'All right.'

Peglar loosened his grip and Yalka pulled away, turning to face him and rubbing her wrists. She was panting. Her knees were grazed and her face smeared. She picked at a splinter in her hand, drew her legs up and pulled her smock over them. Although it was only a few weeks since he'd last seen her, she seemed to have changed. Her hair was bound in tight corn-rows and her face looked more grown up. Peglar watched her cautiously in case she thought to take off. He knew how quickly she could move.

'All right.' she said wearily. Her voice sounded a little deeper and slightly husky. 'Say what you've got to. I won't run.'

He took a deep breath and relaxed. Then, without warning, there was an explosion of light and he felt a sharp, stinging blow on the back of his head. Yalka sprang up and vanished around the corner. Peglar made to go after her but he was dizzy and he fell back onto the ground. What had happened? Who had hit him? Where were they? He looked about but could see no one. He touched the back of his head. It felt wet. He looked at his fingers, smeared with blood, and cursed. Somebody had struck him from behind, Yalka had run off and he had no idea where. There were a hundred places to hide in this warren. He wouldn't find her now.

He was wrong. Yalka couldn't have gone far, because a few moments later she returned. She was holding Verit very tightly by the arm. She plonked him down and made a sign that he was to stay put.

'I'm sorry,' she said, looking at Peglar with concern. 'He's sorry too. He thought you was going to hurt me.' She shrugged. 'I look out for him and he looks out for me.'

Peglar kept his hand on his head, which was now throbbing painfully. There was a sharply pointed flint on the ground nearby; Verit was holding a sling. He glared at Peglar. He didn't seem sorry. Yalka shook her head at him and he looked away.

'He won't do no more,' she said. Peglar didn't know if she was talking about Verit or him. 'Here, let me look.'

She squatted down beside Peglar, and cautiously he bent forward. Her fingers were firm but gentle.

'It's not too bad. Bit o' blood, that's all. You're lucky. He can kill with that thing.'

Lucky? Was he supposed to be grateful? He felt like strangling the little ratbag.

'You need something on it. Come on.'

She grabbed his hand, jerked him to his feet and led the way out of the alley. Peglar followed her through the broken buildings towards higher ground, Verit stalking them like a small, opportunistic animal.

They came to a small yard. 'This is where I live,' Yalka said.

32

A PLAN

On the outside Yalka's home looked just like the other shacks: a broken gate, rotting timbers, peeling paint. She led the way and Peglar stooped under the lintel. When he straightened up he was astonished. He was in a little room with bright paintwork and multi-coloured rugs. The furniture was old but clean and well cared for. It was a pretty and tidy, but it was so small. The ceiling was low and the walls pressed in. The three of them, Yalka, Verit and Peglar, filled it. There was nowhere to move and Peglar felt hemmed in. How could anyone live in a space like this?

The surprising thing, though, was the pictures. There were so many of them. They were on the walls, on the side of a cupboard, propped on shelves. Many were of plants, some were sketches of the Settlements, the rest were likenesses. Yalka had told him she couldn't do people, but these were good. There was one of Verit that was exceptional, catching perfectly the boy's foxy face and turned up nose.

'Not what you expected, is it?' As always, Yalka

seemed to have a knack for knowing what was in his mind. 'People think that 'cos we're poor we live like pigs. They think that 'cos our houses look like shit outside they're shit inside. Same as they think we're all thieves and whores.'

There was nothing Peglar could say. That was exactly what people in the city thought. It was what he himself had thought before he met Yalka.

There was an open door through to a further room. Peglar could see that in the corner there was an old man seated on a wooden chair. He was not dressed in the simple clothes of a peasant but wore a blue gown elaborately embroidered in red and gold, and his white hair fluffed out from under a matching cap.

'That's me granddad,' Yalka said, following his gaze. 'Syramos, the Rhymer.' There was pride in her tone.

The old man sat very erect. His face was wrinkled, with smile lines at the corners of his eyes. Peglar went up to him and held out his hand. The old man took it, and instead of releasing it hung on. He began a slow, rhythmical chant.

'When the night had passed and the sun was high
A handsome stranger was passing by.'
'Pardon?'

Syramos didn't answer, but gave Peglar a knowing smile. His eyes were clear and an intense blue, like Yalka's. His voice was a rich, smooth singsong and he spoke in a quiet, cultured voice. Why did Yalka herself speak so badly if she had learnt from this man?

'He came to ask for the maiden's aid,
He needed her help with a plan he'd made.'
Peglar snatched his hand away as if he'd touched something hot. He was shocked. Was Syramos talking

about him? How did Yalka's grandfather know the reason for his visit?

'Pay no attention,' Yalka said tersely. 'He goes on like this all the time. Now you just shut up granddad. Enough rhyming. Leave our guest be.'

Her grandfather watched Peglar steadily, his eyes never wavering. He looked at him the way Verit did, with total attention and intense concentration.

Peglar turned to the old man. 'You seem to know my business, sir. I'm impressed. Please tell me how you know it, and what you mean.'

Syramos didn't reply, but the ghost of a smile played at the corners of his mouth. His unblinking gaze was disconcerting and Peglar had to look away. Yalka squatted at the old man's side.

'This is Jathan Peglar,' she said to him. 'He's Lord Karkis's son.'

'Lord Karkis,' Syramos murmured. 'The Master of Chamaris. We are indeed honoured.'

Was he being sarcastic? There was a dreamlike quality in the way he spoke. He leant forward and put one hand on Peglar's arm, while he raised the other and pointed ahead. His eyes were distant, as though regarding something far, far away. Automatically Peglar looked to see what he was pointing at, but it was only the wall. Although the pointing hand trembled the grip on his arm was firm. Peglar wanted to pull away, but the old man began a soft chanting, tapping his foot on the floor to keep a beat.

'Look! Blind dancers!
See how they glide,
Every move perfect,
Every step tried.

See the blind dancers!
Don't they look fine?
Keeping the beat,
Holding their time.'

As he continued his voice became stronger, louder, the rhythm faster.

'*See the blind dancers,*
Moving as one,
Pacing their lives
To the beat of a drum.
Watch the blind dancers
Swagger and preen,
Gallant and grand,
Living their dream.'

Peglar had no idea what the words meant but they were hypnotic, spellbinding and he was mesmerised. He looked at Yalka. 'What's he saying?'

It was Syramos who replied. 'The House of Karkis, The House of Styron, The House of Mostani, The House of Lembick. Blind dancers, all of them.' He cackled.

'*Sad blind dancers,*
Thought they were free.
Poor blind dancers,
Thought they could see!'

He laughed again.

'I don't understand.' Peglar looked to Yalka for help. 'What's he talking about? What does he mean?'

Yalka shook her head. 'Take no notice of him,' she said dismissively. 'He won't tell you no more. He just comes out with it when he wants to, and he don't never explain.'

Syramos pursed his lips, then murmured,
'*The rhymer speaks for his hearers' gain*

They must interpret, they must explain.
The truth may be veiled but it's there to be found,
Mine your own mind, reap your own ground.'

Yalka turned to Syramos and spoke sharply, as if to a naughty child. 'Now that's enough, granddad. No more rhyming. You're making our guest feel uncomfortable. Stop it.'

Peglar felt dizzy and his head throbbed. He touched where the stone had hit him. It was tender and there was a lump. Yalka took his arm and sat him on a low stool.

'Come on, let's see to that.'

She started by giving him a drink, a golden liquid from a stoneware bottle. It was thick, sticky and very sweet. 'There,' she said, soothingly. 'That'll make you feel better.'

Almost at once it did. The drink seemed to have a numbing effect and Peglar wondered if she'd drugged him, but he didn't care. For the moment there seemed to be nothing beyond this small, comfortable room, the mystical Syramos and his equally mysterious granddaughter.

Yalka washed her hands in water from a jug, took a knife – it looked like the one she'd had at the Citadel – and carefully trimmed away the hair around Peglar's wound. She tipped the rest of the water into a bowl and began to bathe his head. When she'd finished she dabbed it dry and folded a strip of cloth. She fetched a small jar from the cupboard and poured some liquid from it onto the pad she'd made. It was strong smelling and the vapour made Peglar's eyes water. Yalka held the compress to his head. It stung like a wasp and he winced.

'It'll stop it going bad,' she explained, 'help it heal.'

Peglar leant against her as she worked, resting his forehead on her stomach. It was a pleasant feeling and he closed his eyes.

'You've got a nasty bump but it'll be all right,' she said soothingly. 'Your hair'll look daft for a bit, but it'll soon grow back.' She smoothed it with her fingers. 'You've got long hair anyway. You can easy hide it.'

She took a longer strip of cloth, wound it around his head and pinned it to stop it unraveling. She did everything methodically, efficiently, competently, as though treating people wounded by Verit was routine. When she'd finished she stood back and surveyed her work.

'Why did you run away from me?' Peglar said. 'I thought you were my friend.'

'I was scared. I thought you was coming after me.'

'Why did you think that? I wouldn't harm you.'

There was a silence. Yalka looked at the floor.

'Anyway, I didn't mean just now,' Peglar explained. 'I meant before. When we used to meet at the Citadel.'

'I didn't.'

'You did. You stopped coming to the Citadel. I looked for you but you didn't come. I missed you.'

She looked up sharply and smiled. For a moment her cheeks dimpled and her eyes shone before her expression became serious again. She spoke slowly.

'When I said that to you about, you know, doing it for you, it's 'cos I'd heard that's what rich boys do. They find a poor girl, and they give her stuff, and that's what they want in return. I pretended I'd done it before but I haven't. I thought that's what you'd expect, and if I didn't say I'd do it then you wouldn't want to see me no more.' She frowned and sighed.

236

'Then, after I seen the look on your face I could tell I'd said wrong. That wasn't why you'd given me the stuff at all, and I felt stupid and wished I'd never said it. I thought you'd think I was a whore or something, trying some trick to get money off you. So I kept away. I was scared of going back to the Citadel 'cos I didn't know what you'd say. Then, after, I thought you'd understand, and I went back. But you wasn't there. Lots of times I went back and you wasn't there. I thought it must be 'cos you didn't want to see me no more. Then when I saw you just now with that big bloke, I was scared.'

She'd been to the Citadel, and so had he. It was just that they'd never been there at the same time. Chance, fate, luck, whatever you call it had played a trick on them.

'I'm sorry,' he said.

There was a long pause.

'Friends?' Peglar held out his hand.

'Friends,' she said. She held her own hand upright in front of her. He put his palm against hers and they entwined their fingers.

Still holding his hand she beckoned to Verit, who was lurking in the corner of the room. He slunk over, eyes down.

'He's friends too,' she said. Verit suddenly snatched Peglar's other hand and yanked it towards his mouth. Peglar tugged back, afraid he was going to be bitten, but before he could pull his hand away the boy licked it, a big, wet, lolloping lick, like a dog. Then he let go. Peglar looked at his damp palm. He was touched. He patted the boy gently on the shoulder and Verit looked up at him with his piercing eyes, and smiled. Peglar had never seen him smile before. It was like the sun coming out and he couldn't look away.

Yalka released Peglar's hand. 'You said you wanted me to help you with something.'

'Yes, I do.' Where to start? How to put his idea so that it seemed sensible, attractive, the right option? Yalka waited patiently. 'First of all, you were right when you said my half-brother and some of his friends from the upper city were behind the child killings. I couldn't believe it, but you were right. Ragul and his Companion have been caught and punished, but others have taken over and the killings are continuing. I want to stop them.'

Yalka watched him and waited. Peglar was aware that what he'd said was almost meaningless, akin to saying something like 'I want to be good'. But he was sure his idea was sound. If the Settlements were no more, if no one lived here, Scorpion couldn't use the area as a base. Of course, he could move his operations to the harbour town or to one of the villages on the plain, but they were further away. It would be more difficult for him to work from there and harder to hide.

'Chamaris is at the end of its tether,' Peglar continued. 'People are fed up. They're fed up with the thefts and embarrassed by the killings, and that's all tied up with other problems they think come from the River Settlements.' She made to protest but he held up his hand to stop her. 'I'm just telling you what they say. The pressure on my father is growing. He has enemies who are using the situation to harm him. Soon he'll be driven to doing something drastic. There's already been one punishment burning. There'll be more. Chamaris will send in the army. They'll go through the River

Settlements from top to bottom. They'll clear everybody out shut everything up, and torch the place.'

Peglar looked at the neat little room. The idea of it being the target of a punishment burning was sickening.

'That would please my father because he wants you all out anyway. He wants to clean up the area, rebuild, and make it like it was in the old days. A pretty place for tidy people.' The snag was that nobody who lived in the Settlements now would be able to afford one of the new places. He didn't say that, but he knew Yalka was smart enough to work it out.

There was an expression on Yalka's face that Peglar had seen when she felt something was unjust or unfair. 'But we can't stop Scorpion,' she protested. 'What can we do?'

'No, you can't stop him, but if nobody lived in the Settlements any more he couldn't carry on. Neither could he if the place was rebuilt and there was nowhere for him to hide.'

Yalka looked at Peglar as though he was mad. 'How could we not live here. Where would we go?'

'You could live in the city.'

She sighed. 'We talked about that,' she said wearily. 'I told you: you can't live in the city unless you're a citizen.'

'So we'll make you all citizens. If I could promise citizenship and a home to anyone who agreed to move out of the River Settlements, do you think people would go for it?'

'I dunno,' she said, thinking aloud. 'There'd be some good things. Nice houses, clean streets, no mess. But it wouldn't be that easy. Living up there would cost a lot. And people in the city are busybodies. Bossy too. Nosey and bossy. Lots of rules and people telling you what you can do and what you can't. Here we please ourselves, do what we like, be free.' She looked at Peglar and shrugged. 'I dunno. They'd need money.'

'How much?'

She thought for a minute and said a figure. It must have been a lot to her, but to Peglar it didn't seem very much at all. He did a quick mental calculation, multiplying what Yalka had asked for by the thirty or forty families he guessed must be the present population. The result was less than the profit made by one of his father's ships on a single trading voyage.

'For each family?'

She nodded.

'All right,' Peglar said, cautiously. 'Do you think you could persuade your neighbours to accept that?'

She thought some more. 'I can try. I'll talk to the women. The men would just think it was giving in to Scorpion, well some of 'em would, and that would turn 'em against it. But the women will see it as a chance to make a new start, to get their kids back from where they've sent them and make a proper home again. I think so. Yes.'

'But it's got to be everybody. The whole of the River Settlements has to go. If one family, one person, just one, refuses to move out the deal's off for everyone. Understood?'

'Yes,' she said. 'We can't have a meeting, Scorpion would find out about it if we did, so I'll have to go round and talk to everybody. separately.'

'How long do you think that will take you?'

She pursed her lips. 'A week.'

A week was too long. Feldar had warned about

Ragul plotting something. As far as Peglar knew he was in Rasturoth, but he could be back in a day if he rode hard, together with some cronies from the army. Time was precious. 'I'm worried about what might happen. Can you do it in five days?' he said.

Yalka looked doubtful. 'I don't know. I'll try.'

'Meet me in five days and tell me what people think. At the Citadel. In the afternoon.' He grabbed both her hands. 'This is serious. You must persuade them. Please.'

She could see he meant it. She nodded slowly. 'All right then,' she said. 'You promise we've got five days?'

'Yes.' It was a promise Peglar would come to regret, but he had to convince her.

Verit squatted at their feet. In the next room Syramos spoke again, so softly that Peglar had to strain to hear him.

'Fine was the offer and good the intent,
The maiden knew what the young man meant,
But their days will be hard and troubled their sleep,
For what use are promises no one can keep?'

33

TONIC

Peglar had no idea whether his scheme would work. It was simple enough. The settlers would leave their homes and move into the city. Once the area was clear the slums would be demolished. The river would be cleaned up and new houses built, modern places with gardens and open spaces. A new community would be created. Everything would be properly regulated and effectively policed.

Despite Yalka's cautious reception he was sure his plan would prove tempting to the settlers. Why would anyone not give up a rat infested hovel for somewhere inside the safety of the city walls? Surely it wouldn't take them five days to consider it. It was frustrating, but all he could do was wait. What had Syramos meant when he'd rhymed about promises no one could keep? Peglar had asked him, but Yalka was right; he wouldn't explain. He simply stared in that disquieting manner until Peglar was compelled to back away.

The settlers agreeing to the plan was one hurdle; another, and perhaps even more difficult, was persuading his father to pay for it. That would be complicated. Each citizenship would have to be bought, and that would be expensive because the fees were steep. Ironically it was his father who had increased them a few years ago by a substantial amount in order to ensure that the privilege of citizenship was available only to those with enough money to appreciate it. Then there would be payments to the lawyers who would have to prepare the paperwork. There would be inducements to administrators and officials to ensure that the whole business proceeded smoothly and didn't get snagged in some bureaucratic backwater. Such sweeteners, Peglar had come to realise, were an inescapable part of every deal in Chamaris, even those championed by The Master. Finally, there would be the cost of rebuilding. So although the settlers themselves weren't getting much, the whole package would be expensive. Even so it was surely preferable to what was happening now.

Peglar's first call was on Feldar, and he was relieved to find that the Steward's response was encouraging.

'You've done well,' he said. 'And your girlfriend, you think she can deliver?'

"Girlfriend?" Peglar couldn't help blushing and remembered Yalka's taunting when she'd seen him blush. What had she called him? "Blush baby." Did Feldar really think there was something between him and Yalka? It was ridiculous. Or was it?

'I don't know,' he said. 'I'm sure she'll try and I think there's a good chance. She's very persuasive. It's my father I'm worried about. Will he agree to pay?'

'All right.' The steward thought for a moment. 'You know what impresses your father? Figures. You need to show him that he will get back the money your scheme is going to cost. Look at these.'

They were in Feldar's office and the Steward reached for some rolled papers that were on the shelves behind his desk. He unfurled the first, putting a book on each end to hold it flat. It was a coloured drawing of square, white houses sitting among neat gardens on sloping terraces filled with bougainvillaea and oleander. They were tidy, bright, like the homes of better off merchants in the middle part of the city.

'What are these?'

'They're plans your father had drawn up for some houses he wanted to have built.'

'Where?'

'The River Settlements.'

'No!' Peglar was amazed. He could see no connection at all between the squalor he'd visited and these neat doll-houses. Feldar spread out another roll, this time of interiors. They were in cool colours, with pale walls and marble floors, sparsely furnished with a few elegant pieces. He tried to imagine the walls covered in Yalka's drawings and Syramos in his bright robe seated in a corner. He couldn't. What was proposed seemed cold, sterile. He doubted Yalka would like it, although there was no denying that living in one of these places would be more wholesome and healthier than enduring what the Settlements had now become.

'When were these done?

'Years ago. It was all set to go ahead, but other things came up and the plans were set aside. Do some calculations, a balance sheet.' Feldar rolled up the plans and pushed them across the desk. 'Take these with you. There are some notes that will help you to work out how much it would all cost and how long it would take for your father to recover his outlay. Be realistic. Don't bend the sums just to make it look good. Your father's eyes may be going but his mind's as sharp as a tack. He'll know straight away if you're trying to bamboozle him.'

Peglar went to his quarters and spent the afternoon doing what Feldar had said. He was pleased and surprised to see from the first set of calculations he produced how quickly the investment could be repaid, even at what Feldar's notes quoted as medium rents. Then he remembered how Feldar had urged caution, and he reworked some of the figures. The end product was better, he thought; encouraging without being over optimistic. He made a copy of his work, took it to his father's study and left it with a servant.

He didn't go straight back to his quarters but turned from the Atrium into the women's wing.

He expected that again someone would block his way, but there was no one at the entrance to his mother's suite. That must mean her infection was gone.

Chalia's bedchamber was dim and smelt of sickness. She lay with her face to the wall. Beside her bed sat Forta, next to a table loaded with bottles and jars.

'You're Forta.'

She nodded. 'Yes, sir.'

'You are one of Lady Vancia's women. Why are you here?'

'Your mother's attendants were sent away when Physician Narvil's people were brought in to nurse Lady Chalia. Now they're gone Lady Vancia has made me available again.' Forta had a formal, rather affected way of speaking.

Peglar didn't like it. Why couldn't his mother have her own women back? They were people who had served her for a long time. She knew them and they knew her. It was further evidence of what Feldar had suggested to him: Vancia was trying to isolate his mother. But why was she doing that? He could understand her scheming against him because in her eyes he was Ragul's rival, but what threat was his mother?

'How is she?'

Forta shook her head. His mother had heard his voice and turned towards him. She smiled weakly. Although the curtains shut out most of the light, Peglar could see that her face was drawn, her eyes sunken. Worst of all was her colour. Even in the gloom she looked a sickly yellow.

'Has she eaten anything?'

'No,' said Forta. 'She's had nothing for three days now. She gets a lot of pain, you see.' Even as she spoke Chalia was convulsed. Her face twisted, her body spasmed and she moaned through clenched teeth. Peglar took her hand and she gripped it with a fearsome desperation.

'Where's it hurting you, mother?'

There was a moment before she could speak. 'Everywhere. It's like a rod driving through me.' It was almost beyond her to squeeze out the words.

Forta took a scented cloth and gently wiped her brow. Then she took one of the flasks from the table.

'What's that?'

'It's a tincture Lady Vancia prepares.'

'Vancia?' Peglar was alarmed. 'Vancia brought this?'

'Oh yes. She's been so kind. She's very concerned.

She comes to see your mother several times a day. She brings this.'

Peglar sniffed it. It smelt sour, like decaying vegetation. 'Ugh, what is it?'

'I understand it's an old recipe from Lady Vancia's family.'

Peglar held the flask to the light. It was dark yellow, like horse piss. He sniffed it again and put a spot on his tongue. It tasted bitter and made him think of rotten cabbage, but in the background was a nutty sweetness. It wasn't as bad as he'd expected, but he still didn't know how anyone could swallow it. Forta watched him with an anxious expression.

'Does Physician Narvil know she's taking this?'

'Oh, yes sir.'

'And he's seen it? He knows what it is?'

'Yes, sir. Physician Narvil says that if it makes her feel better she should have it.'

Peglar was doubtful, but if Narvil said it would do his mother good he supposed it was all right. He put his arm around her shoulders to raise her enough to drink. She lifted a trembling hand to steady the flask and sipped weakly, sighed, and sank back on her pillows. It seemed that the potion did indeed help.

With a little bob Forta withdrew, leaving Peglar and his mother alone. He sat beside her bed, watching her drop in and out of sleep. She was restless and seemed unable to find a position that was comfortable. Peglar felt her forehead. She was very hot. There was a bowl of water beside her that smelt of roses, far better than Vancia's 'tonic'. Peglar dampened a cloth and gently bathed her face, her neck, her arms.

'Peglar?' Her voice was weak, her face drawn.

'Peglar, I'm frightened. I don't think I'm going to get better from this.'

Peglar felt as though a column of ice had formed in his spine.

'No, don't say that. You're going to be all right. Narvil says so. You're going to to be fine.'

She gripped his hand and bit her lip. Tears wet her cheek.

'You will be well again soon, it's just taking time. Then we'll walk in the gardens, we'll talk. You can sing to me and I'll accompany you on the baglama.'

His mother managed a wan smile. 'You can't play the baglama. You haven't got one.'

'I'll get one, I'll learn!' Peglar held an imaginary instrument in one hand and air strummed it with the other. Chalia made a face at him.

He continued to sit with her but she was too tired to talk. In the end she drifted into sleep, and after a while he crept out of the room. He left instructions with Forta that she was to tell Narvil to come to see him.

Narvil never came, and what happened that night and in the days that followed prevented Peglar ever finding out why.

34

BURNING

The first Peglar knew of the fire was the smell.

It was late summer and temperatures had been building for days. The sun had raged from cloudless skies, plants dried and died, grass browned, earth cracked. Then a parched, sullen wind set in from the west, and made things worse.

Peglar lay on his bed. He was too uncomfortable to stay still, but the more he moved the hotter he got. Eventually he propped himself on a pillow and watched the stars through the open window. At some stage he fell asleep, then he woke with a start. He could smell burning.

He leapt from his bed and raced out through his day room, thinking something in the Palace was alight. He scanned the corridor but it was deserted and silent, no sign of smoke. He went back to his bedchamber and stuck his head out of the window. The odour was stronger. Whatever was burning was definitely out there.

It was an offensive smell, not sweet like a grass or a

wood fire but acrid. Peglar slipped on a tunic and some sandals, swung his legs over the windowsill and dropped to the stone path below. He expected to see a section of the Palace in flames, windows an orange glow, fire licking the roof, but there was nothing. Some way off he could hear a commotion. It seemed to be in the street outside the front gate. He ran across the yard and into the courtyard.

The gate was wide open and beyond it three or four men were hurrying along the avenue.

'What's going on?'

They didn't stop, but one turned and yelled as he trotted backwards, 'It's a fire. A big one. Great show.'

'Where? What's on fire?'

'The Settlements.'

The Settlements? The *River* Settlements. Yalka! Peglar had only one thought; Yalka, Verit, Syramos needed his help. He rushed along the street in the direction taken by the men, to the end of the avenue and down the hill towards the Port Gate. As he neared the bottom more people were gathering, all keen to see the spectacle. There was noise, smoke hazing the buildings, sparks freckling the air. There was a red tinge to the sky over the west wall.

'Peglar, stay with me.' It was Feldar. He must have come up behind him. 'It's the slums. It looks bad. If the west bank catches the blaze could spread to the old city wall. This way.' He pushed through a knot of milling people and vanished into a gap between buildings. Peglar followed.

Feldar knew short cuts and they zigzagged through pinched lanes. The smoke was worse in the narrower streets, stinging Peglar's eyes and catching his throat.

Suddenly they burst from the maze of alleys into the square behind the Great Gate. One of the barriers was yawning wide, on the other side an orange glow, more smoke, angry, swirling firebrands.

Peglar ran behind Feldar towards the opening. Guardians were striding about, unsure what to do. One of them moved towards them to check their exit, then decided this was not the time to be officious about the curfew and turned away. They passed through the gate and skirted to the left until they rounded the edge of the wall. Then they saw the full horror of what was happening.

The fire was an animal, ravishing the ravine. It growled, snarled, hissed. It lashed its tail and its eyes sparked. All the way up the river bank the wooden shacks were burning. Some blazed fiercely, others smouldered and spat. The air was heavy with smoke and soot. The noise was deafening: roaring, crackling, crashing, the cries of stricken people. Murky figures flitted between buildings, black shapes emerging briefly from the smoke, then vanishing again.

Below them an old man sat at the edge of the river. He held out trembling hands. Even from above Peglar could see that they were badly burnt. Feldar scrambled down the bank and plunged the man's scorched limbs into the cold water.

'Keep them in the river,' he said to him.

He wetted two cloths and tossed one to Peglar, signalling that he should tie it over his face. Peglar hesitated, remembering the reputation of the filthy channel and the foulness of the water he'd seen when he visited, but the smoke was choking so he knotted the rag around his neck and pulled it over his mouth and nose.

Feldar took off towards the heart of the fire and he followed. As they got in amongst the buildings the heat became more intense.

They worked together, moving from house to house, doing what they could. Peglar's mind was numb and he was oblivious to time, fatigue, pain. People were hurt, some badly. One man lay under a fallen timber. Feldar squatted to examine him. He said nothing, but shook his head and gently pulled the man's cloak over his face. They got those who were able to move to the river so they could find relief for their burns in the water. There was nothing more they could do.

All the time Peglar was looking for Yalka. The fire obliterated buildings, the smoke hid reference points. It was impossible to know where they were. Feldar turned back towards where the flames were fiercest and Peglar waded across the river to look for Yalka's home. As he climbed out he heard a scream, a drawn-out, piercing cry. He ran in the direction he thought it came from. The fire didn't seem so bad in this part of the Settlements, but there was a lot of smoke. He blundered across an open space and there was the scream again, closer, above him.

He looked up and saw a child, a girl, at an upstairs window. The downstairs of the shack was alight but it didn't seem too bad. He kicked the front door. It swung open and a fog of bitter fumes billowed into his face, driving him coughing and choking back into the street. When he could regain his breath he saw a pile of smouldering rags in the middle of the room, some tied to a wooden stick. He dashed in, grabbed the stick and flung it from the door, kicking the other rags apart and stamping them out.

The cry came again from over his head, terrified and urgent. There was a ladder in the corner of the room, a trapdoor above. The ladder was old and rotten, and as Peglar climbed one of the rungs snapped and his foot slipped. The splintered wood gouged his leg but he barely felt it. The door was fastened with a heavy bolt. He wrenched it aside and heaved open the trap. It was heavy and it fell back against the floorboards with a dusty thud that shook the ladder. He thrust his head through the hole.

The child was standing with her back to the window. She was terrified, her eyes streaming and her face contorted by smoke and fear.

'Don't be afraid,' Peglar gasped, between coughs. 'I've come to help you.'

He clambered off the ladder and moved towards the girl but she shrank away. He had a sudden horror she was going to topple over the windowsill and fall into the street. 'I won't hurt you,' he called. 'I'm going to get you away from the fire.'

There was a crash and a shout from downstairs, and a flicker of flame lit the wall by the trapdoor opening. It was no time for talk. Peglar made a lunge for the child and managed to get hold of her wrist. She struggled, tried to pull away, then gave in and he swung her onto his shoulder. She clenched his tunic tight in her fists and they squeezed through the hole. They almost fell when Peglar's foot got to the broken rung, but he held on to the child with one hand and the ladder with the other, and they were down.

There was another stick with burning rags in the middle of the room, replacing the one he'd kicked out. Some idiot must have thrown it back through the door.

Why would they do that? He swerved past it and out into the air, lowered the girl to the ground, and fell beside her, coughing and spluttering.

'What's your name? Where's your mother?' He asked her when he could speak again.

The girl looked at him vacantly, then pointed towards the shack. Peglar struggled to his feet. He hadn't noticed anyone else in there but he had to check. He readjusted his face cloth and, crouching as low as he could, peered in through the doorway. Had he missed something? There looked to be a shape in the corner. Could that be a person? No, he was sure there was no one there. Then he noticed a door at the back of the room. It was impossible to get past the blazing rags to it. He went back to the girl.

'You're safe now,' he said to her. She looked up at him, grubby, smeared face, wide, frightened eyes. 'Stay here. Please. Don't go away. I'll be back in a minute.'

He went to the rear of the house. There was a single, dark window in the wall. Peglar looked through into what seemed to be a small scullery. There were no flames yet and only a little smoke, although he could see a yellow flicker in the gap under the door to the other room. There was the body of a man on the floor. Peglar banged on the window but there was no movement. Was he dead? He tried again, harder. Still no response, so he picked up a stone and smashed the glass. The wooden frame was rotten and half the window collapsed inwards with a splintering crash. Even then the man didn't move. Peglar swung himself through the hole, scarcely noticing when a shard of glass nicked his arm.

The man was not dead, but he was inert. There was

an overturned jar beside him. Peglar sniffed it and recoiled from the raw and dizzying smell. He shook the man's shoulder but there was still no response. He slapped his face. The man groaned and stirred.

'Your house is on fire!' Peglar yelled in his face. 'Wake up! You've got to get out.'

He pinched the man's cheeks and slapped him again, harder. This time he showed some life. His eyes opened and his fists clenched.

The room was getting hotter and smoke was seeping under the door. Any minute now the place would erupt in a frenzy of flames.

'There's no time,' Peglar shouted. 'We've got to go. Now.'

The man seemed at last to grasp what was happening because he tried to claw himself up, but it was too much for him and he fell back. Peglar got his arm under his shoulder and hauled him to his feet. He was big and heavy, and Peglar's knees buckled under the dead weight but he managed to get the man to the window. Then he bent him over the sill so his head and upper body were in the open air, lifted his legs and tipped him out. He fell heavily onto the ground, where he lay moaning.

Peglar followed him through the window. The man was unconscious again, and Peglar dragged him by limbs, clothing, anything he could get a grip on, until he got him to what he judged would be a safe distance. The whole shack was now well alight, and the loft where the child had been was engulfed by flames. He ran back to the front. The girl was where he had left her, and he was relieved to see two women with her.

'Is she all right?'

The women looked up. 'Who are you?' one of them said.

'I'm a friend. Are you her mother?'

The woman nodded.

'There's a man round the back,' Peglar said. 'He's in a bad way, passed out. I think he's drunk.'

The other woman snorted. 'I expect he is. Arsehole. That'll be her dad. I'll go get his brother.' She straightened up. 'You're from the city, aren't you?'

'Yes,' said Peglar.

'Well I'd piss off if I was you. His brother's bigger than him, and he don't like city folk. If he finds you here he'll kill you.'

She made off round the side of the house. The girl's mother looked up at him. 'Thank you,' she said, nodding towards her daughter. 'You'd best go now.' Her voice was gentler than her companion's.

Peglar left them and trudged wearily up the ravine until he reached the edge of the Settlements, where the last few tumbledown dwellings petered into scrub. He sank down on a tree stump and pressed the heels of his hands against his streaming eyes. He dabbed at the wound on his leg where he'd scraped it on the ladder. He wiped his face on the hem of his tunic, got to his feet and started back down the hill. The smoke was even thicker now, and he couldn't see more than a few paces ahead.

Then the swirling clouds parted and she was there. Her smock was torn, her yellow hair loose and filthy, her face streaked with soot and blood. She had a glistening gash on her arm. She was standing frozen, dazed. Suddenly she saw him, and howled.

'Jathan Peglar!' she screamed. 'You said we'd got time!'

'Yalka, I'm sorry.' He moved towards her but she backed away. 'I didn't know this would happen.'

'You're a liar!' she shrieked. 'I trusted you but you lied.'

Peglar was bewildered. How could she blame him for what was happening?

'You tricked me, you used me. I hate you, Jathan Peglar, I hope you burn!' She spat the words, brim full of venom and loathing.

She backed away, but before the smoke closed around her again she shouted one more thing: words that, despite the raging inferno, froze Peglar to the bone.

35

RECOVERY

He neared the surface several times, clambering towards consciousness only to slip back again into a void. The pain was never far away. The slightest movement would set off a hammering inside his skull that compelled him to lie still until it ebbed. Eventually thirst forced him to sit up. His lips were cracked, his throat tight and shrunken and it was almost impossible to swallow. He tried to drink from the metal cup beside his bed but each sip was an ordeal. His eyes watered endlessly in the dark.

When he slept he dreamt of fire, of a face twisted in a rictus of agony, of burning people running through the streets with the flames snapping at their heels like angry dogs. He dreamt of Yalka floundering in the river, her arms beating the water. She cried to him to help her and he reached from the bank, stretching as far as he could, but she was too far out and their hands remained achingly apart.

He drifted again, and when he woke next he was aware of bright light, a white space. There was a tall window and an arched doorway. The light assaulted his eyes and he shut them again. Sometimes he thought he heard mumbled voices, distant and indistinct. Another time Verit was standing in the doorway and watched, scowling under his brows, until Peglar had to turn away. When he looked back the boy was gone.

But it couldn't have been Verit. Gradually strands of memory emerged, each one almost beyond bearing. He remembered waking to the smell of smoke. He remembered following Feldar to the fire, the burning homes, the seared flesh, the stench. He remembered Yalka screaming that he'd betrayed her, that the fire was his fault, that she hated him. And he remembered the final words she'd hurled at him just before the smoke took her again.

'Verit's dead.'

'What?' He had been stunned.

'He hid under the floor, to be safe. When the house burnt the fire took all the air. He couldn't breath. He suffocated.'

Dead? No, it couldn't be. There was such finality in the word, such despair in her cry. Verit, the little, brown-eyed, fox-faced boy, dead? How could he be? Peglar felt again his tongue on his hand, rough like a cat's. He saw his smile and remembered the way it had lit his face. Peglar wanted to say he couldn't be dead, was she sure? He wanted to put out a hand to her but he could do nothing, say nothing. He was helpless in the face of her grief and rage, and he could only stand and stare, dumb as Verit had been until with a final, outraged scream Yalka ran into the curtain of smoke.

For a long time he lay on his back in the white room,

silent tears running down his cheeks and on to the pillow.

He remembered other things too, things almost as unbelievable, things that perhaps no one else had seen. He had been staring at the spot where Yalka had been and was about to turn back down the hill when two murky figures emerged from an alley opposite. They wore black cloaks and hoods, and he thought for a second that they might be more men from the city come to help fight the fire, but it was soon apparent they were not. One of them held a pair of blazing torches, the other a bundle of rags. They kicked open the door of a shack, hurled some rags inside and threw one of the torches after. The rags caught at once, flaring fast. The men ran to the next hut and did the same. Then others arrived. Peglar backed into the woods, and watched as the men moved up the hill systematically firing the few remaining buildings.

That explained it: how the fire had started, why it had spread so widely and so quickly. With the last shack ablaze the men gathered on a patch of waste ground. They were laughing and shouting as they looked down the ravine, clapping their hands together in celebration and hugging each other. He saw that one of them was circling the group, embracing each man and handing him a small bag. He looked to be in charge. He was familiar, his build, the way he strutted. Then, to mark that their job was done, the men tore off their hoods and with a cheer flung them into the air. The leader was in the middle of the group with his back turned, and as he revolved, raising his clenched fist to each member, Peglar saw who it was.

Paid and thanked, the men broke up and melted into

the trees, leaving just their leader and one other behind. Together the two looked down the slope at the smouldering remains, admiring their handiwork. Then Ragul put his arm around Burian's shoulder and they, too, left.

It made no sense. Ragul should have been miles away, with the army in Rasturoth. Then he remembered Feldar saying how quickly he could get back if he needed to.

Hours passed, not that Peglar had any idea of time. He lacked any notion of how long he slept, how long he was half awake. Although his heart held a heaviness that seemed to be constantly dragging him towards a dark pit, his body began to feel better. The spells of wakefulness grew longer, and in them he thought about what he must do. He must find Yalka. She would have lost everything. He must talk to her, help her, explain that he knew nothing of the fire, that he could not possibly have prevented it, that it was not his fault. Where was she? How could she bear the loss of Verit, who looked out for her, and who had defended her by firing a stone at Peglar's head?

He reviewed his condition. The good thing was that his headache had eased. There was a bump on his forehead, a cut on his arm and another on his shoulder. These had been loosely bandaged. He had a gash on his leg, and he remembered the jolt as the ladder rung snapped when he climbed to rescue the girl. The wound had been left uncovered and looked clean, with a neat scab formed over it. The worst of his injuries were his hand and forearm. He couldn't recall them being burnt, but they were. They'd been left open to the air and painted with something yellow that worsened their raw appearance. There didn't seem to be any other damage. It was only the burns that really hurt, although his throat was sore and every inward breath produced a wheezy rattle in his chest. He could still taste the fire.

Tentatively he swung his legs off the edge of the bed and sat still while he waited for the pain brought on by the movement to subside. He was naked. He must find his clothes. They were not in the room. Apart from the bed and a single chair it was empty. Cautiously he stood up and took a few weak steps. From the window he was able to look down on a neat square: some trees, stone benches, a fountain. Opposite was a row of low buildings, and behind them the impressive outline of the Academy tower. He knew where he was: the City Sanatorium.

From behind him he heard voices and the sound of footsteps. He hurried back under the bed covers, wincing at the havoc this stirred in his arm and his head. The sound drew closer and two figures appeared in the shadowed archway. One of them came forward into the light. It was Feldar. Peglar was overjoyed to see him and relieved that, although he looked tired, he seemed unhurt.

'Welcome back,' the Steward said as he approached the bed.

'Back?'

'Yes. I visited you yesterday, and the day before, but you were out of this world.'

'Yesterday? How long have I been here?'

'Three days.'

Three days? He had been in the Sanatorium for three days? He had no idea it was so long. If he was to find

Yalka he had to get out. He started to get up but Feldar gently pushed him back.

'Not so fast. Let's see what's going on here.'

He looked at Peglar's head and his shoulder, easing aside the bandages, and he examined his hand and arm.

'Right,' he said, 'it looks as though you'll live. Don't worry about the burns. I know they hurt now, but they're not as bad as they look, or as bad as they might have been. Everything else is fine. Narvil's done a good job. The wounds all seem clean and should heal quickly, but you need to stay put, get some rest and give them chance.'

'How did I get here?'

'I brought you. With a bit of help from your friend here.'

The other visitor came forward. It was Cestris.

'You were in quite a state,' Feldar said. 'Burns, bruises, cuts, but most of all you were exhausted. We had to carry you here.'

'You were babbling, too,' Cestris said.

'Babbling?' Peglar shook his head. He could remember none of this.

'Yes. Something about a dead boy, and you were sorry, and the fire was not your fault. I think you were delirious.'

'No, there really was a dead boy. Did anybody find him? A little boy with reddish hair, about seven or eight.'

Feldar looked sombre. 'We found two dead children. One of them might have been a boy.'

'There was a girl, too,' Peglar said urgently. 'Skinny, about my age. Yellow hair, nose piercing, a mark on her cheek.'

266

They both shook their heads.

'Your friend from the Citadel,' said Feldar. 'No, we looked for her but we didn't see her.'

'I need to find her. The dead boy was her brother.' Again he tried to get up and again Feldar restrained him.

'Where would you look?' he asked gently. 'The Settlements are gone. Everything's gone, there's nobody left. The area's dangerous and the Guardians are stopping people from going there. There was no one like you describe among the injured, or among the bodies.'

He was thrown. A moment ago his course had been simple: get his clothes, go to the Settlements, find Yalka, make it right. Now it seemed that all the settlers had vanished, and he was certain that if there were Guardians around Yalka would not be. But where could she have gone?

Feldar's voice broke into his thoughts. What was he saying? '...get you some fruit and some books. Stay here and rest. There's uproar at the Palace. You're well out of it.'

The visit exhausted Peglar, and after Feldar and Cestris had gone he slept again. When he next woke the sun was lower and, thankfully, the room less bright. He was troubled. Where might Yalka be? He managed to get his leg and arm comfortable and was again bobbing on the margins of sleep when he became aware of someone standing at the foot of the bed.

She was a vision: dark, tumbling curls; smooth, olive skin; huge, brown eyes. Malina smiled and he felt himself smiling back, he couldn't help it.

'I've come to see how you are,' she purred, glancing back at the doorway to where one of her women waited.

She glided towards him, trailing her hand along the bed. 'You're rather a hero. Everybody's talking about what you did, how you saved people's lives.' She sat, not on the chair but on the edge of the bed, close to him. 'Tell me about it,' she pouted.

She was looking at him with an expectant smile. Had he saved people's lives? He didn't know. There was the girl in the loft, and her drunken father. He supposed the man might have died if he hadn't got him out, but somebody would surely have heard the girl and helped her. He was ambushed by a sudden memory of Verit. He hadn't saved him. Verit was dead. Malina saw the tears in his eyes and took his hand, stroking it gently.

She noticed his arm and grimaced. 'You're hurt,' she said, examining it more closely. She straightened up and smiled again. 'Come on,' she said playfully. 'The story is you saved somebody's life. Tell me about it. Don't be shy.'

'It was nothing,' Peglar said gruffly. 'I just helped somebody out of one of the buildings.'

'They say it was a child.'

'Yes, but she was all right, she could walk. All I did was show her the way.' He didn't say anything about carrying her down the ladder, or the bolted trap door.

'Modest,' she said. Then her tone changed. It was slight, only the merest shift, but it was noticeable. 'Were there any others at the fire? Did you see anyone else from the city there?'

'Feldar,' he said. 'Cestris was there too, although I didn't see him, he came later. Feldar did most of it. The rescuing, I mean.'

She shook her head. 'No, I mean apart from them. There's a rumour that the fire was started deliberately. I wondered if you knew anything about that, if you'd seen anybody doing that.'

Peglar didn't know why she was asking this, but he retained enough of his wits to hold back and give as little information as possible. He was certainly not ready to tell her about Ragul. He hadn't even told Feldar, not yet. So he said, 'No, I didn't see anything like that. Just the fire, and the people trying to save their stuff.'

'"People trying to save their stuff,"' she mimicked. 'You've even picked up some of the Settlements way of talking.' For a moment then her tone had taken on a hard edge, like Vancia. She thought for a moment. 'Well, that's good,' she said more gently, tossing her head and flicking back her hair. 'It's best if the blame for the fire can be put on stupid carelessness by some of the Settlers.' She leaned forward till her lips were close to his ear. Her voice was soft and he could feel her breath on his cheek. 'If you did see anyone else there, it would be as well not to mention it.'

She kissed him on the forehead, then rose and moved towards the doorway. She looked back over her shoulder. 'I'm so glad we're friends now,' she whispered.

36

A MESSAGE

Half way down the hill Peglar stopped. He'd discharged himself from the Sanatorium that morning, very much against Narvil's advice.

'Are you all right?' It was Cestris. Peglar was desperate to see the Settlements, survey the damage, and Cestris had offered to go with him.

Peglar nodded. 'Just about, I think. I should have done what Narvil said and stayed put.'

Cestris didn't say he'd told him so, although he had. 'Do you want to go back?'

Peglar shook his head. 'No. I must keep on. I have to find Yalka.'

He had expected the sight to be bad but it was far worse than he'd imagined. The River Settlements were gone. Nothing remained standing, not a single stick. It was impossible in the chaos to see where tracks and streets had been. Piles of blackened timbers were all that remained to mark where the shacks had once stood. Even after several days the fire still smouldered in places, and here and there an occasional puff of wind stirred embers into a sullen glow. However, its days were told; there was nothing left to burn. Clouds of ash swirled in the breeze, covering everything in grey dust. A rim of scorched trees marked the edge of the holocaust, breached in places where fingers of fire had probed the woodlands. Given the dry conditions, Peglar was surprised they had not all caught.

Feldar was right. The area was protected and Guardians were stopping anyone approaching. Peglar and Cestris pushed their way through a clutch of morbid gawkers. Peglar was ready to use his father's authority to insist on closer inspection, but it was obvious there was nothing more to see. Everything had gone. No one could still live here. It was impossible to work out where Yalka's home had been. She and her grandfather were certainly not here now.

What use are promises no one can keep? Syramos had rhymed. Well, Peglar thought, he hadn't been able to keep his, and that meant Yalka couldn't keep hers either. He looked up to see Cestris watching him. His mouth was set firm and his face concerned.

'It's terrible,' Peglar said. 'Worse than I remembered. How many bodies were found?'

'Two children and three adults. A man and two women.'

'Were they recognisable?'

'The children were too badly burnt. The man had been struck on the head.'

'Yes, it was a falling beam. Feldar and I found him soon after we got here. What about the women.'

'One middle aged, one older. There wasn't a girl.'

They returned to the gate and started back up the hill. Peglar felt hollow and weak and sore.

'Cestris, was there anyone else from the city at the fire?'

'What, you mean apart from you, Feldar and me?'

'Yes.'

'I don't think so. There were a few who'd come to have a look, but the Gate Guards weren't letting anyone out, so most people had to stay inside the city and watch from the walls.'

In a stone city, where the fabric of most of the buildings offered little to burn, fires were rare and easily contained, so the spectacular conflagration that had destroyed the Settlements was a rare drama. It was not surprising people had been curious to see it.

'Nobody else?'

'There were a few higher up the hill working to stop the fire spreading to the old city walls, the wooden section. They did a good job. Those timbers are coated in pitch and if they'd caught it would have been very nasty. At the bottom of the hill there was a detachment of Guardians trying to pump water from the river, but by the time they got themselves organised the fire had got too good a hold and they didn't make much of an impact. Anyway, they didn't look to be trying very hard.'

'Does anybody know how it started?'

'There are plenty of rumours. Some people say it was deliberate but no one knows who might have done it or why. The official line is that the settlers did it themselves, although I can't see why they would. Nobody knows for sure. One thing is certain, though. If it was intentional, whoever was responsible did your father a good turn.'

'How do you mean? They've destroyed his property.'

Cestris laughed. 'All they've destroyed is a few old shacks that he wanted to knock down anyway.'

'A few old shacks,' Peglar repeated, and he remembered Yalka's home. 'No, they destroyed more than that.'

Peglar returned to the city, not to the Sanatorium but back to the Palace. Although he felt exhausted his burnt hand hurt and that meant he couldn't rest. As well as that his mind was in turmoil.

After an hour or so he left the Palace by the passage Vancia had used and dragged himself up to the Citadel. Of course, the old fortress was deserted. He hadn't expected anything else. He clambered onto the top of the Great Stone and looked over to the bushes where Verit used to hide. He half expected to hear the tell-tale rustle in the vegetation that was usually the only indication of his presence, but everything was still. He fingered the place on his scalp where the boy's stone had hit him. There was still a lump. It was heartbreaking that this living evidence of Verit's life should remain after the boy himself had gone.

For a long time Peglar sat looking down on the city, as he and Yalka had done so many times before. What had been the Settlements was now no more than a dark smudge, a dirty thumbprint on the edge of the plain. By asking around he had found out that several people from the city claimed to have seen, or knew somebody who had seen, shadowy figures haunting the flames and bearing brands. The speculation was that these were pirates, or even raiders from Semilvarga, although no one seemed to question what either of these had to gain from setting fire to the River Settlements. Peglar never heard Ragul's name mentioned and said nothing of what he had seen. Ragul had talked about punishment burnings. Was this one that had got out of hand, or had he intended all along for the whole area to be destroyed?

He looked towards the wall where Yalka had made the shrine for her sister, and something caught his eye, a patch of brown. He slid off the rock and went to investigate. It was a fabric bag, dirty and scorched. As he turned it over something fell out. It was the remains of the pad he had given her. The scarlet cover had been ripped into pieces, but there on the first page was her name, written by him and copied by her; the first, imperfect attempt and then several more versions done with growing confidence and control.

With the cover came scraps of paper, lots of them, fluttering like leaves. They were her drawings, torn and torn and torn again into tiny fragments. The savagery of the destruction was chilling. He imagined her face as she mangled her work, teeth bared, chin jutting forward, snarling, shredding. There was something heavy in the bag and he shook it out. It was the pencil box. He slid back the lid. Every pencil had been broken, every single one, snapped into short, useless splinters.

The message was clear. Yalka had deliberately put the bag there so he would find it. This was proof that she had survived the fire and was still alive, but that didn't dull the pain of what her gesture meant. She was returning his gift, and its destruction was symbolic of what had happened to whatever there had been between them. She wanted nothing more to do with him. She wanted to obliterate all trace of their friendship, and she wanted him to know that.

Peglar gathered the scraps of paper, put them and the bits of the pencils back in the bag, and tucked it under his arm. His spirit was heavy and his steps slow as he walked back to the Palace.

37

A WARNING

It was the next day when Feldar called. Peglar was in his day room. He'd been half expecting – dreading – a visit from Sainter but he hadn't seen the little man since he returned from the Sanatorium. He was relieved that the visitor was Feldar.

'How are you?'

Peglar shrugged.

'It will take time,' Feldar said. 'Anyway, no rest this afternoon. Your father has called a meeting, in the Library at the third bell.'

'What's it about?'

It was Feldar's turn to shrug. 'I don't know, but I think it concerns you and your brother.'

Was it the Sharing? Surely not the Sharing at last. Now, in the middle of all this turmoil? It couldn't be.

Peglar didn't want to be late so he was in place much earlier than he needed to be. He thought when he entered the Library that he was the only person in the room, but then he saw Sainter. He was sitting at a table in the bay at the far end and he looked up crossly as Peglar approached.

'Yes? Did we have a meeting? I was not aware that one had been arranged.' He put down his pen and frowned. Sheets of the yellow paper that he always used for his notes were strewn across the table.

Sainter's greasy skin looked waxy in the faint sunlight coming through the window. Peglar took in his double chin and the rolls of fat around his neck and his stomach and thought again what an unappealing spectacle he was.

'No, no meeting,' he said. 'Not for you, anyway. However, my father has called one and he'll be here in a few minutes.'

'But I always work here, at this table,' Sainter whined, 'every afternoon.'

'You'll have to go somewhere else,' Peglar said.

Sainter noticed Peglar's bluntness. He gathered his papers, gave a huffy grunt and waddled towards the door. At the entrance he met Feldar, and made a point of standing still and waiting until the Steward stood back and allowed him to pass.

'What's the matter with him?' Feldar asked.

Peglar shrugged. 'He doesn't like being disturbed.'

'Were you having a tutorial?'

Peglar laughed. 'No. I can't remember when I last did. Not that I want one,' he added quickly.

Feldar sat down at the long table which ran down the middle of the room. 'How are your burns?'

Peglar looked at his hand and arm. 'All right, I suppose. A bit sore sometimes.'

'Cestris tells me that you and he went to look at the River Settlements.'

Peglar nodded. 'Yes. Or what's left of them.'

'Any sign of the girl you were looking for?'

'No.'

There was a long pause. Then Feldar said, 'Why do you want to find her? I know you used to meet her on the Citadel, but if you want a girl for sex there are plenty in the middle city who'd jump at the chance of a roll with the Master's son. What's so special about this one?'

Peglar hadn't planned a confession to Feldar. Neither had he realised how much of what he felt about Yalka was bottled up inside him, how desperately he needed to talk to somebody about it, and as soon as he began the whole story spilled out. He told him what they talked about at their meetings. He told him about her sister being forced into the city by the thing who called himself Scorpion, and about her murder at the hands of a gang, and of the shrine Yalka had made. As he spoke the visions flooded back. He remembered her yellow hair and her bright, blue eyes. He remembered her feelings for other people, her fascination with stories, her honesty, her exceptional drawings. He described being wounded by Verit, his visit to her tiny but spotless home, meeting her grandfather, the rhymer. Finally he described how he'd seen her on the night of the fire, and how she had held him responsible for that and for the death of her brother.

When he'd finished Feldar didn't speak straight away. Instead he stood up, came over to where Peglar was standing at the window and put his hand on his shoulder. Then he said, 'I'm sorry. You obviously think a lot of this girl. She and her family seem remarkable people. But you have to face it, she's gone. She trusted you, and she thinks you've let her down. Even though she'll learn sooner or later that the fire was nothing to do with you, the damage has been done. I don't think either of you will be able to forget what's happened.'

He was right, Peglar knew it, but it didn't make it any easier.

'Anyway,' Feldar said gently, 'even without that, you have to accept that you have no future with her. You can't pair with her, certainly not yet and probably not ever. Your father will want you to pair with a noble girl from a high family. Having someone from Yalka's class as a mistress is possible, but not till you have two or even three noble wives. Would you both be happy with that? Are you prepared to wait that long? Is she? Stop torturing yourself and try to move on. Find yourself a pretty, rich girl that your father would approve of, and see if she can take your mind off things.' He smiled.

Peglar hadn't finished but they couldn't talk any more because at that moment Uncle Mostani and Styron came into the room, followed by his father, tapping with his staff. The three men sat down and two Household Guards stood at the door. Karkis motioned to Peglar to sit and Feldar took up his usual stance behind the old man's chair.

'I want to know about the fire,' Karkis said, almost immediately. 'Tell me what you saw.'

Peglar was puzzled. Surely Feldar must already have given him a full account. 'I woke up in the middle of the night and I could smell smoke. I ran down to the city gate and on the way I met Feldar. We went round the…'

'Yes, yes, yes,' his father interrupted tetchily. 'I know all this. But what did you *see*? Did you see things that Feldar didn't? For example, what did you see of the fire?

There are rumours that it was started and spread deliberately. Did you witness any evidence of that?'

Peglar thought quickly. Malina had warned him against mentioning the fire raising, but surely that didn't apply to their father. Besides, he had the feeling he already knew.

'Well yes, sir.'

Uncle Mostani and Styron were watching him keenly. 'Tell me about it,' said his father.

'I was in one of the houses when somebody threw some burning rags in through the door.'

'Did you see who? Did you see any of the arsonists?'

'Yes, father. I saw all of them. At the end, when they'd finished and all the buildings had been set alight they gathered at the top of the ravine.'

'Did you recognise any of them?'

'Yes sir. They wore hoods but at the end they took them off. I recognised several of them, two in particular. One of these was their leader.'

'Who was it?'

'It was Ragul, sir. The other was Burian.'

There was silence. Then Uncle Mostani said to his father, 'It's true, then.'

Karkis nodded. 'So it would seem.'

There was another long pause while his father and the other two seemed to be thinking and Mostani made some notes. At last he looked at Peglar and spoke.

'There is a problem. What you have told us confirms what we had already heard: that the fires were started by your brother and some of his army pals. The trouble is, some of them have been boasting about it, shooting off their mouths in some of the city taverns, saying how they'd taught the Settlers a lesson, removed a blot from the city, snuffed out the child thieves, that sort of thing. The story has got around.'

'I challenged both my sons to find a solution to the problem of the River Settlements,' said Karkis. 'You, Peglar, devised a plan which was not a bad idea. There would have been some financial cost, but it could have worked. Your brother took – how shall I put it? – a more direct route.'

'Yes, he burned the wretched place down,' said Styron, with a hollow laugh. 'Which might have been all right if the idiots involved had kept their mouths shut about it.'

'And if it were not for Ormard,' added Uncle Mostani.

His father turned to Feldar. 'Tell him, Steward.'

'Ormard is a lawyer, who has a practice in Auric Park,' said Feldar. He paused for a moment to let what he'd said sink in. Auric Park was a fashionable district which attracted ambitious and successful young professionals. 'He has a growing business. Apparently he's very good.'

Peglar didn't understand. 'But what does this have to do with Ragul?'

It was Styron who answered. 'Nothing, at present. However, it will have a great deal to do with him if Ormard has his way. Do you know what a Notice of Litigation is?'

He did. A Notice of Litigation was a document presented to the City Authority giving warning that somebody was intending to bring a lawsuit. Its purpose was to notify the City Court of impending cases so that it could plan its business. It was a simple document,

stating what the suit was about, who was bringing it and the sum being sought.'

Uncle Mostani picked up an official looking paper. 'The subject of this one is compensation sought from those responsible for loss of life, injury and the destruction of property caused by the deliberate burning of the River Settlements. It's been filed by Ormard on behalf of the people living in the Settlements at the time of the fire.'

He pushed the paper across the table to Peglar. Ormard's name was followed by a list of others. Half way down was a name that jumped out at him. Yalka. No addition, simply Yalka. Peglar had taught her to write it, and he could see her now, head bent forward, a frown of concentration on her face as she steered the pencil. At the bottom of the page was the sum that Ormard was seeking. Peglar whistled at the size of it. It was many times more than the Settlers would have received if they'd taken the offer he had tried to arrange.

'Yes,' said Styron. 'I can see you're surprised. The figure is so high because of the loss of life.'

Karkis spoke again. 'If Ormard wins it could ruin us. The best strategy is to strangle it now, choke it before it can get any life.' He spoke firmly, and Peglar had a vision of the old warrior strapping on his sword for one last battle. 'I have told Ragul and Burian to stay low, and they've gone to the garrison in Halish-Karnon. It will keep them out of sight while my agents spread a rumour. This is your idea, Mostani. Tell him.'

Uncle Mostani gave a self-satisfied smile. 'The rumour your father's people will put about is simple. On the night of the fire Ragul and some colleagues from the Army were engaged in a night exercise. They were near the harbour when they noticed a fire in the River Settlements. They hurried there and as they drew closer they saw a number of people, hooded and masked, moving between the shacks and setting fire to them. When they arrived the fire raisers fled. They pursued them but they got away. It is because of the prompt and courageous action of Ragul and his comrades that the fire didn't spread to the old city walls which, as you know, in that area are built of timber, and that there wasn't even greater loss of life.'

There seemed to Peglar to be plenty of holes in the story. He started with the most obvious. 'But people will have seen them. I did, and others will have too.'

'Ah, they may have seen *someone*,' said Uncle Mostani, 'but that was not Ragul or any of his men. That was the others, the ones who were chased away. If Ragul and his men were hooded and masked all the time any witnesses can't possibly have seen their faces. They won't be able to say who was spreading the fire.'

'But what about the people who heard the story in the taverns?'

'What they heard was young men showing off and exaggerating, very drunk young men,' Uncle Mostani said soothingly.

'Suppose the men who were boasting do it again.'

'They won't,' said his father. 'I've ordered the rest of Ragul's team to Rasturoth. By the time their tour of duty is finished all this will be forgotten.'

'If they come back at all,' added Uncle Mostani. 'There's been some trouble with rebels refusing to pay tithes. We've lost five men from that posting in the last six months.'

Peglar could still see difficulties. 'Who are these

others supposed to have been? Who is supposed to have started the fire?'

His father gave a slight smile. 'Here's the clever part. In a few days from now we start another rumour: that it was the settlers themselves who did it. Ormard was behind it, and came up with the idea as a way to make money by claiming compensation. That will be believed because Ormard has agreed with the settlers that he will only get his fee if the suit is successful. If he loses they will pay him nothing. The final proof of Ragul's innocence comes when Thornal releases the report made by Ragul to his commanding officer.'

Peglar was puzzled. 'Won't it be a bit late for that? People will wonder why it didn't come out straight away. And what about Ragul's commanding officer? He'll know there was no such report.'

Karkis leant back in his chair, smiling to himself. 'Ragul's commander is an old friend of mine. Besides, he is under investigation over some missing mess funds. I think he will want to show his gratitude if I arrange for that problem to go away. There is little that cannot be resolved with careful planning and the right contacts.'

And enough money, thought Peglar.

His father rose, and Uncle Mostani and Styron helped him from the room.

Peglar felt depressed, and very tired. He looked at Feldar. 'What do you think of this?'

The Steward shrugged. 'It will probably work. Anyway, it's the way things are done. Your father will stop at nothing to protect his House and his position.'

'So this is what's normal in Chamaris,' Peglar said dejectedly. 'Truth is immaterial. So called facts are invented to support what those who have power want to be believed.'

'Yes,' said Feldar, 'that's how it works.'

Peglar was dejected but it was seasoned with anger. 'It could be so different. Chamaris has so much. It could be wonderful, a paradise. Instead it's withered, like a garden that could be beautiful but all the plants have died.'

Feldar nodded. 'And until someone emerges who has the conviction and strength to change it, that's how it will remain. A word of warning, though: watch out for Ragul.'

That surprised Peglar. 'What is there to fear from Ragul? He's in Rasturoth, and anyway I would have thought he's got enough on his plate for now.'

Feldar shook his head. 'He's now more dangerous than ever. Think about it. Your father was planning to hold his Sharing very soon. He set you both a challenge, and he was very pleased with the way Ragul had responded, solving the problem at zero cost. He would have awarded him the lion's – or should I say, the leopard's – share.' He laughed at his own joke. 'Now it's all up in the air again. Your father and Mostani have had to take some quick action to cover up the indiscretion of Ragul's pals, and Ragul himself has to keep his head down.'

Peglar recalled the look of pleasure on his father's face as he described what he was doing. 'My father seemed to be enjoying the situation.'

'Yes, I'm sure he is. He's always liked a bit of plotting. But he knows that this whole thing is risky. A lot of people will be in the know about what's going on, about what really happened on the night of the fire. Your father has to rely on them all being sufficiently in debt to him or frightened of him to keep quiet. Some of them will realise that they now have a hold over the Master of the City, and sooner or later one of them will want to exploit it. In your father's eyes Ragul may have seemed the man of action yesterday, but today he looks more like an impulsive hothead. Your plan seems to have been the best idea after all. The wheel has turned, and Ragul is at the bottom once more. Vancia knows this, and she won't let it stay that way.'

'What do you think she'll do?'

'I have no idea. All I can say is that a plot hatched by Vancia will be clever, devious and subtle. It will attack you where you are weakest. Be on your guard. And there's one more thing. You may hate your half-brother, but don't assume that everyone feels the same as you do. Some people love him. I don't mean just his mother and Malina. His army commander thinks he's wonderful and the men in his company worship him. They got into some trouble in Rasturoth when they were ambushed, and they reckon it was only Ragul's courage and quick thinking that got them out of it. As far as they're concerned he can do no wrong. Make no mistake, he'll be back.'

38

GOODBYE

The Palace was morbidly quiet. Ragul and Burian were absent, gone south, as ordered by Karkis. Vancia and Malina, too, seemed to be in hiding. Chalia seemed to be a little better but remained in her rooms. Feldar spent the day either in his office or at the Karkis counting house in the city. There was no news at all of Yalka, although there was gossip that some of the settlers were living in the harbour town a couple of miles away.

Peglar found most days boring. The dismal parts were the sessions with Sainter, which he strove to minimise and where possible escape from altogether, but which couldn't entirely be avoided. The highlights were his training sessions with Cestris. They were hard, and his trainer made no allowances, but Peglar could feel his performances were getting better and he took pleasure in the feeling these advances brought. He began to relish his own strength. He remained in awe of Cestris. His bronzed, muscular body, his head of golden hair, the way he seemed to find everything so easy, made him seem like a hero from one of the old stories. A couple of times Cestris caught Peglar studying him when he was oiling himself or bathing, and he had to look away in embarrassment. Cestris had smiled, as though he was used to such admiring looks, from men as well as from women.

Peglar thought a lot about Yalka. Feldar had been right, the sensible thing was to forget her, but he couldn't simply switch off his fascination with this puzzling girl. He missed her laughter. He missed her direct, honest gaze. He missed her surprises. He missed her sense of fun. There was a space inside him where she should be. Was that what being in love was like? And what happened if you lost the person you loved? Feldar had said move on. How did you move on? What exactly did you do to move on? How long did moving on take? Something decisive was needed, some action that would make a definite break by demonstrating that at last he really had brought this part of his life to a close.

He had kept the charred bag Yalka had left at the Citadel; now he tipped it open and spread out its contents on the desk in his day room. He tried to fit together some pieces of the drawings. He reassembled a couple of the broken pencils. Then he reached a decision and stood up. It was over. He had no idea where Yalka was. She and her grandfather might be living in Maris Partem, the harbour town, or they might have left for another city across the plain. She could be far away, building a new life and meeting new people. If she had wanted to see him she would have sought him out, or at least got a message to him. The only message she had sent was contained in these broken remnants, and its meaning was clear: she was done with him. There was no future in moping about and waiting for something to happen; it already had.

He scooped up the vandalised fragments, put them back in the bag and slowly trudged up the hill to the Citadel. It would soon be evening, and an edgy breeze was whipping up the hillside and rustling the dry grasses. Autumn was keening the wind, sharpening it for winter. He stood for a moment beside the Great Stone, where he had been that day when he first saw the girl with yellow hair. He remembered her accusation of spying, and her wonder at the telescope. He looked out over Chamaris, as they had then, and picked out the landmarks: the Ceremonium, the Assembly, the Sanatorium, the Academy, and far away the burnt out Settlements. He would not come here again.

'Yalka, I'm sorry,' he said aloud. 'I'm sorry about your sister. I'm sorry about Verit. I'm sorry about your home. I'm sorry about the part my family has played in the things you have had to endure. Wherever you are, I wish you well.'

He turned away from the city and crossed to the rearmost wall of the Citadel. The view here was very different. The low, broken rampart topped a near vertical drop. He leant over until he could see the rough path that zig-zagged steeply to a narrow gate. Across the chasm the steep shoulder of the next hill looked very close.

Peglar scrambled onto the wall. The uneven stones wobbled and the wind threatened to unbalance him. He looked down and imagined his body diving, tumbling, bouncing. Would he be killed straight away? Would he die before he hit the ground, as people said you did when you fell from a great height? He gathered himself on the lip of the dizzy drop and took a deep breath. Then he swung his arm and hurled the bag, Yalka's bag, as far as he could. He almost lost his footing as he let go but he steadied himself and watched it curve away in a slow arc before it hit the rocks far below, bursting and scattering its contents. He watched as a gust of wind caught the scraps of paper and whirled them in a spiral before smearing them across the far hillside.

'Goodbye,' he called. The canyon took his cry and tossed it back at him. 'Goodbye, goodbye, goodbye.'

He had shut the door. He had moved on. He jumped down from the wall and went back to the Palace.

39

A MEETING

A few days later Peglar was working on some papers for his father when a servant delivered a note. It was obvious who it was from. The untidy handwriting and the yellow paper were unmistakable. There would be nothing there to interest him so he didn't open it straight away and it was some time before he looked at it again. When he did he was surprised. It was brief, and intriguing.

My Dear Peglar

I have a confidential matter of the utmost importance to discuss with you. It is imperative we talk urgently. I await you in the Library. Please join me as soon as you are able.

Your Companion and friend,

Abriul Sainter

P.S. This is private business and I would appreciate it if you do not inform anyone of our meeting.

P.P.S. Forgive me if I reiterate the urgency of this request. Please do not delay but come at once.

He had seen Sainter only the previous day but he had said nothing. What important matter could have come up since then? Confidential? He and Sainter never had confidential discussions. If it were not a tutorial, why meet in the Library? Why didn't he come here, to Peglar's quarters? Later he remembered these questions and realised that he should have paid more attention to the misgivings they provoked, but at the time his curiosity won. He put aside his father's papers and went to the Library.

Even though it was midday the place was in darkness. The drapes at the far end of the room were closed and it was hard to see anything, but there seemed to be no one there. Sainter must have grown tired of waiting and gone. Someone had been there, though. He could smell perfume. Warm and sensual, it was a scent he knew. He moved a few steps further into the room, and heard a whisper behind him.

'Peglar.'

'Malina?' Malina was the last person he expected to find in the Library. 'I'm sorry,' he stammered. 'I didn't mean to... I was looking for...'

'Me,' she said softly, stepping between him and the door.

'...Sainter. Sainter asked me to meet him here.' Peglar looked around to see if somehow he'd missed him. 'He wanted to talk to me. I thought he would be here. It must be a mistake.'

He made to go, but she was in his way.

'No, please stay.' She was standing very close. He moved back but she stepped forward, narrowing the space between them. She put her hand on his arm and looked into his face. 'It was me. I asked Sainter to get you to come here. I need your help. Will you help me? Please?'

Help her? Whatever did she mean? How could he help her? She looked at him with huge, pleading eyes. If he had not been beguiled by the impact of her presence he might have questioned what was happening. Why meet here? Why involve Sainter? Why not simply come with one of her women to his quarters? Where were her women, anyway? None of this occurred to him. All he registered was her serious face in its frame of dark curls, her red eyes and her tear streaked face.

'What's the matter?' he said.

'Oh, Peg,' she said, shaking her head and using the name she'd called him in the nursery. 'Please help me. I don't know what to do.'

'What is it? What's wrong?'

She looked as though she was going to cry again, and she dabbed her eyes with a handkerchief. She bowed her head and stared at the floor.

'How can I help you?' There was no reply. 'What do you want me to do?'

She took a deep breath. Whatever she had to say to him seemed to be an effort. 'I don't know where to begin. It's father.'

'Father?'

She nodded, choking back a sob. Peglar was lost. What was going on? 'What about father?'

She regarded him steadily for a moment, her eyes heavy with tears, and then slowly looked away. She spoke so softly he had to lean towards her to hear. 'He wants me to pair.'

Was that all? It was no surprise. Many girls of her age were already paired, and it would be remarkable if a pairing were not being arranged for her. In fact, the surprise was that it hadn't been done already.

'So? Isn't that what you expect?'

'Yes, of course. But he wants me to pair with…' her voice dropped even further, '…with… Lembick.'

'Lembick?' It was unexpected. He was not a family friend. As far as Peglar knew he had ambitions to take over himself as Master of the City. But Peglar knew that their father was devious, and trying to work out his reasons was never simple. There must be a rationale for such a pairing. Perhaps he saw it as a way to neutralise Lembick, to bring him into the fold.

'Well, it may be a good thing. He doesn't have a pair. You would be his first wife. You would always be senior.'

Malina sobbed again. 'But he's old,' she wailed. 'He's as old as my mother.'

Again that wasn't unusual. Older men from the rich families often took much younger wives. He thought of his own mother, Chalia, many years younger than Karkis.

'When did you hear this?'

'My mother told me last night. She said that Lembick likes me and has asked father for me. He's promised that if the pairing goes ahead he will agree not to oppose father. He'll support him as Master of the City in any way he can.'

It made sense, but it didn't. Lembick was ambitious, unscrupulous, and a known enemy. Why would he want a pairing that would bring him closer to the House of the Leopard? On the other hand, he had seen Lembick looking at Malina in a particular way – although when he thought about it, that was not unusual, a lot of men did.

Malina broke into his thoughts. 'There's the bride gold, too. He's offering a large sum for me.'

Lembick was reputedly very wealthy, and he knew from the papers he'd seen that the family businesses were not doing as well as they had. A handsome pairing settlement would be helpful. Removing Lembick as an opponent and at the same time filling the family coffers made a lot of sense.

Malina was watching him anxiously. 'Help me, Peg. Please.' She leaned forward and took the front of his tunic in both her hands, resting them on his chest. 'You're the only one who can.'

He felt flattered by her confidence in him, but he didn't see how he could change their father's mind. 'If that's what our father has decided, what can I do?'

'I have to see him tonight, at the seventh bell. Talk to him before that.' The hands gripping his tunic clenched into two tight fists. 'Persuade him that this pairing is wrong. Think of obstacles, I'm sure you can. He'll listen to you. Save me from this, please.' Another tear rolled down her cheek.

Peglar felt sorry for her but was reluctant to get involved. He and his half-sister had never been close. She had always been on Ragul's side against him and had often joined in the teasing and the tricks. 'I don't know,' he said. 'You know how stubborn father can be. If he's made up his mind he wont listen to me.'

That was the moment at which everything changed. Suddenly, and without any warning. At one moment Malina was gazing at the floor, sobbing and dabbing her eyes. The next she looked up, straightened her shoulders and stared Peglar in the eye. The tears and the frailty were gone. Instead there was her mother's calculating coldness.

'He won't listen to you,' she said, in a voice quiet but hard as iron. 'That's exactly what I wanted to hear.'

Peglar froze, unsettled by the change and then horrified by what she did next. She reached to her throat, seized her garment and with a savage jerk tore it away. The thin material ripped and fell, baring one breast. She looked at Peglar for a moment with an amused expression, then she opened her mouth and cried out. 'No. No. Get away. Peglar, no.'

Peglar took a step back and she turned and ran from the Library, covering her breast with her arm, knocking over a chair, screaming.

At once the room flooded with light. Peglar leapt as if stung and spun round to where the drapes had been flung back. Sainter was beside the window, staring at him.

'Malina!' Peglar called, and started after her.

He got to the doorway and saw Malina, hair and gown flying, as she ran down the passage, calling. When he turned back Sainter had left by the other door.

40

TAKING STOCK

Peglar steadied himself against the door frame. His head was thumping and he took several deep breaths to try to calm himself so he could think about what to do. He wanted to go after Malina and find out what was going on, but the sensible thing was to follow Sainter. He needed to know how long he had been in the Library, and what he had seen and heard. Malina was behaving as if he'd tried to attack her. That was ridiculous. She'd gripped the front of his tunic but he hadn't touched her. Sainter would have seen. He could say what really happened.

He hurried in the direction of Sainter's quarters. He knocked on the door but there was no reply. Perhaps he'd gone to Peglar's own rooms to wait for him. Yes, that was it, that's where he would be. But he wasn't there either. There was no Sainter. There was no sign of even the usual servants.

Peglar sat at the desk in his day room and went over what had happened. The note about the meeting had definitely come from Sainter. It wasn't just the yellow paper, the handwriting proved it. Where was that note now? He had been sitting in this same place when he read it and he was sure he had left it on his desk, but it was not there now. He looked in the basket he kept for discarded papers in case he'd thrown it away. It was empty, there was nothing there.

Was Sainter involved in what Malina had done? Was this what Feldar had warned him about? Was it a plan of Vancia's? Or was it a trick, some sort of sick joke that Malina had cooked up with Ragul to embarrass him.

He was too agitated to stay in his room so he went back to the Library. It was just as he had left it, the drapes at the far end askew, the tumbled chair. Where was everybody, though? It was the end of the morning and the Palace should have been heaving. There should have been callers paying their respects, petitioners begging his father for favours, clerks bringing reports from the various family businesses, there should have been servants, but there was nobody. He tried some of the other public rooms: the Atrium, the Great Hall, the Waiting Room, the Audience Chamber. All were deserted.

He went back to his bedchamber and sat on the bed, his head in his hands. Not only had Sainter disappeared but everyone else seemed to have vanished too. Something was wrong. He had not seen a single soul since he'd watched Malina running down the corridor. The image of the fleeing girl was burned in his mind, her hair flowing, her gown falling off her shoulder, her backward glance towards him as she ran.

He rang the bell for a servant. No one came. He took off his sandal and hurled it across the room. It hit the door with a hollow thump and dropped to the floor.

'SERVICE. GIVE ME SOME SERVICE HERE!'

There was no response.

Peglar's head was aching. He needed to talk to Malina. He didn't want to face her, didn't know what he'd say to her, but he must try to neutralise whatever she was up to. He went to the women's wing.

That was as deserted as everywhere else. Malina was not in her quarters, although he did at last see another human being. A waiting woman was tidying the Women's Parlour. She told him that Malina had left the Palace.

'Left?'

'Yes, sir, with her mother.'

'When?'

'A little time ago, sir. They seemed in a hurry.'

The woman did not know where they had gone, or when they would be back.

'Did she leave a message for me?'

The woman looked surprised. 'No, sir. I am sure she did not.'

He walked slowly back to his own quarters. Left with Vancia? That didn't sound good.

His small bedchamber was cosier than the vast day room. Peglar lay on his bed and stared at the ceiling. He concentrated on taking deep breaths, in and out slowly, trying to kill the unease he felt. Where had Malina gone? Why? Where was Sainter? Could Peglar rely on him to give an honest account of what had really happened? He was a respected man, a scholar, so surely he'd tell the truth. But as he'd remarked to Feldar, the truth was what people in power made it. How much power did he have?

The answers to that question came at around the

third afternoon bell. There was a noise in the day room and Peglar leapt from his bed and rushed through, hoping it might be Sainter. It was not. Instead it was Feldar. He looked grim, and there were two men of the Household Guard with him. They had pointed staffs and wore their helmets low over wooden faces. Peglar was pleased to see Feldar, but the Steward's greeting was cold.

'Your father wants you. Come with me.' Peglar turned towards the bedchamber to tidy himself but Feldar snapped his fingers. 'No time for that.'

The guards took up positions one on each side of him, and with Feldar in front they marched quickly out of the room, along the corridor and through the Atrium towards his father's study.

Peglar started to speak but Feldar held up a hand. 'Your best course for now is to say nothing.'

They walked in silence, the only sounds their tramping feet and the men's staffs rapping the marble floors.

Malina must have complained. In a way this was good because it would give him the chance to explain what had really happened. Surely no one would believe he'd attack Malina. He wouldn't assault any girl, least of all his half-sister. He wasn't like that. And Sainter would bear him out.

By the time they reached Karkis's study Peglar was feeling excited and was looking forward to the opportunity to settle the incident. However, it didn't work out like that.

41

A HEARING

The last time Peglar had been in his father's study it had been pleasantly cool. Now it was restored to its customary breathless heat. Also it was crowded. Karkis was at his desk, his face in shadow. Beside him sat Uncle Mostani. On the other side was Vancia, who glared at him. He was surprised to see her. She and Malina must have returned. Sainter was standing at his father's left shoulder. He didn't look at Peglar. Another surprise was that Ragul was on his right. What does any of this have to do with Ragul? Peglar wondered. And why wasn't he in Rasturoth with the Army?

Peglar was nudged into the centre of the room. There was no chair for him, so he had to remain standing, a guard on each side.

His father raised his head and Peglar saw his expression. He looked to be in a state of shock. For a long time he gazed in his direction and his jaws moved, as if he was chewing something. Peglar wondered if he could see him at all, the room was so dim, and he edged forward to get into a better light. One of the bodyguards brought his staff down sharply, stopping him going further. Peglar felt threatened. Something was seriously wrong.

At last his father spoke, using his formal name. 'Jathan Peglar, your sister has brought an accusation against you. A terrible accusation. What she alleges is so appalling that I would not myself believe it, except that your Companion here,' and he gestured towards Sainter, 'witnessed the incident she described and he corroborates her account.'

Peglar's heart sank. What did Sainter think he saw?

Sainter stepped forward, as if on cue. He cleared his throat and began to speak. He seemed uncomfortable and still avoided looking at Peglar.

'Earlier today I had cause to be in the Library,' he said. 'I often go there to undertake reading for my research.' His voice, usually smooth and viscous, was high and unsteady. 'I wanted to avoid being disturbed, so I took my books to a small table in the bay of the window, and for added privacy I closed the drapes behind me.' The room was silent. Everyone was fixed on his story. 'After I had been there for some time,' he continued, 'I heard a cry. I pulled aside the drape and saw Peglar with his sister, Mistress Malina.'

'What was Peglar doing?' asked Uncle Mostani.

'He had his sister by the wrist and was pulling her into the room.'

'No!' Peglar protested, 'Malina was already in the Library when I arrived.'

'Be silent!' his father growled. He turned to Sainter. 'Resume your account. What followed?'

Sainter gave him a fawning smile. 'Thank you, my lord. It all happened so very quickly and was so very shocking, I can barely bring myself to describe it.' He dabbed his brow with an embroidered handkerchief and made a show of composing himself. 'Peglar pushed his sister into the corner of the room just inside the door and started... started... groping her and, er, pulling... at her... clothing.' He stopped and patted his face again, as if too distressed to go on.

Peglar shook his head violently. 'No, no, no. That's ridiculous!'

'Silence,' bellowed Karkis. 'Interrupt again and I shall continue this hearing without you.'

Hearing? Hearing? thought Peglar. Was this some sort of lawsuit?

Karkis nodded to Sainter. 'Please continue.'

'Yes, of course. I apologise. Just... so very upsetting.' Sainter gave the appearance of forcing himself back to a disagreeable duty.

'What exactly was Peglar doing?' This was from Mostani, who seemed to have taken over the interrogation from Karkis.

Sainter paused just long enough to give his words the impact he wanted. 'He was trying to get his hands... inside his sister's robe. He was trying to...force himself on her.'

Vancia gasped.

'What was Malina's reaction?' asked Mostani.

'Oh, she was distraught. She was resisting him, trying to push him away, struggling and sobbing. It was terrible. Terrible.' He shook his head, too upset to go on.

'What did you do? Did you not intervene?'

'Oh yes! Of course. How could I not? At first I was too shocked, I couldn't believe what I was seeing. Then I called out and came from behind the curtain.'

'What happened then?'

'His sister took advantage of the distraction to tear herself free and escape.'

'Did Peglar follow her?'

'No, not at once. He turned on me. He was very angry. He shouted at me, used the foulest language. He told me that I'd better keep my mouth shut. He said that if I didn't he would have me thrown out of the Palace. Then he ran after her.'

There was silence. The air of disgust was palpable. Everyone was looking at Peglar, who was in a state of shock. These were terrible lies. Why was Sainter saying this? Why would they believe it? He had to explain, to say what really happened.

'Where's Malina?' he said. He was sure that when faced with it Malina would be unable to lie. She would tell them that Sainter's story was not true.

His father answered, his voice leaden. 'Malina is extremely upset. Her mother has been comforting her and she is now with one of her women. She will shortly go to stay in another house, where we hope she can begin to recover. You have hurt her dreadfully.'

'You must talk to her,' said Peglar. 'You must see her. She'll tell you that it didn't happen the way he said. It's not true.'

Karkis turned to Sainter again. 'Do I have your word on oath that you yourself witnessed the events you have described and that they occurred exactly as you have told us?'

'Yes,' said Sainter, his voice shaking. 'It was exactly as I have told you. You have my word.'

Peglar could contain himself no longer. 'He's a liar!'

The reaction was immediate. His father banged his

fist on the table, Uncle Mostani stood up, Sainter looked as he'd been struck. It was one of the worst charges Peglar could make, to accuse a citizen of lying under oath. Even as he shouted the word he realised that in the eyes of his opponents he was putting himself further in the wrong, but he had to make them see.

His father looked coldly at him. 'Sainter is your Companion and might have chosen to stay silent, but he behaved honourably by reporting what he saw. He does not deserve your insult, which is simply another example of your shameful conduct.'

Sainter looked prim. 'I had no choice,' he purred. 'I love Peglar, I truly do, but his sister, really, I had no choice.'

'Don't I get a chance to speak?' said Peglar.

'If you have anything to say,' his father replied. 'I doubt there is much you can add, but fairness demands you be given an opportunity to put your case.'

Fairness. The word had a hollow ring but Peglar tried to calm himself. This was his chance to convince them he had not done what Sainter, and presumably Malina too, had said.

'This is what happened,' he began. He spoke slowly and deliberately. He described receiving the note from Sainter, the handwriting, the yellow paper, its contents.'

Sainter started to protest but Karkis quietened him. 'You have this note?' he asked.

'Well no, not here, but I'm sure I can find it. You could ask the servant who brought it. I could point him out.'

Vancia looked skeptical. Sainter smiled.

'Continue,' said his father.

'When I got to the Library, Sainter wasn't there but Malina was. She was waiting for me.'

'Why would she do that?'

'She said she wanted my help. She wanted me to persuade you not to pair her with Lembick.'

'Pair her with Lembick!?' His father exploded. 'Have you lost your mind? Mostani, what on earth is the boy talking about?'

Uncle Mostani shrugged. Vancia laughed.

It wasn't going well but he had to get to the climax and he hurried on. 'You want to pair Malina with Lembick to get him on your side, so he won't oppose you and will support you as Master. And for the bride gold he will bring.'

Karkis appeared to choke. Mostani snorted.

Vancia got to her feet and came from behind the table to stand in front of Peglar. 'You have heard my daughter's account of what happened. Are you saying that she's a liar too?'

'I didn't do what she's accusing me of,' Peglar said.

Before he realised what was happening Vancia drew back her hand and slapped him hard across the face. There was a clap like a bag bursting, lightning flashed and his ear rang. Ragul, who this whole time had said nothing, grabbed her arm and pulled her away. Then he turned back to Peglar and shouted in his face. Peglar heard him bawling but it made no sense. It seemed to be the same word over and over again.

'Challenge. Challenge.'

Their father held up both his hands, Mostani banged the table. Slowly things calmed down.

Karkis spoke. 'I cannot begin to understand why you

did what your sister and your Companion have described.'

'It's one of the worst things I've heard in a long time,' said Mostani.

'He's not only weak, he's evil,' Vancia hissed. 'I always told you so.'

'Sir,' said Ragul, raising his hand, 'May I speak?'

Their father nodded.

'Peglar's wicked behaviour is an insult to our House.' He came towards Peglar, who backed away, thinking he was going to be hit again. His nose was bleeding from Vancia's blow, blood oozing down his chin. 'Jathan Peglar,' Ragul spat, 'you are accused of assaulting my sister. You have insulted your Companion, an honourable man. I challenge you to a Trial of Veracity. I challenge you to settle the truth of this business in combat.'

Everyone was silent. Peglar couldn't speak. He didn't understand what was going on. He had no idea what to say, how to respond to this terrible situation, how to make himself believed. 'I haven't. I didn't,' he spluttered. He gestured towards Sainter. 'Why do you say this? It's not true.'

Karkis stood up. 'He accepts the challenge,' he said, and walked from the room.

42

VERACITY

Peglar slumped onto a chair and put his head in his hands. His nose was bleeding and slow, heavy drops hit the floor. Everyone had left when his father stormed out. Only a single guard remained, standing woodenly at the door.

He had never felt so wretched. What had happened? How? Only that morning he had trained in the gymnasium with Cestris. He had gone back to the Palace and read some papers from his father. He had gone to the Library, and then within a few minutes his world had disintegrated. He had always known that Malina disliked him, but he'd never imagined she hated him as much as this. Sainter too. They hardly knew each other, so why was he working to hurt him in this way. He'd snubbed Sainter, at times ignored him, and that had been rude. But did that deserve such terrible revenge?

The door opened and Feldar came in. He took Peglar's chin and pushed his head back, pinching the bridge of the nose and holding it while the bleeding stopped. Then he released his grip and gave him a cloth to wipe his face.

'Here. Dab it, don't rub. And don't blow your nose.'

He placed a chair directly in front of Peglar, turned it round and sat down, his arms resting on its back. He leant forward and turned Peglar's head, examining his bloody face.

'Mm. She must have caught you with her rings, but you'll be all right.' He let go. 'Now, I want you to listen carefully. I've heard two conflicting stories, yours and Malina's. I think I believe yours, but I have to be sure so I'm going to ask you some questions and I want you to think before you answer. Consider what you're saying very carefully, and tell me the truth. Understand?'

Peglar nodded.

'All right. Firstly, did you go to the Library today?'

Peglar nodded again.

'I want to hear you say it.'

'Yes, I went to the Library.'

'At what time?'

'I'm not sure of the exact time. I was back from training with Cestris and I'd done some work after that, so it was late morning.'

'Why did you go to the Library?'

'A servant brought me a note from Sainter asking me go there to meet him.' Peglar looked over to the guard on the door.

Feldar snapped his fingers. 'Look at me. Look at my face.' Peglar turned his head back to the Steward. 'Right. Tell me about this note. What did it say?'

'Just to meet him in the Library.'

'Did it say why Sainter wanted to meet you?'

'No, only that it was important. And confidential. I wasn't to tell anyone about it.'

'Mm.' Feldar thought about this. Then he said, 'Where is the note?'

Peglar shook his head. 'I don't know. I left it on the desk in my day room, but when I got back it wasn't there.'

Feldar frowned. 'What did you do when you got the note?'

'Well, I was in the middle of studying some papers that had come from my father. I knew the note was from Sainter because I recognised his writing but I didn't think it would be anything important, so I finished what I was doing before I read it.'

'And then you went to the Library?'

'Yes.'

'Did anyone see you?'

Peglar considered for a moment. Had he passed any of the servants on the way to the Library? 'No. I don't think so.'

Feldar nodded. 'Did you meet Sainter in the Library?'

'No, he wasn't there. I mean, I know now he was there, but I didn't see him.'

'Did you meet Malina?'

'Yes, but it wasn't…'

Feldar held up his hand. 'One answer at a time. Pay attention to my questions. This is very important. Did Malina tell you that your father wanted to pair her with Lembick?'

'Yes.'

'Why did she tell you this?'

'She said she wanted me to get father to change his mind.'

'And you believed her?'

'Yes.'

'Why?'

Peglar hesitated. Why had he believed her? It seemed stupid now, but at the time she had sounded so convincing. And he supposed he was pleased that with Ragul away it was him she'd come to for help.

Feldar lifted his eyes skyward. 'Lembick! I ask you. Didn't you think that was just a little bit odd? What happened next?'

'She shouted out. Screamed. And she pulled at her gown, ripped it down the front so it showed one of her breasts.'

'And then?'

'She ran away. Ran out of the Library, shouting and yelling.'

'What did you do?'

'I went to follow her but she'd knocked a chair over as she ran out and that slowed me down. By the time I got to the door she was way down the corridor.'

'Did Sainter see and hear all this?'

Peglar thought for a moment. 'I don't know how much he saw. He must have been where he says he was, in the bay behind the drapes, all the time. I don't know if he heard what Malina said, but he must have heard her yelling.'

Feldar leant back and looked hard at Peglar, weighing him up. He seemed satisfied. 'Well, Ragul's challenged you to a Trial of Veracity. Do you know what that means?'

Peglar shook his head.

'It's an ancient tradition that used to be followed by the old families as a way of settling a dispute about who's telling the truth. There hasn't been a challenge of this sort since I can't remember when. What happens is the two parties fight it out. The winner is credited with being the one telling the truth, the loser is held to be the liar.'

It was unbelievable. If he were to fight Ragul he would certainly lose, but Ragul was the liar, not him. 'That's insane.'

'Yes, it is, isn't it. Might is right and all that.'

'So what will happen?'

Feldar described how, when and where the trial would take place. The more Peglar heard the more desperate his situation seemed. Was there no way out of this?

'Of course,' said Feldar. 'You can refuse the challenge and walk away. But if you do you'll be saying that Malina and Sainter are right. You'll be arrested, tried for attempted rape, flogged, and imprisoned. You won't inherit any of your father's property. How does that sound?'

'Will the same thing happen if I lose the contest?'

'No. Honour will have been satisfied and there can be no further action against you.'

'It doesn't sound as though I have any choice.'

'No, I don't think you do,' said Feldar. 'You'll need a second. Normally it would be your Companion, but you don't have one so it had better be me.' He stood up. 'Come on, let's get that mess off your face, change your tunic and see what we can do to get you ready.'

Peglar was grateful beyond words that Feldar was prepared to help him. They walked to his quarters in

315

silence. While Feldar bathed Peglar's face and helped him find clean clothing he ran over the procedure.

'There's a strict etiquette to be followed. Ragul will issue the challenge formally and I, as your second, must register your acceptance. The names of the combatants must be lodged with the City Marshal, and he'll fix the time and place for the combat. It will probably be early tomorrow, in the Arena.'

'So soon?' Peglar was alarmed. This left him no time to prepare.

'Yes. The whole thing moves very quickly. In the olden days a delay meant there was a danger that the combatants might kill each other before the thing started, so nowadays it happens straight away. You'll meet at the Arena, and Ragul will state publicly the reasons for his dispute with you, and you will have to say why you reject them. The combat will start at once, and the winner will be judged to be in the right and telling the truth, and he will set the penalty for the loser.'

'What penalty?'

Feldar shrugged. 'It's up to the winner. In times past the contest was the main thing and once that had settled the matter the penalty was usually something trivial, like a donation to the City Library. Often when it was over the two protagonists would go off to the tavern together, but I can't see that happening in this case.'

'He'll want me out of the way.'

'Yes. So we'd better make sure you don't lose.'

During the past few hours events had swept Peglar along and he'd had no time to stand back and think about what was happening. Now he could see that this was exactly what Feldar had tried to warn him about.

Everything fitted: Ragul's cockiness and his confidence that he would triumph over Peglar; Vancia's recommendation of Sainter as his tutor; Malina's behaviour in Ragul's bedroom and in the Sanatorium, when she'd been testing his reaction to her. It all connected. They must have been working on it for months.

He put his hands over his face. 'I've been such a fool!'

'Yes, you have. But you can't have expected your half-sister to be so savage, or your Companion to be on her side.'

Peglar had another thought. 'Does my father believe them? Does he think what Sainter and Malina say is true?'

'I don't know. Perhaps, perhaps not. It doesn't matter now. If things had been left he would have had to make a judgement. By challenging you Ragul has taken it out of his hands. Your father has no choice in the matter, events must take their course.'

Peglar recalled the alacrity with which his father had agreed to Ragul's challenge. He had sounded almost relieved that the combat would save him from having to choose between them.

When Peglar was clean and dressed Feldar produced a flask from his bag and poured something into a glass. It was thick, sweet and sickly and Peglar didn't like it.

'Drink it. It will give you energy.' Feldar watched while Peglar drained the glass. He took it back and looked at him earnestly. 'Right. Let's get busy.'

43

PREPARATION

Peglar had played combat games when he was a boy, using toy clubs and paddles to mimic the contests of the heroes in the stories. Then when he was older he'd been given some proper training. He wasn't very good at it. He'd managed to develop a decent feint and parry, but his height and his skinny frame made him gawky. He was heavier now and had more muscle, but he wished he'd done more training with Cestris. He was under no illusion. Ragul was a trained soldier; he would be a much better fighter.

Once he was cleaned up he went straight with Feldar to the Gymnasium. As expected, Cestris was there. As far as Peglar could tell he seemed to live there. He was shocked when he heard what had happened, and immediately offered his help. Peglar was overwhelmed that someone like Cestris would come to his aid when everyone else apart from Feldar had abandoned him. Cestris asked nothing about the accusation. They embraced and Peglar started to explain but he brushed it aside.

'Time enough for that later. Whatever you say, I believe. We must concentrate on getting you ready for the fight.'

First Peglar had to be equipped with a club and a paddle. It was vital to get these right. The club was almost the length of his arm. It was heavy, cased in leather, and weighted at the end. Cestris helped him to find one that was the right size and balance, light enough for him to swing freely but solid enough to do damage when it landed.

Next, the paddle. This, too, was made of leather, a sort of heart shaped board with a thick, hide face. It had to be strapped to his left hand, so it was important to get one that he could grip tightly and wouldn't slip. The paddle was a shield so the fighter could defend himself against blows from his opponent's club by parrying and glancing them aside. If done properly this would throw the opponent off balance and make an opening for a counterattack with his own club. But the paddle was also a weapon in its own right. Used flat it could deliver a painful blow. Being struck by an effectively wielded paddle was like being whacked with a plank of wood. Used edge on, with a chopping action, it could hack flesh and break bones. Peglar tried a number before he found one that suited him.

When Cestris was satisfied with his choices, he and Feldar strapped training guards on him – pads to protect the shoulders, knees, groin, stomach and arms - and lastly a helmet.

'You won't wear any of this stuff for the actual combat, it's just to avoid injuries while you practice,' Feldar explained.

The sparring sessions were hard. It wasn't easy to move wearing all the clobber, and soon Peglar was sweating like Sainter. Feldar fought him first, then Cestris. Feldar kept yelling at Cestris not to go easy, to go after Peglar harder, and he did. He took some hits that rocked his skull, even inside the helmet, and twice he was knocked over, but he also landed some good blows in return.

All the time Feldar was keeping up a commentary, getting Peglar to read his opponent's moves and anticipate attacks. 'Watch his turn. Look out for his foot. He's feinting, hang back. Now lunge. Again. Now crack him. Chop.' Between bouts he was given more of the sweet drink, and some tips: watch his eyes, see where he's looking, pick out his weak spots, don't be squeamish about hurting him. 'You're there to damage him, so that's what you've got to do. If you don't finish him, he'll finish you.'

Afterwards Peglar bathed. Then, while he lay on the training table and Cestris rubbed oil into his arms and legs, Feldar talked to him about Ragul.

'Make no mistake, he's strong. But he'll be cocky. He thinks he's so much better than you that winning will be easy, so he'll be tempted to underestimate you and that will make him sloppy. Go in hard from the start. Don't let him settle. He's heavy and not as fit as he thinks he is. Try to knock him off balance early on. He'll be surprised how strong you've become. If he starts to have doubts, then you've got a chance. He's a show-off and he'll act up to the crowd. When his attention strays, that's the time to attack.'

All this time Cestris was kneading Peglar's limbs

and shoulders, easing the muscles and joints. He described Ragul's preferred moves – rapid jabs with the club followed by a sharp slice with the paddle – and demonstrated how to neutralise them.

'You're a better fighter than he thinks,' said Feldar. 'He won't expect you to be able to stay with him and that gives you an advantage. The longer the fight goes on the better your chances, so hang on. Wear him down, and when you're able to land your key blow, what then?'

'Follow up hard,' Peglar said. 'Catch him while he's off balance, hit him on the fall.'

'Good,' said Feldar. 'Good. One more thing: keep your temper. Forget what they've done to you. He'll try to rile you, so ignore anything he says. If you lose your temper you'll also lose your judgement. Oh, and if he hurts you, don't be afraid to go down. The Marshal has to give you reasonable time to recover. Use it. Don't be tempted to act the hero by getting up too soon.'

Eventually Feldar and Cestris decided that they'd done as much as they could and Peglar needed to sleep. Feldar walked with him back to his quarters. 'Sainter won't be back, so I'll sleep in his room. I'll call you an hour before dawn. Try to get some rest.' He started towards the door.

'Feldar,' Peglar called after him. 'Why did Malina do this?'

'What do you mean? We talked about why.'

'No, I mean, why all the pantomime? Surely Vancia could have got the same result just from Sainter's lies. Why go through all the performance in the Library?'

'It's obvious. They had to get you and Malina in the

Library together. It was important for the story that you were both there at the same time. This house is full of watchers. Both of you will have been seen going in that direction. Also, it was essential that nobody saw you anywhere else. An alibi for you would have ruined their plan.'

'Yes, but why the rubbish about Lembick?'

'Sainter's story was that you molested your sister, but on its own that wouldn't have been enough for what they wanted. You wouldn't be the first young man to lust after his half-sister. In some of the old houses incest is practically a family pastime. If that was all, just you pawing at Malina, your father would have given you a lecture, you'd have apologised, he'd have sent you away for a few weeks to do something nasty on one of his farms, and that would have been the end of it. They needed more than that. They want you out of the way so that Ragul gets the whole of the Sharing, and they want your complete destruction. They want everyone from now on to think of Jathan Peglar not only as a lecherous lout, but also as an idiot and a liar. They want to ensure that nobody will ever trust you or accept your word again.

'Malina told you an outrageous lie about Lembick. She knew that anyone with any sense would see that her story was ridiculous. She gambled on you being dumb enough to believe it. She knew that if you repeated it people would think you were a fool. Ragul was ready and waiting for you to blurt it out so he could jump in with his challenge.'

Peglar understood. Why hadn't he seen it at the time? But was Malina really so cold and calculating?

Peglar took in the bleakness of this and added it to his other woes. He knew Feldar was right. He also knew that Yalka, a girl from the slums his family thought worthless, a girl that his father would have had whipped and that his brother would cheerfully kill, would never do what Malina had.

44

THE ARENA

Although it was early there was already a large crowd outside the Arena, with some sour looking Guardians keeping the entrance clear. There was a stirring as Peglar followed Feldar and Cestris through the path they made.

'Sister shagger!' a voice yelled, and the crowd surged forward. The Guardians used their batons and shoved the throng back.

'One of Ragul's crew,' Feldar said in Peglar's ear. 'There'll be a lot of that kind of thing. Take no notice.'

Peglar held his head up and looked to the front, ignoring the onlookers. He kept repeating to himself that whatever they shouted he had done nothing wrong.

They made their way to one of the changing rooms. It was big and chilly, with painted walls and wooden benches, and it smelt of liniment and sweat. Peglar sat down and Feldar squatted beside him.

'Ignore what you heard outside. You're going to get plenty of insults,' the Steward said. 'Ragul's cronies have had time to go round the city and they'll have planted people in the crowd to unsettle you. Try to forget it. Just concentrate on what you're here to do.'

Peglar looked down and shook his head. Feldar had misinterpreted his silence. It wasn't that he was unsettled by the taunts, it was that he felt disconnected from it all. It was as if none of this was happening to him but to someone else, another Jathan Peglar, and he was just a bystander. He didn't care who shouted what.

'Don't worry,' said Feldar. 'There'll be support for you too. Some of Cestris's pals have spent the night making sure that at least some people in that crowd know what really happened. The heckling won't all be on Ragul's side.'

'Thank you,' Peglar said. It didn't seem enough. He wanted them to know how grateful he was for what they were doing. He wanted Feldar to know he was concerned for him. This was the second time he'd taken Peglar's side against Ragul. The first time he had won. If this time he lost, things would not go well for him. 'I'll do my best,' was all he could manage.

Cestris helped him off with his tunic and started to rub his arms and back, while Feldar got to work on his legs. Then he bound Peglar's left hand, wrapping it in strips of cloth until it was a tight fit under the strap of the paddle. He could still feel the traces of his burns but they were almost gone. While they got him ready Peglar limbered up, hopping from one foot to the other, bending his knees, twisting from the waist, stretching. The crowd noise was starting to build, an indistinct hum punctuated by bursts of shouting and chanting.

There was a rap on the door and Thornal came in. He was in his full regalia as City Marshal and wore a golden sash over a long, green robe that was studded with emblems to mark his years of service. He didn't acknowledge Peglar and spoke directly to Feldar.

'This is a sorry business,' the Marshal said. 'Family disputes are the very worst, and they're never resolved by combat. Is there no other way of settling this?'

'This quarrel is not of Peglar's making,' Feldar replied. 'It's Ragul's business. If he and his sister withdraw their accusations and apologise, then I'm sure Peglar will be willing to make peace.'

'Yes, I will,' said Peglar.

Thornal shrugged, as if he'd expected this answer and knew it was of no use. 'Very well, then. Let's get it over with. Are you ready?'

'Yes,' Peglar said, 'I am ready,' and with that all his feelings of calm vanished. He felt a surge of nausea, and a pitch in his stomach enough to make him want to run through the door, down the street and away from the Arena and the city and whatever the next hour might hold. He tried to pull himself together by bouncing on the balls of his feet but his legs were wobbly and he had to sit down. Feldar busied himself with a box of bandages and ointments, the paraphernalia of a second, and pretended not to notice. Peglar wished with all his heart he had more time. There had only been a few hours since Ragul's challenge. If he had more time to train, more time with Feldar and Cestris, he might stand a chance. If only this could be put off.

Cestris smiled and held up his fist in a salute, and Peglar and Feldar set off down the long, dark tunnel towards the Arena.

45

THE CAGE

The tunnel was a cool oasis before they emerged into the brightness and the din. Peglar stood in its mouth and blinked. Facing him were tiers of seats, rows of faces. Above him on a raised platform was the cage, a circular, barred pen twice as high as a man and twenty or so paces across. A place of pain from which he would not be able to escape. He and Ragul would be locked in it and they would fight until one of them was incapable of carrying on. Only then would they be allowed to leave. Peglar felt as though his stomach had been hollowed out and the space filled with cold, damp air.

'Where's Ragul?' he muttered to Feldar.

'He'll come in from the other side. You'll see him soon enough.'

The Arena was almost full. A little way up was a row of seats grander than the rest, where the nobility sat. Peglar could see Uncle Mostani, Lembick, Styron and in the centre, occupying the Master's throne, his father. At his side was Vancia. Peglar looked for his mother but she wasn't there, and he felt a pang of guilt that the troubles which had befallen him over the past twenty four hours had taken his whole attention and he'd not been to see her. Was she still ill? Malina was absent too, and there was no sign of Sainter.

A cheer had gone up when Peglar entered. Now there was a louder one as Ragul and Burian appeared. Ragul was showing off to a section of the crowd, dancing on his toes and making shadow lunges. His club and paddle looked as though they'd seen some service, not new and unmarked like Peglar's. There was a group of twenty or so young men close to the front, and every time Ragul performed one of his moves they cheered and he preened.

'They're some of his cronies from the Army,' Feldar muttered.

Peglar wondered if any of them had been at the fire. Were these men the ones who had torched Yalka's home? Were they the people who had killed Verit? He felt a surge of anger.

Thornal led the way up the wooden steps onto the platform. Ragul and Burian followed. Ragul sneered at Peglar as he and Feldar fell in behind. Two Heralds brought up the rear. At the top they all turned, faced the dignitaries and bowed. Although Peglar knew that there was no possibility his father could see him from that distance, he stared the old man in the face with a directness of which Verit would have been proud.

Karkis flapped his hand to signal to Thornal that the proceedings were to begin. The Marshal held his mace aloft and the crowd became quiet.

'My Lord Master, Elders of the City, Members of the Council, citizens,' he began. 'We are here today to witness the settlement of a dispute. The issue is who, between an accuser and a defender, is telling the truth. Do we have the accuser?'

Ragul stepped forward and bounced some more. Peglar thought he looked cocky, confident and dangerous. He was well muscled and shining with rubbing oil, but he was also carrying some fat. He raised his paddle and there was wild applause from the group at the front.

Thornal waited for quiet. 'What is your name?'

'Morat Ragul.' There was another cheer. Ragul waved, swaggered, and bounced again.

'Morat Ragul,' the Marshal called, 'whom do you accuse?'

'Him.' Ragul thrust his chin forward and pointed his club at Peglar. 'I accuse him, my half-brother, Jathan Peglar.' There was booing, but Peglar was encouraged to hear some cheers too. His stomach heaved. He needed a lavatory. He concentrated on trying to still his trembling legs.

'Of what do you accuse Jathan Peglar?'

Burian held up a paper. Ragul looked at it and frowned. 'I accuse Jathan Peglar of two instances of dish... dish... dis-honourable conduct.' He read slowly, stumbling over the words. 'In the first instance I accuse him of ass-aulting our sister and see-king to force himself on her.'

Much booing and angry yelling. Some of the crowd pointed at Peglar and shook their fists. Thornal banged his mace for silence and Ragul squinted at the paper again.

'In the second instance,' he read, 'I accuse Jathan Peglar of see-king to conceal his actions by lying.'

Hubbub. Cries of "liar", mixed with other yells of

"horse shit" and "you're the liar". The Marshal pounded angrily, and once more the clamour died down.

Ragul limped on. 'These actions by Jathan Peglar are contemp... contemp... con--temp-itable,' he paused, triumphant at having mastered the word, 'and are unworthy of a citizen. I call upon him to ack... nowledge these charges and make repa... repa... ration.' Burian lowered the paper, to Ragul's clear relief.

'If he fights as well as he reads we've got nothing to worry about,' Feldar said to Peglar, loud enough for Ragul and the front rows to hear. Some of the nearer spectators laughed and Ragul glared.

Thornal waited for everyone to settle again. 'Jathan Peglar, under City Law you must accept this accusation, or reject it. What do you say?'

Peglar's legs were shaking so much that he thought everyone must be able to see them. The Arena was hushed, waiting for him to speak. He cleared his throat and prayed that his voice would hold. It did, and the sound came out stronger than he felt.

'This accusation is false. It is without foundation and I reject every part of it as lies.' Some people shouted his name and a small section of the crowd took it up as a chant, "Peg-lar, Peg-lar."

Thornal held up his staff until the chanting stopped. 'An accusation has been made, and it has been rejected. As Marshall of the City of Chamaris I direct that the truth be established in the traditional manner by a Trial of Veracity. Seconds, are your principals ready?'

'Yes,' said Burian.

'Ready,' said Feldar.

'The combat will take place now,' Thornal intoned, 'before these citizens assembled here. The parties will fight with club and paddle. All blows are legal and there are no fouls. The combat will begin on my signal and will continue until one of the parties yields, or I judge that one or other is unfit to continue. At that point the remaining combatant will be judged the winner. By these means this matter will be settled once and for all, and it will be held for ever after that the winner has the true version of the disputed events and that the loser's version is false. Jathan Peglar, you are the defender and may choose your colour.'

Peglar looked at the painted circle that filled the floor of the cage. One half of it was black, the other white.

'Black,' he said without hesitation. Feldar had told him to choose black because it would not show his blood in the way that the white area would. Ragul would have to have white. These were now their 'homes'.

Thornal opened the gate to the cage. Feldar gave Peglar a drink, wiped his face and shoulders and slapped him on the back. He went in.

46

THE FIGHT

The cage seemed much smaller now he was inside it. He stood in the black semicircle; Ragul in the white was only a couple of steps away.

'You've got it coming, runt-boy, he snarled. 'You're going to be sorry your miserable whore-mother ever had you.' He made a few experimental twirls with his club, swinging it from his wrist. Peglar wanted to reply, to shout back at him, but Feldar had told him to say nothing. He held his head up. He was taller than Ragul and that pleased him. He turned to see Feldar signalling at him through the bars.

'Remember what I told you,' Feldar said when Peglar moved closer. 'He can hit harder than you, but you have the longer reach. Keep him at bay with jabs. Keep the contest going till he tires.' He reached through and gripped his arm. 'Good luck.'

'Take your positions,' called Thornal. Ragul and Peglar faced each other across the line between the two semicircles. The crowd was silent. One of the Heralds slammed the gate of the cage shut and slid the bar across, locking it. Peglar was imprisoned with someone who hated him, somebody who he was convinced wanted him dead.

'Begin!' barked the Marshal.

It was a slow start. Feldar had warned that Ragul might rush, charge like a bull to get the thing over with quickly. Peglar was prepared for that, but it seemed that despite his cockiness Ragul didn't want to risk the first move. So they eyed each other and edged along the black/white line, each staying in his own half of the circle. Ragul made a couple of swipes but they were only experimental, there was no force behind them and Peglar easily dodged. Gradually they began to venture out of their own territory and to rotate around one another, seeking openings. Both jabbed, but neither managed to land a blow. The atmosphere was tense, the crowd silent, waiting for the action proper to begin.

As they moved, Peglar realised that his brother had contrived to get him into the centre of the circle while he went round the outside. This meant that Peglar had to keep turning to face him. He was whirling faster and faster, forcing Peglar to spin and spin more and more desperately. He couldn't move quickly enough, he was becoming dizzy. Ragul was going to get behind him and clobber him from the rear. It was "Fool's Twist", an old trick that an experienced fighter might try against a rookie. Cestris had warned him about it. He had also shown him the way to get out of it.

Peglar made a sudden lunge to the left, counter to the direction they'd been turning, and at the same time he leapt forward. Ragul was taken by surprise and momentarily unbalanced. As Peglar dodged past he aimed a back-handed chop with his paddle at his brother's kneecap. He felt a jar as it connected, and Ragul howled and doubled up. As he bent, Peglar swung his club at the back of his neck. Ragul knew the move, though, and ducked so that the club caught his shoulder instead of his head. It hurt him but it was not the killer blow Peglar had intended.

Ragul staggered into the white semicircle and collapsed, clutching his knee. He was sucking air through clenched teeth and his face was twisted in pain.

The Heralds on opposite sides of the cage were holding ropes, and as soon as Ragul fell they let them go. A net dropped from the top of the cage, crossing the dividing line between the semicircles and effectively keeping the two combatants apart.

Thornal had said there were no rules, but there were a few. If a fighter had more than two points of contact with the floor it constituted 'going down'. If he went down on his home colour the contest was suspended, his opponent had to withdraw and the net was dropped between them to keep them apart. It was up to the Marshal to decide how much time to allow for recovery, how long the net should stay down. As the contest went on, and if the Marshal was lenient, it was possible to take quite long breaks in this way. If, however, a combatant went down on his opponent's colour the contest would continue; there was no net, no respite and he may be struck. The way to win was for a fighter make his opponent go down on the colour that was not his own and prevent him from crawling or rolling to his home, while attacking him with paddle and club.

A small section of the cage on Ragul's side slid back and Burian scuttled in, knelt beside his master and started to work on his knee. Peglar leant back against the bars in front of where Feldar and Cestris sat. Feldar reached into the cage and held a flask to Peglar's mouth. 'Well done, that was a good move. Pity you couldn't land the follow up. The knee was a beauty, though. It will slow him down. Try to hit it in the same place again.'

Peglar looked across the ring to where Ragul was still on the ground. His knee seemed hurt and he squealed in pain as Burian tried to flex it. A few of the crowd began a slow handclap.

'This is taking much too long,' Feldar muttered. He shouted to Thornal, who had gone into the cage and was standing beside Burian. 'Marshal, is he out? We demand he continue or yield. If he can't go on you must award the contest to Peglar.'

Thornal ignored Feldar, and Burian helped Ragul to his feet and steadied him while he tested his knee. The rule stated that once a fighter was on his feet his opponent could attack him again, but the net was still across the cage, keeping Peglar back.

'This is a farce,' Feldar fumed. 'He's on his feet. Lift the net,' he shouted to the Heralds. 'He's been given far too much time.' Some of the crowd were now becoming angry, and there were boos and shouts of "swindle" and "fix". Just then the Marshal raised his arm and the Heralds hoisted the net clear as Thornal and Burian left the cage.

Ragul was breathing heavily and it looked as though his knee couldn't bear his weight. He hobbled a few steps and swung his club. He rotated his shoulder, the one Peglar had caught, and bit his lip.

Peglar glowered, but Ragul was avoiding looking directly at him. He felt a surge of elation. He was going to win. He would be vindicated. Vancia's plot would be exposed and Ragul would be disgraced. He rushed forward, seeking an opportunity to finish it off quickly, and he jabbed his club at Ragul's midriff. It was not a heavy blow but Ragul winced. Peglar jabbed again, harder. His brother seemed scarcely able to move, unable to dodge effectively. If he could just catch that knee again with another blow like the first it would all be over.

He was looking for an opening when he caught from the corner of his eye what Ragul had been planning all along, a savage and frighteningly fast scything slash with the edge of his paddle. Peglar dived and the blow missed his neck, but it struck his left side, just below the ribs. There was an agonising, tearing pain, as though he'd been sliced in two. He couldn't breath and he gasped at the air like a beached fish. Ragul swung the club at his thigh. Peglar saw it coming and tried to jump aside but the club struck his leg, chopping it from under him and he fell heavily.

He made to get up but the flat of Ragul's paddle hit him again, clattering the side of his head and he fell back. Ragul lifted his club and whacked it down with all his might. Peglar had just enough about him to twist aside and the weapon bounced on the platform, booming like thunder. He tried to roll away but Ragul hit him again. There was a burst of light, everything spun and a red mist filled his vision. The club came down again. This time Peglar parried with his paddle, but the force of the blow almost dislocated his shoulder.

Peglar's head was spinning and he could scarcely think. He was in the white section, with Ragul between him and the black. There was no net to save him. If he stayed there he would be finished. Everything seemed to be happening in slow motion. Ragul straightened up and raised his paddle for the killer blow. Peglar summoned all his strength and hurled himself out of the way. Ragul's miss threw him off balance, and Peglar swung his club as hard as he could at the damaged knee. It connected, knocking against the hinge of the joint. Ragul screamed and crashed to the floor.

Peglar clawed his way into the black area and the net came down. He lay on his back while the Arena spun around him. The crowd noise sounded as though it was coming from the bottom of a well shaft. There was an agonising pain as Feldar's fingers probed his side. Someone else was applying a cold compress to his face and ear.

'Come on,' said Feldar. 'You've got to get up before Ragul does.'

Peglar struggled to a sitting position. Movement was torture.

'No major damage, by the look of it,' said Feldar, 'but you might have a broken rib.'

Peglar's head was still ringing and it hurt when he breathed in, but his vision was clearing and he was sure he could go on. He had felt a crack when he hit Ragul's knee. If something was broken he wouldn't be able to stand up. If he couldn't stand up and Peglar could, he would win. He took a gulp of water and gathered himself to rise when he became aware of the Marshal standing over him.

'The net has been lifted,' he said to Feldar. 'Your man's not on his feet. Isn't he able to carry on?'

Feldar was appalled. He pointed towards Ragul, who was still sitting in his half of the circle, with Burian kneeling beside him. 'Ragul's not up yet, either! The net should still be down.'

The Marshal ignored him and bent over Peglar. He looked at the side of his face and his ear, which was bleeding. Then he poked Peglar's ribs, hard, forcing him to yelp with pain.

Thornal straightened up. 'Peglar is hurt. I judge that he's unable to continue and I rule him out. I award the contest to Ragul.'

'This is outrageous!' Feldar shouted. 'Peglar's on his feet and Ragul's not. You can't declare a man who's down the winner.' The Marshal tried to move away but Feldar blocked his path. 'No,' he shouted in Thornal's face, 'this is not right.'

'Step aside,' the Marshal snarled, holding up his mace.

'No! You can't rule Peglar out! He's standing. He has won.'

Feldar could barely be heard over the din from the crowd. Two Guardians grabbed him by the arms and dragged him away. Peglar tried to move forward but a Herald blocked his path.

Thornal stepped out of the cage and faced the crowd. 'Neither combatant is able to continue, but Jathan Peglar went down first. I therefore rule that Jathan Peglar is out, and I declare Morat Ragul the victor.'

He could hardly make himself heard; the racket was

incredible. Some people were leaving their seats and climbing down over the rows in front of them. Guardians were on every exit, while Karkis's bodyguards were clearing a path for him and Vancia to leave.

Thornal shouted. 'Under the laws of our city, Morat Ragul is deemed by this victory to have demonstrated that his version of events is true. I therefore decree that the accusation is proven and that Jathan Pedlar is guilty of the crimes of which he has been accused.' All the upper tiers of the Arena were by now empty and there was a sea of faces in front of the platform, with Guardians struggling to keep them back.

Thornal motioned Ragul to come forward. His face was white and twisted in pain, and he had to lean heavily on Burian. It was plain that he couldn't stand without help.

'The victor will now set the penalty,' Thornal announced.

The crowd went quiet to hear what Ragul would demand. 'I want him flogged and then exiled,' he grunted. Ragul's army cronies burst into wild cheering.

'That is two penalties,' Thornal said. 'You are entitled to state only one.'

Ragul thought. He clearly wanted to see Peglar flogged, but that would soon be over. He wanted more than that, he wanted him gone. 'Then exile,' he said. 'I want Jathan Peglar exiled.'

Ragul's pals took up the cry: 'Exile, exile, exile.'

Thornal didn't bother waiting for quiet and he pressed on. 'By the powers vested in me as City Marshal I confirm the penalty.' He turned to Peglar. 'Jathan Peglar, you are now and forever banished from

Chamaris. Your rights as a citizen are forfeit. You must leave the city at once and you may not re-enter. You may not take with you any money, and you may remove only such goods as you are able carry. You must have no further business with the city or with any of its citizens. It will be the duty of any citizen finding you within one day's journey of here to slay you. Any citizen giving you aid or comfort will be subject to the same punishment. Your exile is effective from sundown today. Go.'

47

LEAVING

Feldar's advice was simple: take the back road to the Port Gate, because that way would be quieter. In the end it probably didn't matter. Word of Peglar's ordeal had got around and small clusters of people were gathered to stare at this phenomenon: a member of the highest family in the city being turned out. A few of the onlookers shouted, but most were silent, either dumbstruck or just too curious to utter. As he made his way down the hill Peglar remembered the last time he had come this way, the night he had followed Vancia and Forta. Blossom Yard must be around here somewhere. If he was allowed a detour the apothecary might be able to give him something for his wounds.

On the whole his injuries were not as bad as he'd at first thought. The worst one was his side, where Ragul had driven the edge of the paddle into him. According to Feldar, if the blow had landed with its full force it could have burst his spleen, and it was as well that he had seen it in time and managed to dodge. The muscles he'd built up in his training with Cestris had helped to protect him, too. So yes, his wounds were not as damaging as they might have been but even so, they hurt. Cestris said he might have a broken rib, but even if he had there was nothing that could be done; the only thing was to wait for it to mend. His ear and the side of his face had stung, but a liberal application of salve soothed them. He seemed to have lost the hearing in one ear but Feldar was sure it would return.

Peglar was frustrated and he was angry. He had not been seriously harmed, and if he'd been given only a little more time to recover he would have been able to carry on. On the other hand, it was obvious to any impartial observer that Ragul's knee wouldn't bear his weight. Feldar was convinced that Thornal had been paid by Vancia to make sure Ragul won, and he was talking about an appeal. That wouldn't help Peglar now, though. He had to leave the city today, by sundown.

After the combat the two Guardians who now marched on either side of him escorted Peglar to his quarters. They hadn't left him since. It was their job to make sure that he didn't slip away somewhere to hide, and they would stay with him until they'd seen him safely out of the gate. They were sturdy and taciturn; not hostile, just two men doing their job. They wanted to see the back of him as soon as possible so that they could get back to their normal lives.

When Peglar had first returned to his quarters he'd been confused and unable to think. His head was still spinning, his side hurt with every breath and his face throbbed. His ear felt the size of a cushion. He couldn't take in what was happening and he had no idea what to do. Feldar took charge. First he cleaned Peglar up, bathing his face while Cestris strapped his side. Then he gave him a drink and applied salve to his ear. The drink had been bitter but the balm eased the pain. Then he motioned to a servant, who began to pile some of Peglar's possessions on the bed.

'You can only take with you what you can carry, so we're going to pack you a bundle.'

Feldar started to pick out things that might prove useful and put them in the middle of a large rectangle of blue cloth he'd spread on the floor. The idea was to choose first those items that were essential, then the merely useful, and last of all the personal.

'Leave behind anything of value,' Cestris advised. 'Even if you were able to sell it you'd most probably be swindled, and the chances are it would be stolen first.'

Choosing was easy. There was little Peglar wanted to take: a few clothes, spare footwear, a head covering to protect him from the cold and shield him from the sun. There were a few books, a leather bound notebook, a belt with a silver buckle, a timepiece, a flask, and the small carving of the leopard from his mother. He was unsure about this. It was special because it was a gift from her and because it represented for him a minor triumph over Ragul – he stole it and Peglar got it back. However, the leopard symbolised The House of Karkis and it would remind him of much that he would rather forget. He held it in his fist for some time before deciding to take it.

Peglar thought he was being restrained, but the finished bundle was heavy. Feldar looked at it critically and went through the selection, weeding out some of the things: timepiece fine, two of the thicker books impossible. Peglar took out the belt with the silver buckle. 'It's too valuable to take, I'd worry about it being stolen. I'd like you to have it.' At first Feldar refused, but Peglar insisted and the Steward clipped it around his waist, clearly moved.

Finally, Feldar surveyed the much reduced collection and was satisfied. Then, almost as an afterthought, he took from under his cloak a zirca in a sheath and placed it on top.

'You're not allowed to carry a weapon in the city, but as soon as you're through the gate get this out of the bundle and strap it on. Hide it under your clothing and don't take it off, even when you sleep. Especially when you sleep. And don't be afraid to use it.'

He folded the corners of the cloth into the centre and tied them together with a cord. 'Nothing too fancy. You don't want to mark yourself out as someone who has anything worth taking.' He demonstrated how to knot the cord to make a loop that could be used to swing the bundle onto his shoulder.

It was afternoon by the time they finished. There were two things left to do, one from choice, the other because he was obliged to. The obligation was to see his father. He didn't want to but it had to be done, and he left his quarters with the two Guardians following him like faithful dogs. However, instead of carrying on across the Atrium to his father's study he halted at the mouth of the women's wing. The Guardians glanced anxiously at each other but must have realised that there was no way out of the building in that direction. They nodded and followed Peglar to Chalia's door.

The room was dark, and at first Peglar didn't think

she was there, but when he peered into the shadows he saw her in a chair near the curtained window. She winced as he eased back the drape to let in some light. What he saw filled him with dismay. His mother's skin was sallow, her face jaundiced. Her eyes were yellow, the beautiful, blue irises dull, and her lips were purple and swollen. He had never seen anybody look so dreadful.

'Hello, mother,' he said softly as he bent to kiss her cheek. He took one of her hands. It felt clammy and limp. 'I have to say goodbye.' She smiled weakly and the answering squeeze from her hand was feeble. He felt tears prick his eyes.

'You know why I have to go?'

She managed a slight nod, and sighed.

'What they say I did, I swear to you I didn't. I was tricked. Vancia and Sainter set it up. They tricked me, and Malina helped them. I promise you.'

Her hand came up and stroked his cheek. Her touch was moth light and he hardly felt it. 'I know,' she said, barely audible. 'Vancia has been plotting for a long time. Now she has her way.'

Peglar leant forward and hugged her gently. The bones of her shoulders and back were hard and sharp. She felt so fragile, as if a good squeeze would break her.

'For now,' he said. 'Vancia has her way for now.'

'Oh, Peglar,' she murmured. 'Vancia has won.'

'No, she hasn't. It's not finished yet. I'll find a way to get back at her, and Ragul, and even Malina too. I don't yet know how, but I will.'

She managed a smile. She knew that was what he wanted to do, but exiled from the city, how could he?

There was so much Peglar wanted to say to her, so

much he wanted her to tell him. Instead he sat quietly beside her, holding her hand and thinking about how things had reached this stage, why he had let them and what he could have done to stop it.

The Guardians had remained outside the door. Now one of them took a step inside and pointed down the corridor. It was time to go.

'I have to leave,' Peglar said. 'But I will come back. I will come back and look after you. I promise.'

That was what he said, but in his heart he feared that this might be their last meeting. He could hardly see for tears as he left his mother's room.

Peglar was feeling the familiar anxiety, a hollowness in the pit of his stomach, long before he arrived in the lobby outside his father's door. It seemed only moments since he had waited there with Ragul, and their father had announced his Calling. Even though he knew that making a favourable impression on Karkis no longer mattered, he smoothed down his hair and checked that his cloak hung neatly before he advanced into the lobby. There was a Household Guard on the door. He opened it and preceded him into the room.

'My lord, here is Peglar,' the Guard announced. Not "Lord Peglar", as it should have been, or even "Master Peglar", as it was before his initiation. Just "Peglar". If he had wanted a demonstration of the scale of his loss, this was it. Well, he would not be intimidated. He squared his shoulders, took a deep breath and marched in.

It was all he could do not to make an immediate about turn and walk straight out again. Behind his father's huge desk sat not Karkis, but his half-brother.'

'Well, runt-boy. At last,' said Ragul. He reclined and

threw one arm across the back of his chair. 'I can't tell you how much I've been looking forward to this.'

Peglar noticed several things about Ragul. He noticed that his face looked puffy. He noticed that although he tried to hide it he winced when he moved. He noticed the zirca flat on the desk no more than two inches from his right hand.

'What are you doing here? Where's father.'

Ragul smiled smugly and took his time answering. 'My father,' – he emphasised the "my" – 'has asked me to stand in for him. He said that meeting you himself was too painful, given what you've done. As you are disinherited and I am his sole heir, it seemed an appropriate opportunity to start my future role as Head of the House by taking on this meeting. Besides, there's nothing I wanted more.'

Peglar was silent.

'Yes,' Ragul continued pensively, 'it looks as though it's only a matter of time before I take over as Master of the City. With a little help from the Household Guards the Council will agree next week a Declaration of Inheritance, which will mean that a serving Master may be succeeded by a named son without the city having to bother with the inconvenience and expense of a formal selection procedure. In this case the named son will be me.'

'And you think Lembick will allow that to happen?'

'Lembick.' There was scorn in Ragul's voice. 'Lembick's a nobody. I shall offer him Malina, and she'll have him eating out of her hand. And mine.'

Peglar could scarcely believe it. Was Malina a party to this? Had she known about Ragul's plan all along when she'd ambushed him in the Library? Ragul's plan, or his mother's? Peglar recalled Vancia's show of incredulity and indignation when he told their father what Malina had said. It had been a pretence. He'd been duped, taken in, misled from the start. He had been a fool.

Ragul smiled in a self-satisfied way and stretched, but he couldn't hide from Peglar the pain that this movement caused him. Peglar looked at the zirca. The Guard had not come in with him and he and Ragul were alone in the room. He wondered if he could reach the sword before Ragul responded, but Ragul saw where he was looking and quickly put his hands back on the desk.

'How's your knee?' Peglar asked with a show of concern. It was not the response Ragul had written into his script and he was for a moment thrown, but he quickly recovered.

'How thoughtful of you to ask, little brother. My knee is just fine. How's your face? And your head? And your side, where I think I broke your rib?'

Peglar ignored him. 'It will be good experience for you, finding it hard to move, having pain whenever you walk, having people stare at you. After all, if you're going to rule people you need to know how even the most unfortunate of them feel.'

Peglar could see he was taken aback. This was not how would have planned for the meeting to go. He would have imagined that he would berate Peglar for a while and turn him out suitably cowed. He was not prepared for defiance and he sought to regain the initiative.

'Don't think we're finished. I am going to kill you, Peglar.'

'Oh yes?'

'Yes. Any citizen finding you within a day's journey of the city has an obligation to execute you. It doesn't matter where you go – Halish-Karnon, Semilvarga, Rasturoth or farther – my men will find you and bring you back to me, and I shall carry out my duty to kill you.' He ran his fingers along the blade of his zirca. 'The stain your mother brought to The House of the Leopard when she paired with my father will be eradicated.'

'My mother brought no stain. She brought beauty, and gaiety, and laughter. Things you wouldn't understand.'

'Your mother was a whore from a low family in Rasturoth. She brought no bride gold. She bewitched my father and tricked him so that by the time he brought her back here they were already paired.'

Peglar waited. He felt detached. He watched, as from a distance, his half-brother's face becoming more florid, the spittle flecking his lips as he worked himself up.

'But it's all dealt with now. You will be gone and so will Chalia. You won't see your mother again. Either you will be dead, or she will, or both of you. I hope you took a good look at her when you made your farewells. Hasn't she gone the most attractive colour? A delicate yellow, just like those flowers that grow all over the Citadel. What are they called, now? Oh yes, that's it: Leopard's Bane.'

Peglar felt an almost intolerable pain as everything fell into place. He cursed himself for his stupidity and his obtuseness. Leopard's Bane, the powder Vancia had obtained from the apothecary. Of no medicinal value but a slow poison causing damage to the liver. Liver failure resulting in jaundice and eventually proving fatal. His mother had been and still was being poisoned. He'd known it at the back of his mind from the first, but it had seemed so improbable. Narvil had insisted that what troubled his mother was an infection, and that with his treatment she would recover. The Physician must have been in on the whole thing too. Why hadn't he seen it before?

'I can understand why you would want to remove me,' said Peglar, hardly able to speak. 'I'm a threat to your position and far too clever for you.' Ragul snorted. 'But why my mother? What has she done to you?'

Ragul looked at him with disdain. 'Really Peglar, for somebody who puts himself forward as clever you really are blind. How old is your mother?'

Peglar had to think for a second. 'Thirty six.'

'Exactly.'

Then he saw it, and once more marvelled at his own stupidity. His mother was still young enough to have children, to provide Karkis with yet another child. If she did, and if it were a boy, that would enhance Chalia's standing but worse, it would dilute Ragul's share of the inheritance. Through stratagems and poison, actual and verbal, Vancia had managed to keep Chalia and Karkis apart, but as long as his mother lived there was a possibility that she might conceive. As far as Vancia was concerned that must be prevented at all costs. Why had he not seen what they were doing? It was so obvious.

'Time for you to go,' said Ragul, waving him away with his hand in a gesture he had obviously copied from his father. 'It would be a shame if you were not out of the city by sundown. You would have to be killed straight away, and that would save me the pleasure of hunting you down and doing it later.'

Peglar took one last look at his half-brother and left.

In a way he was sorry his father had avoided him. What was it Syramos had called him? A blind dancer, choosing neither the music nor the moves but taking both in an uncomprehending embrace while thinking he knew what he was doing. Thinking he could see.

48

THE HARBOUR ROAD

Halfway down the hill the cord holding the bundle was biting into Peglar's shoulder and he stopped to change sides. He fingered the small leather purse hanging from a cord around his neck, hidden under his tunic. Feldar had pressed it into his hand as he left.

'What's this?' Peglar had asked.

'Money, cock head. What do you think?'

'But I can't. You've done too much for me already.'

'Of course you can. Besides, it's yours.'

'What do you mean?'

'It's what's left of the money I won from Ragul. I didn't hand all of it over to Crestyn. I put some aside in case it might be needed someday. Now it is. Keep it close, don't put it in the bundle, but don't let anyone see. You're not allowed to take money out of the city.'

Feldar kept his body between Peglar and the two Guardians to conceal what he was doing.

'I don't know how to thank you for all this,' Peglar said. Feldar and Cestris were the only people who had been prepared to stand up for him. Feldar had become a true friend, Cestris the Companion that Sainter could never have been.

'Well then, don't thank me. Just take it, and take care till we meet again.'

'What about you? Won't you be in trouble for helping me?'

'Don't worry about me. I've been around long enough to know how to look after myself. Besides,' he whispered, leaning closer, 'I know enough about The House of the Leopard to keep me safe.'

One of the Guardians tapped Peglar on the shoulder and pointed to the sun. It was low in the sky and would soon touch the horizon. By then he must be gone.

If the Guardians had expected him to try to avoid leaving they were mistaken. Peglar had no reason to remain in the city. The events of the last few months had demonstrated some lessons about Chamaris that made it impossible for him to live there any longer.

The first lesson was about the truth. He had always thought that there were only two alternatives: truth and lies. Now he knew it wasn't so simple. There was a third possibility. There was the truth, there was the lie, and there was also the story. The story was not the truth, but it was not a lie either.

Peglar knew the truth of what took place on the night of the fire. For him to have said anything different from what he had seen and heard would have been to lie. But his father had paid for a different version of events. He and Uncle Mostani had invented a story and used their power to spread it. Many people now thought that this story was what had really happened. The more the story was repeated, the more it would become the credible version. Although the story was not true, the people who believed it were not liars. For them the story was the truth.

The story about the fire had been bought and paid for, but a story didn't have to be bought; it could also be imposed. Trial by combat was an ancient custom. It came from the days when it was thought that truth had such power, possessed such might, that those who fought for it could not fail to win against an opponent who was lying. As one of the heroes in the stories that Yalka loved so much was supposed to have said, "To have the truth on your side is worth a thousand men." So over the years it had come about that the victor in a combat was credited with telling the truth, and the one vanquished was held to be a liar, and it had been a way of doing things for so long that nobody questioned it any more.

Peglar wasn't proud of what he'd done, in fact he felt a fool, but he'd given his father an honest account of the events. The story told by Malina and Sainter was a lie and Ragul knew it, but he had challenged Peglar, Peglar had lost, and without further thought just about everybody accepted Ragul's version and rejected Peglar's. So another thing Peglar had learnt was that money and power could subvert the truth, and force could polish a lie until it shone as bright as the evening star. Yalka had made him realise that Chamaris, the golden city on the hill, the queen of the plain, was more corrupt than the River Settlements could ever have been. The beautiful garden had been poisoned, and the ownership of its ills lay with those who had allowed it to happen: men like Styron, Uncle Mostani, and his father. If the House of the Leopard was the greatest of the city's great families it must take the largest slice of the blame for any failings in the society it had created and sustained. Peglar could do nothing to change this, at least not yet. Until he could it was better for him to make a life somewhere more wholesome, where he could begin again without the shackles of custom, position, wealth, privilege or power.

At the Port Gate a wooden fence had been put up and more Guardians were keeping onlookers behind it. The clamour rose as Peglar approached and his escort steered him to the centre of the gateway. The sun was hanging over the rim of the horizon and a bell sounded from the Gatehouse Tower. It marked the close of day.

One of the Gatekeepers mounted a stone block beside the wall. 'The gate of Chamaris is closing,' he intoned. 'All persons who have no business in the city are ordered to now leave. In one hour the curfew will commence and no one may then be on the streets.'

Peglar looked around. He seemed to be the only one going. A Guardian shoved him in the back and he stumbled forward, across the threshold and out of the city.

He turned and watched as the huge gates swung behind him, slamming with thunderous finality. There was a drawn out rattle and a clank as the locking bars were slid into place and secured. They would not be unlocked until dawn.

Peglar looked up at the towers, at the city rising behind them, at the trees – pine, palm, eucalyptus – clumped in grey-green blotches. Square, white houses clambered up the hill towards the Citadel, their windows yellow with the promise of evening. He imagined the people, the chatter, the wine, the laughter, the smell of food being cooked. Had the murdered children seen this view before they crept in to their deaths?

For a moment he felt a tug back to what he knew, what had been his home. It only lasted a second, then he turned away. Chamaris was no longer his home. It was no longer a place he knew; it was a place he had never known.

He squatted, opened his bundle, and took out the zirca. He strapped it to his waist and fastened the thong binding the sheath to his leg. He hoped that there were people watching from the walls. Lifting the bundle back onto his shoulder, he turned his back on the city and set out along the darkening, dusty road towards Maris Partem, the harbour town. He would use some of the money Feldar had given him to buy food and lodging for the night. Then, in the morning, go. His best option would be to take a boat and get as far away as possible, to a place where he could plan his next moves and work out how to rid Chamaris of the vermin that fouled it.

He unsheathed the zirca and took a savage swipe at a tall thistle by the roadside. The blade was sharp and the result spectacular, the flower jumping from the stem like a thing stung. There was a whole patch of them further along the track and in a blur of rage Peglar attacked. He swung his blade as he had the paddle when he'd fought Ragul, and the plants tumbled. 'That one's for slime-ball Sainter,' he shouted as he chopped. He slashed again. 'That one's for Styron the slime-ball.' Then again. 'That's for Thornal the fraud. That's for mealy-mouthed Mostani. That's for Ragul the arse. That's for Burian the turd. That's for Vancia the witch. That's for Malina the cock-teaser.' He hacked and sliced in a frenzy until the clump was razed and he looked down at the destruction he'd caused. 'Blind dancers, all of them,' he snarled, breathing hard. 'Shit-smeared, piss-stained, pox-faced, blind dancers.'

He stood still and studied the destruction he'd caused. The zirca swung loosely from his hand.

'There, feel better for that?'

He knew the voice at once, and although it was getting dark and she was hooded he knew the speaker too. He glanced beyond her, half expecting to see Verit but even as he did he knew that was impossible.

'What are you doing here?' he said.

'Well that's a fine way to say hello. I'm here to meet you.'

'Why?'

She didn't answer straight away, she made him wait for a moment. Then she said, 'I know. I know what happened to us in the Settlements. I know what happened to you. And I know who done it, all of it.' The hood fell back from her head and she tossed her yellow hair. Peglar started to speak but she held up her hand to silence him. 'There'll be time for us to talk about it all later.' She jerked her thumb over her shoulder, towards the lights and fires of the harbour town. 'For now, me and granddad have got a place near the harbour. It's small and we've not got much, but you're welcome to share what we have.' She held out her hand. 'If we hurry up we can be there before it's properly dark.'

Peglar hesitated, then took it and they walked on towards the distant lights.

The story continues in *Leopards Bane* book 2,
A Smouldering Torch

With his life threatened by Ragul's thugs, Peglar must get away fast. He has no contacts and little money, and his only option is to sign up as crew on a ship leaving for Semilvarga. However, the journey is dangerous and half way through disaster strikes.

Yalka and her grandfather begin to rebuild their lives and at first things go well. However, trouble comes and they too must flee.

In the city of Chamaris its ruler, Karkis, becomes increasingly feeble and Vancia extends her plot to seize power. But Malina is not content, and others too are restless. Meanwhile in the background Scorpion lurks.

Yalka and Peglar start to recruit allies, but Ragul and his mother are well entrenched. It will take all their energy and all their ingenuity to challenge them.

Thank you for reading my book. I hope you enjoyed it. Would you leave a review on Amazon? Ratings and reviews are very important to authors because they help to get their works known.

If you go to my website - www.phillfeatherstone.net - you can find out more about me and my writing. While you're there please think about joining my email list. When you sign up you'll be offered a free book of my short stories.

Finally, would you follow me on Facebook, Instagram and Twitter? And of course, if you enjoyed my book please tell your friends. If you didn't please tell me so I can try to do better next time!

Phill Featherstone
facebook.com/PhillFeatherstone-author
twitter.com/PhillFeathers
instagram.com/phillfeathers

ACKNOWLEDGMENTS

There are always many people to thank when you complete a book. Traditional publishers have in-house editors, proof readers, book designers, cover designers, print managers, admin staff to handle things like ISBNs and copyright library deposits, and marketers to publicise books and organise launches. An independent author must either do all these things themselves, or persuade or hire others to do them. I'm enormously grateful to everyone who has helped and supported me in all my writing, in whatever capacity. Here are just a few of them. I'm bound to have left some out, and I apologise to those I've missed.

I'm fortunate to have some loyal readers who review and comment on pre-publication drafts of my work: Mags Schofield, Marta Ames, Angel Leonard, Jon Cutcliff, Howard Pierce, Emma Dunmore, Helen Collett, Rod Collett, Theresa Anafi, and of course my dear family John Featherstone, Sarah Featherstone, Kathy Mervis Featherstone, and Jeff Durber. I am grateful to you all.

I'm grateful too to subscribers to Promoting Yorkshire Authors and Book Connectors who are generous with tips and advice, to The Wishing Shelf, Indie B.R.A.G., and Pauline Barclay of Chill for their support, and to Random Things Tours and Love Books

Tours for organising book blogs. Thanks to Cathy Helms for her wonderful cover design for this book.

Finally, there is Sally Featherstone, my wife, my business and creative partner, and my very best friend. She helps me with ideas, reads drafts, suggests improvements, and encourages me to fly, but she also knows when I should keep my feet on the ground. I am endlessly grateful to her for helping me to do what I do.

ABOUT THE AUTHOR

Phill Featherstone began writing fiction after a long career as a teacher, administrator and publisher. His first books were the REBOOT series: *Paradise Girl* (2016), *Aftershocks* (2018), and *Jericho Rose* (2020). These three, which predated Covid by some time, tell the story of a worldwide pandemic and how it affects one family and their wider community.

Phill's next book was *The God Jar* (2021). It describes how the Elizabethan mystic John Dee finds a mysterious object with extraordinary powers, which resurfaces 400 years later in contemporary England, with dramatic results.

In *What Dreams We Had!* (2022) five teenagers are offered a stay at a celebrity villa in Tuscany, but once there discover that the invitation is not what it seemed.

I Know What You're Thinking (2022) is centred on the murky world of illicit organ harvesting. *The Poisoned Garden* (2022) is the first book in the *Leopards Bane* series.

Paradise Girl, Aftershocks, The God Jar, and *What Dreams We Had!* have been awarded Indie B.R.A.G. Medallions. *Paradise Girl, Aftershocks*, and *The God Jar* are Wishing Shelf Award Finalists. *Jericho Rose* is a Wishing Shelf Red Ribbon Winner. *Paradise Girl, The God Jar,* and *What Dreams We Had!* are Page Turner Book Award Finalists. *Paradise Girl, Aftershocks,* and *What Dreams We Had!* have Chill Awards.

Printed in Great Britain
by Amazon

16560354R00214